THE WEREWOLF
DATES THE DEPUTY
NOCTURNE FALLS, BOOK TWELVE

KRISTEN PAINTER

THE WEREWOLF DATES THE DEPUTY:
Nocturne Falls, Book Twelve

Copyright © 2020 Kristen Painter

Published in the United States of America.

Welcome to Nocturne Falls, the town that celebrates Halloween 365 days a year. The tourists think it's all a show: the vampires, the werewolves, the witches, the occasional gargoyle flying through the sky. But the supernaturals populating the town know better.

Living in Nocturne Falls means being yourself. Fangs, fur, and all.

Fire chief and werewolf, Titus Merrow, has a pretty good life. Great family, great job, great friends. No love interest, sure, but he's got too much going on to worry about that. Like the 10k race for charity that he's helping to plan. Too bad the woman he's planning it with is so hot. No, wait. He meant annoying.

Sheriff's deputy and valkyrie, Jenna Blythe, has somehow gotten stuck working on a charity event with her boss's brother. Not only is Titus Merrow full of himself, but he challenges every suggestion she makes about the race. Why are the handsome ones always so smug? She can't wait to beat him in the competition and bring home the trophy for the sheriff's department. Again.

But when they answer a call together and things explode, dangerous magic is unleashed. They're suddenly forced to work together. Literally. And the magic only gets more treacherous as time ticks forward. Not even Jenna's good friend seems to be able to help them as shady forces lurk in every shadow.

Swords and sorcery abound, and Jenna's past comes back to haunt her. She and Titus are left with no choice but to question everything—and everyone. Who's targeting them? Is what they're feeling real? Can love survive against darkness? Can a valkyrie learn to run with the pack?

For my husband, who may or may not
have inspired a few lines of dialogue in this book.

Being the sheriff of a town where Halloween was celebrated three hundred and sixty-five days a year had its ups and downs. Today wasn't an up.

Hank Merrow stared across the conference table at the two stubbornest people on the face of the earth. His brother, Titus, who was also the fire chief, and one of his best deputies, Jenna Blythe, a valkyrie.

The only other person who might be more stubborn than these two was his sister, Bridget, who owned the local watering hole, Howler's. No, wait. Make that their aunt, Birdie Caruthers, the woman he'd foolishly hired in a weak moment of nepotism to work as the sheriff department's receptionist.

Okay, maybe stubbornness ran in the family. But that didn't explain Jenna.

She and Titus stared back at him, waiting on an answer.

He growled softly. "Look, I forgot. It happens.

I have a three-year-old at home. I'm lucky I remember to eat breakfast. Can't one of you just step aside?"

Titus shook his head. "Kind of dirty pool using my niece as an excuse. But I'm not stepping aside. It's high time the fire department got to organize the charity relay 10K. The sheriff's department always does it."

"That's because we do it right," Jenna said.

Titus glared at her. "And you think we wouldn't?"

She raised her brows. "I think you'd make it all about the fire department, and it's supposed to benefit *all* first responders. Plus, you'd probably make people carry hoses or buckets of water."

Titus snorted. "That's quite an assumption, and I don't like—"

"Enough," Hank said. "Since neither of you wants to step down, you can co-chair the project."

Jenna scowled. "What?"

Titus looked fit to chew nails. "Hank, that is not—"

Hank stood. "I'm going back to my office and back to work. The matter is settled. Unless one of you wants to quit." He almost cringed. He shouldn't have said *quit*. There was no way either one of them would do *that*.

The two of them, the werewolf and the valkyrie, went back to arguing. With him or with each other, he wasn't entirely sure, but he wasn't sticking around to find out. He left and shut the door behind him. Their bickering carried through the door—although to be fair, he was a werewolf, so his hearing picked up a lot more than most people's.

He pinched the bridge of his nose.

Birdie, seated behind the reception desk, snickered. "How'd that go?"

He gave her a look. "You can hear as well as I can. You already know."

"Yes, I do." She sipped her caramel-and-cinnamon-scented coffee, if you could even call such a froufrou drink *coffee*. Ripples of white foam remained on the surface, all that was left of the whipped cream that had once topped it. "But I still want to talk about it."

"I don't." He went straight to his office, which necessitated continuing past her desk. "Next year, the sheriff's department is out of that race entirely."

Birdie frowned. "You mean you aren't going to let the deputies enter?"

"They can enter. But we aren't planning it. Not a single kilometer. We'll provide security. That's it." He opened his office door. "Hold my calls. And no visitors unless a serial killer comes to confess."

"That reminds me. Ivy called." Birdie grinned.

He frowned. "Serial killers remind you of Ivy?" Not the most flattering comparison to his wife.

"No, you ninny." Birdie frowned right back at him. "The hold-my-calls part." She smiled again. "Hannah Rose said her first full sentence."

Hank's heart clenched at the mention of his little girl. "What did she say?"

Birdie's grin widened. "Check your phone. Ivy sent a video."

"Will do." Now he had a real reason to hide away in his office. "Thanks."

He went in, shut the door, and picked up his phone off the charger on his desk. He pulled up Ivy's text and hit play.

Hannah Rose appeared on the screen. She was at the side of the couch. Off-camera, he could hear Ivy saying, "Go ahead, tell Daddy."

Hannah Rose laughed and lifted her chubby arm in the air. "I love you, Daddy."

The words were clear and distinct, and Hank had to swallow against the knot of emotion suddenly clogging his throat. The sweet words of his baby girl wiped away all the stress of the last few minutes.

Ivy turned the camera around, her beautiful face filling the screen. He smiled. Was there a more perfect woman than his wife? She blew him a kiss. "I love you too. See you for dinner, honey."

The video ended. With a full heart, Hank sent a text back, telling Ivy he loved her, too, and would definitely see her for dinner and did she need him to pick up anything at the store.

And just like that, Titus and Jenna and the race were forgotten.

* Six months later *

Titus had better things to do than sit down for yet another meeting with Jenna Blythe. She might be a great deputy and one of the tougher supernaturals in Nocturne Falls, but she was also a royal pain in his—

A knock on his open office door made him look up.

"Chief?" Sam Kincaid, Bridget's boyfriend and a

fellow pack member, stood in the door. "Jenna's here."

Six minutes early too. He sighed and nodded. "Send her in."

Sam grinned. "Don't you think she makes that uniform look good?"

Titus narrowed his eyes and decided to torture the younger man a little. "I'm sure Bridget would love to hear that."

Sam's smile faltered. "I wasn't saying that I... I was wondering if *you'd* noticed. I'm all in for Bridget."

"Good to know." Titus *had* noticed. But Jenna's ability to fill out a deputy's uniform didn't negate that she argued with him over every detail of this race. Just like the way she smelled like lemons and sunshine didn't change how she'd double-checked all the flyers and posters to make sure the sheriff's department had equal billing. Oh, sure, she'd claimed it was to look for typos, but he knew better.

What kind of valkyrie smelled like lemons and sunshine, anyway? Shouldn't they smell like... brimstone and sadness?

Jenna walked in. Her dirty-blond hair was back in its usual knot, up off her collar as per regs, but a narrow strand had escaped and now hung down over her right eyebrow. It seemed to point to her lush mouth. He swallowed and made himself stop staring. Thankfully, she tucked the wayward lock back behind her ear. "I brought you the updated sponsor list."

He leaned back in his chair a bit. She did look good in her uniform. Any man would notice that. But he was a red-blooded werewolf. He couldn't be expected to ignore an attractive female. Even if she was annoying. "You could have emailed that to me."

Her crystal-blue eyes narrowed. "This is easier. I'm on patrol today. Not sitting at a desk."

Like some people. Like him. That's what she seemed to be implying. He frowned.

"Besides," she went on, "I wanted to tell you about the two new ones I just firmed up. Big Daddy Bones is donating two seventy-five-dollar gift cards. And—"

"Have you eaten there? I hear the barbecue is pretty good."

She looked up from her notes. "Yes, I eat there every once in a while. Not enough to be a regular, but they seemed to remember me. Probably the uniform. You?"

"No." He knew he should change up his routine a little, but most nights he ate at Howler's, seeing as how his sister owned the place. Okay, almost every night. "I should check them out."

"You should. Especially because they're sponsoring."

Maybe he'd ask her if she wanted to go with him, just to see the look of shock and horror on her face. He snickered at the very idea. Then wondered what she'd look like out of uniform. Well, not *out* of her uniform altogether. But in something different. Although, now the first image was kind of stuck.

She frowned. "Why is that funny? Why are you smiling like that?"

"It isn't, sorry, just remembering something someone said earlier." He realized he was still smiling. He tried to clear his head and focus.

"Good to know I've got your full attention," she snarked.

He sighed. If only she knew what he was thinking about. "You do. Go on."

With a rather stern look, she did. "I also got the DIY Depot to donate a room of flooring."

"Hey," he said. "That's pretty good."

She lifted her gaze to look at him. "I'm very persuasive."

He could see that. Maybe it was a valkyrie thing. She probably ground people down until they gave in. Except, her sister didn't seem that way. But then, Tessa was a librarian and not quite so…direct. "I've been talking to people too."

"And?"

"Guildman's is donating a two-hundred-dollar gift card and two hours of wardrobe styling."

Jenna's mouth bunched to one side. "Nice. I can think of a lot of guys who could use some of that."

"Really? What do you think 'wardrobe styling' is, exactly? I didn't want to ask." As a man who spent every day in a uniform, Titus's nonwork wardrobe didn't go much beyond jeans and T-shirts, with the occasional flannel button-down thrown in for cold weather.

Jenna shrugged. "I suppose Dexter Guildman would help the winner decide what works for them and what doesn't. Or maybe he'll select a few outfits for them to show them how they could dress."

"Oh. Yeah, that's probably it."

She laughed and shook her head.

"What?" Titus said. "You don't like a nicely dressed man? You know what that song says. Every girl's crazy for a sharp-dressed man."

She looked at him, clearly unimpressed with his ZZ Top reference. What did valkyries listen to? Swedish death metal?

"I'm all for a nicely dressed man," she said, "but I care more about what a guy's like on the inside. Who he is, not how he's dressed. Clothes are optional."

He choked a little. "Optional?"

She went slightly pink in the cheeks. "That's not what I meant. I meant character matters. Clothes don't."

He decided to let her off easy. "Well, I agree with that."

But he also thought her head would be turned like every other woman's at the sight of a man in a great suit. Wasn't that what women liked? He wasn't really sure anymore. Since his fiancée, Zoe, had broken things off a few years ago, he'd pretty much given up on having a relationship, deciding to throw himself into work instead.

Work was dependable. And he wasn't interested in getting his heart broken again, no matter how well things had turned out for Hank and Bridget and their significant others. Titus recognized that he'd had his chance at love, and it had gone belly up.

Jenna handed over the paper she was holding.

"You can put that in your race file, or wherever you're keeping things."

"Will do." As he accepted the paper, her radio crackled.

Birdie's voice came over. "There's been a report of a suspicious person loitering at 2310 Batwing. House is for sale and currently unoccupied. Could just be a lookie-loo."

Jenna grabbed her handset and answered. "I'm on my way."

Titus put the sponsor list off to one side to be filed later. "That's only two blocks away."

Birdie's voice came on again. "Hang on. There's also a report of the smell of gas in the same area. I need to call the fire station."

Jenna clicked the handset again. "No need to call. I'm at the fire station right now." She looked at Titus.

He nodded, answering her unspoken question.

Jenna squeezed the handset. "Chief Merrow will accompany me to check for a gas leak. We'll be there in two minutes."

"Roger," Birdie said. "Over and out."

Jenna stood, pushing her chair back.

"I'll kit up and be right behind you."

"See you there." She left his office, going toward the front of the building.

He went right and headed for the back, where his truck was parked. Along the way, he stopped, put on his protective gear, and grabbed his gas meter.

He arrived at the house just as Jenna was walking toward the front door. He joined her, meter in hand.

"What's the plan?"

She looked surprised he'd asked, but this was her call since she was the law. "I'm going to check the doors, see if any of them are unlocked or have been forced open. You want to keep an eye on the front while I circle around?"

"Sure." He inhaled, his wolf senses working overtime. "I do smell traces of what might be gas. It's very faint, though, so if there's a leak, it's not a major one." He pulled the meter out and took a look. "Not enough to register."

"Well," she said, "I'd trust a werewolf's sense of smell over a piece of equipment. I'll be quick, then we'll go in."

He almost rocked back on his heels. That was the closest she'd ever come to complimenting him. "Okay."

With her weapon drawn but at her side, she went up the steps of the front porch and checked the door. It was locked, as was the real estate agent's lockbox secured around the knob. From there, she headed around the side of the house.

A few moments later, she called out, "This is the Nocturne Falls Sheriff's Department. Make yourself known." When there was no answer, she repeated herself.

Titus kept his eyes on the front door. Minutes ticked by. Was she okay? No sounds came from the house, and his hearing was excellent. No sounds was a good thing, wasn't it?

A few more minutes went by. The front door opened, and Jenna came out, weapon holstered.

"House is clear, but the smell of gas is stronger in here. Strong enough I can smell it. You want to bring your meter in and see if you can find out where it's coming from?"

"Yep." He went up the steps. The stink of rotten eggs hit him hard as he walked into the house. His nose wrinkled. "Methanethiol."

"What's that?"

"The stuff they add to natural gas to make it smell bad. Also known as mercaptan."

"Which they add because natural gas has no smell, right?"

"Right." He checked the meter, which showed that gas was still only faintly present. "Weird."

"What is?"

"For as much methanethiol as I smell, the meter isn't reading the equivalent amount of gas present."

Jenna's brow furrowed. "Why would that be?"

"Not sure yet. You've searched the whole house?"

"Yes."

"Is the smell any stronger anywhere else?"

"Not that I noticed."

He looked around. "Is there a basement?"

"Off the kitchen. You want to start your sweep there?"

"Yes, although natural gas is lighter than air, which means it should rise, making the smell stronger up here, but there are usually plenty of pipes to check in a basement."

She tipped her head toward the back of the house as she holstered her weapon. "Let's go have a look."

He held his hand out. "After you."

Jenna opened the door to the basement, turned on the light, and headed down with Titus right behind her.

She wasn't about to admit it to anyone, but there was something kind of sexy about Titus when he was in fire chief mode and not trying to tell her how they were going to organize the race. Not just because she had a thing for men in uniform. Particularly *firemen*. He wasn't hard to look at either.

Not with that slightly feral thing he had going on. Reminded her of the valkyrie's male counterpart, the berserker, which was exactly who she would have been paired with in an arranged marriage if not for the extra two years of service that she'd taken on.

Berserkers were wild warrior men with an unmatched fierceness. All the shifters seemed to have that same look about them, some more than others.

Titus had it in spades, especially when he was passionate about something. Like the race. Or his job.

He'd probably look that way about his mate too. Although she hadn't known him to date since his breakup.

She could only imagine what it would be like to be the focus of that feral energy.

She blew out a breath at the sudden rush of heat that went through her. She really shouldn't be thinking about him like that. Not when he was two feet behind her and smelled like the forest after a hard rain.

Which was a much better smell than the stink of rotten eggs filling this place.

"You okay? You're not feeling lightheaded, are you?"

She glanced over her shoulder. "I'm fine."

He shrugged. "Well, the way you exhaled, I thought the fumes were getting to you."

She narrowed her eyes before turning her head back around. "I'm a valkyrie, wolf. I'm not affected by such things."

"That's probably because your sense of smell isn't as keen as mine."

She snorted as her feet hit the basement floor. She twisted to face him. He was still a couple of stairs up. "Right. Also, *keen*? Really?"

"'Keen' is a perfectly good word." He joined her and held the meter out, scanning the basement.

She watched him, maybe admiring the muscles in his forearms just a little. "You sound like my sister. And she's a librarian."

"You have something against librarians?"

"Nothing at all. But those kinds of words coming out of a fire chief?"

"Would you prefer I growl my words? Maybe grunt a little?"

She laughed, not meaning to.

He smiled.

And her insides clenched. She inhaled, suddenly needing the air. There was something magical about that smile. Which was stupid. Because smiles were just the muscles of the face contracting. Nothing more.

He shook his head. "You've been working for my brother for too long."

"Maybe." She needed to get back on track. "What's your meter say?"

"That there's no gas leak down—"

Something thunked on the floor above them. Well above them. The sound was followed by what had to be footsteps.

"Crap," she whispered. "The attic. There's a set of pulldown steps in the garage, but I didn't check up there."

"Come on," he said. "I'll be your backup. You lead. You've got the gun, after all."

Just like that, they were back to the task at hand. That's how it was with them. Being a first responder meant the job took priority. But Jenna kind of enjoyed how easily they went from banter to business.

With a nod, she took out her weapon and went back upstairs. Titus stayed close behind.

She nudged the basement door open and assessed the room beyond. "All clear," she said softly.

She went toward the garage, cautiously, clearing each room as they went through until they got to the door at the end of the hall that led out. She stopped there, taking up position as she prepared to go through. "Stay behind me."

She expected a thousand different smart remarks, but he just nodded.

She breached the door, her gun leading the way. The garage, like the rest of the house, was empty. She flipped on the light. The access was right above where a car would have been parked. It was closed, just like it had been earlier. But the cord that hung down to open the panel swung slightly.

She glanced at Titus and put a finger to her ear, then pointed up.

He listened for a moment, then shook his head. "You?"

She shook her head as well. She hadn't heard a sound, but it was stranger that Titus wasn't picking up anything. Werewolves had sensitive enough hearing that, at this range, he should be able to home in on a heartbeat.

Had whoever'd been in the attic fled?

He leaned in, putting him so close she could feel his body heat. Wolves ran warm, she reminded herself. Like that fact was going to distract her from his sudden proximity. "I'll pull down the steps. You keep the opening in your sights."

"Okay. On my signal." She went through the door, training her gun on the attic access as she moved into position below.

He followed and grabbed the cord but kept his eyes on her. They were across from each other, separated by a few feet. She nodded, and he yanked the panel down.

The stairs stayed folded up against the panel, and the hinge creaked with disuse. How had neither of them heard the creaking before? The space above was dark, and there was no sign of movement.

She stood there, gun aimed, body tensed for action. "Nocturne Falls Sheriff's Department. Show yourself now."

Nothing. No movement, no sound. With her eyes still on the space, she spoke to Titus. "Can you get the light on up there?"

He tried a few switches. The third one did the trick. Light blazed from the rectangle in the ceiling, and she could clearly see the trusses holding up the roof. No signs of life, though.

"Stairs?" he asked.

She nodded and moved so she was at a forty-five-degree angle from the opening.

He was tall enough to reach the bottom rung easily and pull down the steps.

Once he secured them, she moved forward. "I'm going up."

"Are you sure?"

She frowned at him. "It's my job."

"Right."

But she wasn't just going to climb those steps and make herself a target. Instead, she put both hands on her weapon to secure it, then jumped, landing neatly at the top of the expanded steps. With great speed, she cleared both sides of the attic. "No one up here. But there is a vent on the far wall that could be removed and used for access if the person was small enough."

She moved to see past one of the trusses. "There's also a small box sitting in the middle of the open space on the left side where the floor is finished. And the smell is pretty strong up here."

"How small?"

"About twelve by twelve." She glanced down at him. "I think we've been pranked."

"How?"

"This box might be a homemade stink bomb."

He frowned. "Great."

She lifted one shoulder. "It's almost summer. The kids are wound up from being in school all year. The summer crazies have begun. Or we might have some fledgling witches practicing their spells, that kind of thing. You never know."

"That's just perfect." He rolled his eyes. "The good news is I have a containment bag in my truck."

She made a face at him as she put her gun away. "For real?"

"For real. It's not really for stink bombs, but I'm sure it'll work. We had a skunk incident once." He grimaced and shook his head. "Don't ask."

She laughed. "Oh, I'm going to ask, but later. You want to grab it?"

"Sure. Be right back." He disappeared from view.

A second later, she heard the garage door going up, and natural light filled the space below. He came back in a couple of minutes with a large canvas contraption that was half bag, half box.

He climbed the steps to join her. She moved out of the way to let him go by, although there was so little area in the attic that he still brushed against her.

The nearness let her get a whiff of him again. Definitely a better smell than rotten eggs.

He opened the bag. "You want to hold this open while I lift the box in?"

"Sure." She took the bag from him, keeping the mouth wide.

He put a hand on one of the trusses as he went under it but yanked his hand back suddenly. "Son of a—there must be a nail sticking up."

His palm was bleeding from a long scratch. She frowned. "You caught yourself?"

He nodded. "I'll be fine. Wolves heal fast. Let's just get this thing and get out of here." He reached for the box, but as soon as he picked it up, it started ticking. Eyes wide, he looked at her. "Run."

He dropped the box as they both started to move, but before it hit the floor, it exploded in a shower of white powder and glittering particles.

They coughed and wheezed. Jenna tried to hold her breath, but she'd already inhaled some. It covered them and filled the air.

She was already feeling lightheaded. "We have to get out of here."

He nodded and reached for his radio. "We need help too."

She made it to the stairs, but she was in no condition to jump. Her vision had gone double. She turned around and got one foot on the first rung. Her hands were clammy, and her heart was racing. She squeezed the sides of the steps harder.

The floor below tilted and shifted like a carnival ride.

A thud and a low growl brought her head up.

An enormous wolf lay on his side next to the remains of the box. Titus had shifted. And apparently before he'd gotten to call for help, because she hadn't heard anything, and his radio lay a foot away from him now.

She knew that transforming was a natural response for a lot of shifters when they were hurt. Had the explosion done more to him than cover him in dust and glitter?

She pulled herself back up the steps to the attic floor. "Titus, are you okay? Do you need help?"

The attic light went oddly dim, and the entire space turned sideways.

No, it wasn't the attic moving. She'd fallen. She was too numb to get up. Her entire body was pins and needles and nonresponsive.

At least she could still breathe. The air was thick with the scent of wolf. Maybe because she was only inches from Titus. His fur looked so soft. If she'd been able to move, she would have reached out and touched it. His paws were huge. So were his teeth.

"The better to eat you with," she whispered. Then she giggled, loopy from whatever she'd inhaled.

A second later, the light that remained went completely out.

Titus hadn't meant to shift. He'd been about to call for assistance on his radio when the wolf had taken over, the urge driven by whatever had been in that dirty bomb. So he'd shifted, dropping the radio in the process, and then lost his ability to stand.

Now he lay sprawled on the attic floor in wolf form, paralyzed by the same cocktail of substances that had caused him to shift. He watched helplessly as Jenna came toward him and fell.

She ended up close enough to touch, but he was powerless to do anything for her. A little noise that almost sounded like laughter escaped from her, then she went utterly still.

He couldn't move, and his vision was getting blurry. He couldn't do anything but lie there and growl. Lot of help that was. After a few more seconds, he wasn't sure he'd even be able to do that anymore.

Everything wavered like it was caught in ripples of overheated air. For a moment, he panicked, thinking there was a fire, but he didn't smell smoke.

Then, in the shadows beyond the reach of the attic bulb, something moved. A trick of the light? Or maybe just him seeing things. That was more likely. He tried to lift his head for a better look, but his body wasn't responding to the signals his brain was sending out.

The shape came closer but remained a murky figure, impossible to see clearly. Except for a pair of eyes that glowed like live embers. As it drew near, Titus noted the form was generally human but so dark, it was almost like a shadow come to life. The edges ebbed and flowed as it bent near Jenna.

A hand shape snaked out toward her.

Titus's instinct kicked in. Jenna was in danger. With every ounce of energy and determination he had left, he snarled.

The shadow leaped back, staring at him. Scared? Surprised? Titus wasn't sure, but he wasn't letting up. His snarl deepened into the most menacing growl he could manage. The shadow creature snarled back, eyes blazing like a fire that had been stoked.

Then it disintegrated into little black threads of ether that disappeared like mist into the dark recesses of the attic.

Titus went quiet, breathing with his muzzle open. The spend of energy had exhausted him. But Jenna was safe. Or as safe as she could be with whatever toxins they'd ingested coursing through her.

They needed help. Hopefully, someone would notice them missing soon, because he could feel the contaminants in his system starting to win the battle.

As strong as his wolf was, he wasn't invincible. His eyes drifted closed. He forced them back open, but a moment later, the urge to sleep overwhelmed him again. He clawed against it, desperate not to lose consciousness, but whatever he'd inhaled was too strong.

He blacked out again even as he was thinking that he was failing Jenna somehow by not protecting her and how ridiculous she would think that was because she'd be the first to tell him she didn't need protecting.

The thing that stuck with him as he drifted into oblivion was the sense that her not needing protection was no longer true.

Titus awoke to Deputy Alex Cruz standing over him. At least he thought the person was Deputy Cruz. Hard to tell through the hazmat suit. He turned his head to check on Jenna. Good to know he could move again. She was still out, still lying beside him.

"Jenna," he whispered, throat dry.

"Don't move, Chief Merrow."

Yep. That was Cruz all right. "Why?" Titus asked. Hmm. Speaking meant he wasn't a wolf anymore. His body must have processed the toxins in the bomb faster than Jenna's. Or had he ingested less of it? That didn't seem possible, since he'd been closer to the bomb. Or…something else he couldn't think of.

"You're injured. There's blood on your palm."

"No, I cut myself on a nail." He flexed his hand. The wound was gone, but it still hurt a little. Nothing major.

"Can you tell me what happened up here?"

"Thought it was a prank. A stink bomb. But then the thing exploded, and whatever was inside knocked us out. Is Deputy Blythe all right?"

Cruz nodded. "Her vitals have been checked and they're fine, but we're hoping she regains consciousness soon."

"Me, too." Titus stared up at him, not quite ready to get to his feet yet. "Why are you in a hazmat suit?"

"There's a chemical smell in the air and a lot of white powder on the pulldown stairs and the garage floor. Standard operating procedure in a situation like this."

"Smart."

"Can you give me a few more details?"

"I responded with Jenna on a report of a gas leak, but there wasn't one. Just the smell of sulfur, probably so we'd think there was a leak. My meter picked up a trace of gas, but not enough to justify the smell. We heard a noise up here, came to check it out, and found the box. When I picked it up, it started ticking. A second later, it blew up, covering us with powder. We only lasted a few seconds after that."

"Okay, thanks." Cruz glanced toward the opening to the attic. "EMS is here. They're going to transport you to the hospital for further examination, but they can't exactly bring a gurney up here."

Titus bristled at the idea that he needed any kind of help. Even though he knew he did. "I don't need a gurney."

Jenna stirred and let out a soft exhale.

That was all the motivation Titus needed to move. He turned onto his side and pushed himself upright. A little wave of dizziness hit him, but he ignored it, just like he ignored feeling like he'd been turned inside out. "Jenna, are you awake?"

She didn't immediately respond.

Titus looked at Cruz. "We don't need EMS as much as we need someone who can analyze whatever we were dosed with. There was magic involved in this. Or witchcraft. Or both. Anyone who can take down a valkyrie, and keep her down, knows what they're doing."

Cruz nodded. "Yes, sir. We're actually working on—"

A voice shouted up from below. "Titus?"

Titus answered, "Up here, Hank."

"How's my deputy?"

"Not awake yet. And I'm good, too, thanks for asking." Titus got to his feet, using one of the trusses for support, careful to avoid nails this time. "I'll bring Deputy Blythe down."

"Sir," Cruz began, "with all due respect, you don't look—"

"Don't worry about me. I'm—" The ground beneath Titus's feet canted like the house had slipped sideways. The blackness returned and slid over him before he could get another word out.

Mechanical beeping and the smell of disinfectant woke Jenna. She opened her eyes, a little blinded by the sudden light. She blinked twice before her eyes focused on the concerned face of her sister.

"You're awake," Tessa said with a smile. "How are you feeling?"

"Like I just went ten rounds with a berserker." Jenna rubbed at the throbbing in her head. "Where am I?"

"The hospital."

Jenna looked around. Okay, that should have been obvious. There was no mistaking this room for anything else. How long had she been out? But more important… "Where's Titus? He was hurt too."

Tessa's smile widened ever so slightly. "He's in the next room."

"How is he? I think he took more of the blast than I did."

"He's doing all right. Do you need anything?"

To see Titus. In fact, the desire was almost overwhelming. So much so, it made her uncomfortable. Why should she care so much? She shouldn't. And yet, she did. Eagerly, she changed the topic. "Just for my head to stop throbbing. How long was I out?"

"A few hours. Mom's been trying to reach you. One of your friends from your time in the service called her, looking for your number to get in touch with you."

"Who?"

"I don't know. But I didn't tell Mom the reason you weren't answering your phone is because you're in the hospital."

"Thanks." Tessa was a good sister. "Did they find out who was responsible for that bomb? Do they know what chemicals were used on us?"

Tessa shook her head. "They didn't catch anyone yet, and they don't know what was used to drug you, but samples were taken for analysis. In fact, I brought you some clothes because your uniform has to be cleaned before you can wear it again. It's all covered in that stuff. Your Kevlar vest was okay, though."

"Thanks." She looked down at her hospital gown. "What did you bring me to wear?"

"A pair of my yoga pants and a sweatshirt. I didn't have time to go by your house."

"Okay. Who's analyzing the samples?" Jenna sat up a little, but it took some effort, which bothered her. She didn't like feeling weak, and she was ready to put this whole episode behind her. "Because I'm pretty sure there was magic involved in what happened to us."

Tessa put the bed's remote control in Jenna's hand. "Here, use this to adjust your position. Everyone seems to agree that magic, and probably witchcraft, is a factor. I know one of the samples was sent to Alice Bishop."

Jenna exhaled. "Good. Alice should be able to figure it out." Not only was the woman the most powerful witch in town, she was also the oldest,

27

most experienced witch. It was her magic that imbued the local water so that it clouded tourists' minds to the fact that real supernaturals walked among them.

Alice was the OG of witchcraft in Nocturne Falls.

A knock on the door was followed by a doctor coming in. "Hi there, I'm Dr. Navarro. How are you feeling?"

Jenna shrugged. She knew Dr. Navarro was human but that he'd recently been clued in to the reality of Nocturne Falls. In other words, he probably knew she wasn't *just* a sheriff's deputy. "I have a headache, but that seems to be it."

"We can get you some heavy-duty Tylenol for that, but with your metabolism, I'm not sure it would be effective."

"I'll be all right. When can I get out of here?"

"Whenever you're ready. All your vitals are normal, so we have no reason to keep you. I would strongly suggest you rest for the next day or two while your system rids itself of the chemicals you inhaled. You might have some short-term memory loss, but we expect that to disappear quickly."

Rest wasn't really her thing, but she wasn't going to tell the doc that. "Short-term memory loss, huh? That's interesting. Do you know what any of the chemicals were yet?"

He nodded. "We did find trace amounts of pentothal in your blood work. It'll be a few days before the rest of the labs are back."

She frowned. "Truth serum?"

"That's one of its uses. It's also a powerful sedative. We're pretty sure that's what knocked you both out."

"Wow. Anything else?"

"Nothing yet. We'll be sure to let you know when the rest of the labs are back." He smiled. "You're officially discharged. But remember, a day or two of rest. And if you start feeling unwell again, please come back. I know you're physically stronger than most of my patients, but I'm serious about the rest."

She nodded. "Thanks. I will. I'm sure I'll be fine."

"All right. Have a safe trip home. An orderly will be in shortly to take you downstairs."

Jenna held up a finger. "Just a second. Why do I need an orderly to take me downstairs? Are we talking wheelchair?"

Dr. Navarro nodded. "It's hospital policy."

"Yeah, that's not going to happen, so you can save him the trip."

"Jenna." Tessa's voice held all the signs of an imminent scolding. "It's hospital policy."

"I heard the man, but I'm a sheriff's deputy. What are people going to think if I get wheeled out like an invalid? They need to have confidence in me."

Dr. Navarro crossed his arms and gave Jenna a look that said he wasn't about to give in. "Maybe those chemicals affected you more than we realized. Maybe an overnight stay for observation is in order after all."

Jenna sighed. "Bring me the wheelchair."

Jenna thanked the orderly who'd wheeled her out, then got herself into her sister's car. Her headache seemed to be lessening. She felt pretty good. Especially because the hospital was now behind her. "Thanks for giving me a lift. Wait. Where are we going?"

"Your house. I guess that short-term memory loss is kicking in," Tessa said as she climbed behind the wheel and put on her seat belt. "And you're welcome for the ride. That's what family is for."

"Speaking of, how's Sebastian? Still grumpy?"

"He's not grumpy." Tessa started up her Mercedes SUV, a gift from the man himself on their one-year wedding anniversary. But Jenna wasn't jealous. On the contrary, she was ridiculously happy for her sister. And she really liked Sebastian. After all, he was the reason her sister had stayed in Nocturne Falls. "He's just a serious man."

"Which is why you're so well matched."

"I'm not *that* serious."

"You can be," Jenna said. "You've actually lightened up a bit in the last year or so."

"Thanks." Tessa's sarcasm was thick. "You're not exactly a barrel of monkeys, you know."

"Please. I'm a freaking delight."

Tessa snorted as she drove away from the hospital entrance. "Sure, if you think going to the range or drinking some beers is a good time."

"Everyone should practice their range skills. And excuse me for not liking fancy drinks."

Tessa smirked. "Wine is not a fancy drink."

"It is when it's five hundred dollars a bottle."

"Sebastian has good taste. And as far as range time goes..." Tessa shook her head. "We're valkyries. We have magical swords permanently etched into our backs, ready to be called forth and made real whenever we need them. I don't know about you, but I'm good."

"I'm a sheriff's deputy. Range time is mandatory."

"I know." Tessa stopped at the parking lot exit, looked both ways, then pulled out.

Pain immediately shot through Jenna's gut. She clutched at her stomach, bending over at the sudden onslaught. "Owww. Holy Loki, that hurts."

Tessa pulled over. "What's wrong?"

The pain intensified, leaving Jenna almost unable to get the words out. "I...don't...know. Bad pain. Bad."

Tessa whipped the SUV around. "I'm taking you back."

"No…okay." Jenna groaned, still bent double by the stabbing, searing whatever-that-was happening in her middle. It felt like someone was trying to tear her insides out with a claw hammer.

For a librarian, Tessa suddenly had the driving skills of a Formula One racer. She screeched to a stop in front of the hospital doors they'd just come through, jumped out of the car, and ran around to Jenna's side. "Come on, let's get you inside."

But Jenna's pain was gone. She straightened. "I think I'm okay now. Maybe, um, it was just…gas?"

Tessa's look said no explanation was going to stop her from getting Jenna back into the hospital. "Out of the car, then, and you can walk in under your own power."

"I'm good. Really."

"Do not make me carry you. You know I can."

She could. Valkyries were incredibly strong. "You can't leave the car here. What if there's an actual emergency?"

"This isn't the emergency entrance." Tessa hooked her thumb over her shoulder. "Inside."

With a sigh, Jenna undid her seat belt and got out of the car. "Fine. I'll wait for you while you park." No way was she letting Tessa leave her here. Jenna wanted to be home. Whatever pain she'd felt in the car had to be some residual thing. After all, it had gone away almost as quickly as it had shown up.

She walked through the sliding doors to wait on Tessa.

Just then, an orderly came through the lobby.

"Is there a Jenna Blythe here? Jenna Blythe?"

She lifted her hand. "I'm Jenna Blythe. What's going on? Did I forget something?"

"No. Dr. Navarro would like to speak to you again."

She made a face. "He could have called."

"He tried. Please, if you could just come upstairs with me." The orderly held his hand out toward the elevators.

"As soon as my sis—"

"I'm here," Tessa announced.

Jenna turned to see her. "Apparently I have to go see Dr. Navarro again. Also, do you have my phone?"

"Because of the pain you had? They're really taking this seriously." Tessa dug in her purse. "And yes, I have your phone. I meant to give it to you."

The orderly's brows rose. "Ms. Blythe, did you say you had pain? Was it in your abdomen?"

Jenna took her phone from Tessa, nodding as she looked at the orderly. "Not long after I got in the car to go home."

The orderly seemed pretty interested in that. "We need to get you up to Dr. Navarro immediately."

"Lead the way," Tessa said, looping her arm through Jenna's.

Jenna frowned at her sister. "You seem pretty eager to get me examined again."

"I just want you well, sister dear."

They went with the orderly, who introduced himself as Chuck, back to the floor Jenna had just been on. At the nurses' station, Chuck had Dr. Navarro paged.

The doctor arrived a few minutes later with a worried smile on his face. "I'm very glad to see we got you back. There appears to be a complication we were unaware of."

That caused a slight moment of panic in Jenna. She didn't like complications. "What's that?"

"Severe abdominal pain."

Tessa gasped. "She just had that. Just as I pulled out of the parking lot. She was doubled over."

Dr. Navarro nodded. "Chief Merrow experienced the same thing. Probably right around the same time. We don't know what's causing this, so we'd like to run a few more tests."

Jenna's jaw muscles tightened up. "What you're saying is you want to readmit me?"

"Yes. At least until we can get the results of these new tests."

She got angry, and she wasn't sure why. It was all very logical. If there were complications, what other choice did they have but to try to figure them out? And yet, something was ticking her off in a way that made the sword lying against her spine tingle with the desire to taste blood.

And when *Helgrind* wasn't happy, neither was Jenna.

Then it came to her like a swift kick to the backside. "I need to see Titus."

The day Titus had been in the car accident that had nearly killed him, he'd been pretty banged up and plenty bruised. But shifters healed fast and had a high tolerance for pain, so he'd gotten through it.

Whatever had happened to him up in that attic was nothing compared to that day. And yet, he was grumpy and irritable, and the pain he'd experienced a few moments ago had felt like someone was trying to cut him in half.

Maybe that's what was making him so mad. Pain, with no real reason or explanation, seemed unfair. But then, life was unfair. Proof of that was him in this hospital bed when he should have been at the station, taking care of—

Three quick raps on his door interrupted his line of thought. "Come in."

He expected Dr. Navarro.

Instead, Jenna walked in.

It was like the clouds had parted to allow the sun through. And what a lovely sun it was. He smiled. "Hey. How are you doing?"

She smiled back. "I was just about to ask you the same thing."

Her hair was pulled back in a ponytail, she was wearing yoga pants and a sweatshirt, and she looked beautiful. But then, she *was* beautiful, so her outfit made no difference. He took a breath, much happier than he'd been a moment ago. "I had some pain earlier, but I feel all right now."

"Yeah," she said. "Me too. Apparently, we had it at about the same time. I was discharged, but the pain is why I came back. Dr. Navarro wants to readmit me for some more tests. You too?"

He nodded. "Same. And I'm ready to be out of here."

"Yeah, I'm not a big fan of hospitals."

"Who is?"

"Right?" Jenna sighed. "I just sent my sister home. I figure there's no point in her waiting on me when I have no idea when I'll be able to leave."

"Hopefully, it won't be much longer."

She stared at the railing on the side of his bed, looking very much like she had something else to say. "I'm sorry you got dragged into all of that at the house."

Apologies couldn't be easy for her. That she felt compelled to give him one meant something. "Hey, we were both doing our jobs. And injury comes with the territory."

"It does." She smiled again, but it wasn't as bright or as wide as the one she'd walked in with. "I'm glad you're okay."

"You too." He pushed himself a little more upright in the bed, a fleeting image of something dark and shadowy speeding through his head. It was too quick for him to grasp, but it left him with a question for her. "You have any idea who might have done this?"

"No. Not a clue. I need to talk to Hank. See if they were able to recover any prints off the box or—"

"Did I hear my name?" Hank strode into the room and closed the door behind him. "Glad you're both here. How are you doing?"

Titus answered first. "Well enough to be home."

"Same," Jenna said. "Except I'd prefer to be back at work."

"About that," Hank said. "I have some news."

"Good or bad?" Titus asked.

"Yes," Hank answered.

"Whatever it is, it's better than no news at all." Jenna's brows lifted. "What did you come to tell us, Sheriff?"

Hank took a breath and pulled out his phone. He tapped the screen a few times, bringing up what looked like a long text message. "Alice Bishop completed a partial analysis of the powder sample we gave her. There was definitely witchcraft involved, but not any kind she's familiar with."

"And pentothal," Jenna added. "That was involved too."

"Truth serum?" Titus looked at her with surprise.

So did Hank. "Who told you that?"

"Dr. Navarro," Jenna said. "I guess he hasn't had a chance to share that with you. He thinks it's what knocked us out. And it could cause us some short-term memory loss. Anyway, what else did she find?"

Hank glanced at his phone again. "There were a few elements Alice has yet to identify. The pentothal is probably one of those, since it's of human origin, and she's focused on the organic components. But what she has found so far includes rue, gold, ground rose petals, and mugwort, to name a few. Seems it was a whole cocktail of ingredients, none of which means much to me, but the bottom line from her is the bomb had a lot going on. More than one spell. As best she can tell, it was a love potion and a binding spell."

"A love potion?" Jenna blinked but didn't make eye contact with Titus. "That's random. Except…I'm sure Pandora Williams is the listing agent on that house. I'd like to talk to her, see if she has any ex-boyfriends that might be up to a stunt like that."

"Because of the love spell?" Hank asked.

"And the binding spell. That's a pretty stalkerish combination."

Hank nodded. "That it is."

Titus didn't feel especially in love with Jenna, but he also couldn't remember why he'd ever thought she was annoying. He frowned. "You think Pandora's in trouble?"

"Could be." Jenna looked at Hank. "Maybe we should get someone over to her office. Verify she's all right and hasn't had any unwanted visitors lately."

Hank put his phone away and reached for his radio. "I'll get someone on it, then fill Birdie in."

While Hank made his call, Titus pondered the information about the love spell a little more. Was that why he suddenly thought Jenna was so beautiful? She *was* beautiful. All valkyries were, but he felt like he was noticing her beauty in a way he never had before. Hmm. Was this line of thinking proof that the spell was affecting him?

Hank finished talking to Birdie and looked at his brother and Jenna again. "All right. Deputy May is on her way over there to talk to Pandora."

Jenna chewed on the inside of her cheek. "You said you had good news and bad news. What's the good news?"

Hank thought a moment. "That Alice has started to figure it out."

"Oh." Jenna looked like she'd had hopes for something else. "And the bad is the love spell and the binding spell."

"Right," Hank said.

Titus realized they'd glossed over the second one. "What's the part about the binding spell? Can you explain that?"

Hank glanced at his brother, his gaze lighting up with the most curious gleam. "That's where it gets interesting."

"Like it wasn't already?" Titus frowned. "I don't like where this is going. Tell us what you know."

Jenna nodded. "Please."

Hank took his phone out again. "Whoever set up this little magic bomb apparently intended for the target to not only fall in love with them but be bound to them. Like you said, a very stalkerish combo."

Jenna held out her hands. "We're not bound to anyone."

The corner of Hank's mouth twitched like he was trying not to smile. "But you are. You two are not only under the influence of a love potion, but it seems you're now bound to each other."

Jenna sat down hard on the utilitarian love seat near the window. "Bound. To Titus. By magic?"

"Wait a second," Titus said. "Is that even a thing? I mean, how do you know it's working? There's no magical force keeping us together." Thankfully, because being bound to Jenna would be a nightmare. Planning the race with her was already testing the limits of his good nature. He couldn't imagine having to be around her all the time.

Except that he could. In fact, he was. And the things he imagined were raising his temperature in ways that were only going to get him in trouble.

"Alice said," Hank began, "that if you two get too far away from one another, you'll feel the consequences."

"Consequences?" Jenna looked at Titus with the same panicked expression he probably had on his face. "If that's true…"

Titus nodded. "We already have."

Jenna couldn't fathom what she was hearing. Bound to Titus? The man who'd made her life miserable these last few months? And under some kind of love spell, to boot? She refused to accept that was possible, magic or not. Sure, he was a very attractive guy who was probably a great kisser, but—wow. What was that? She shook her head. "Nope. Don't want that. Don't want the love spell either."

Hank snorted. "I don't think it works that way."

"I don't care. I'm a valkyrie. I have my own magic." She'd just use the sheer force of her willpower to negate whatever magic had been performed upon them. She looked at Titus. She was not going to let herself be influenced by…he really did have the nicest eyes.

Freya on a stick, she was in trouble. She was not falling in love with anyone. Ever again. Love meant heartache. And she'd had enough of that for a hundred lifetimes.

"Good luck with that," Titus said. "Isn't valkyrie magic just swords and stubbornness?"

Jenna glared at him. "Oh, suddenly man's best friend is an expert on valkyrie magic?"

Titus glared back. "I'm a wolf, not a—"

"There's my favorite nephew!" Birdie Caruthers strode into the room with all the calm and quiet of a category five hurricane. She wiggled her fingers at Jenna, making the hot pink fringed handbag hanging off her elbow sway. "Hiya, Jenna."

"Hi, Mrs. Caruthers."

Hank frowned. "Aunt Birdie, you realize I'm standing right here."

"Settle down." She wrinkled her nose at him. "You're my favorite healthy nephew. Now don't be so needy."

"I'm not—" He sighed and shoved a hand through his hair. "I'd better get back to the station, because clearly no one else is there."

Birdie rolled her eyes. "There's someone there. Probably."

"Sheriff?" Jenna stood.

He paused on his turn toward the door. "Yes?"

"Is Alice working on a way to break these spells?"

He nodded. "She is. Or rather, she will be. She has to figure out all the remaining ingredients first, but then hopefully she'll be able to come up with something."

"Until then, what am I supposed to do?"

Hank looked from her to Titus. "That's up to you two. I'll get someone to cover your shifts until you figure that out."

Titus made a face. "I have the inspector coming in this week. I have to be at the station."

Jenna put her hands on her hips. This was a complication she didn't need. "And the race is coming up."

"Like I said, figure it out." Hank turned, lifting his hand in a wave.

Jenna huffed out a breath and sat back down, staring at the door as it closed behind him. "This is unacceptable."

Birdie sat down beside her. "What's that, honey?"

Jenna turned to the older woman. "This whole thing. But especially that your nephew and I are apparently bound together because we were exposed to a magic bomb."

Birdie looked way too amused by that. "Is that right?"

Titus let out a little grunt. "You're kind of glossing over the big one."

"Oh?" Birdie said.

"We're also under the influence of a love spell. Apparently." His gaze shifted to Jenna. "I can't say as I feel particularly amorous, however."

"Good," Jenna said. "Let's keep it that way." But inside, she was the slightest bit miffed. Was he really not attracted to her even the tiniest bit? How was he ignoring the magic's pull when she was definitely feeling it? Of course, she was also ignoring it. Hard. But feeling it all the same.

"So what are you two going to do if you can't be apart?" Birdie asked.

Neither Jenna nor Titus answered right away.

"Well?" Birdie said.

"I guess we haven't thought that far," Titus finally replied.

"What we need is for Alice to work out a way to dissolve the spell." Jenna stood. "Maybe we should test just how far apart we can get." She already had an idea about that based on where she'd been in the parking lot when her stomach had started hurting, but the truth was, she was outnumbered by werewolves at the moment and needed some air. Air that wasn't saturated with the scent of Titus.

He raised his brows. "Where were you when your stomach started to hurt?"

She sighed. He was ruining her chance to escape. "Pulling out of the parking lot."

He looked out the window. "This room is almost directly over the main entrance, so that makes the lot exit about, what? Thirty yards? I think we can use that as a gauge."

Birdie whistled. "A hundred feet? That's it? Doesn't give you two a lot of options, huh?"

Titus made a face. "No. It doesn't."

"So," Birdie said. "Whose house are you going to live in when you get out of here?"

Titus looked at her. So did Jenna. Then they looked at each other. In horror.

Jenna recoiled. "I can't live with you."

He shook his head. "I'm not living with you."

Birdie laughed like it was all a big joke. "You two.

So funny. What other option do you have? You can't be away from each other. Look on the bright side. It'll be easier to work together on figuring out who planted that package."

"That's not the job of the fire department." Jenna paced to the door. "And Alice will have a remedy soon. I know she will." Jenna knew nothing of the sort, but she refused to believe anything different.

"And if she doesn't?" Titus asked.

A nurse came in, saving Jenna from having to answer. "There you are, Deputy Blythe. We're ready to start the new round of tests now. If you could just come with me. Chief, Nurse Lawrence will be in for you shortly."

Jenna hesitated. "Where are we going?"

"Back to your room next door. I have everything set up in there."

"Okay, great." Jenna exhaled, glad she didn't have to explain why she couldn't go too far away from Titus. The hospital was a mix of human and supernatural workers. This nurse was definitely human. "Let's get this testing done so we can get answers."

That was paramount. Because living with Titus could not happen. It was one thing to be stuck in a room with him, but to be with him twenty-four seven? She might be a legendary warrior with the stubbornness of a thousand hellborn mules, but she was also a living, breathing, red-blooded woman with needs and urges and... She swallowed and glanced back at Titus.

Even lying in that hospital bed and wearing that silly gown, he radiated maleness. The kind that turned up her internal thermometer and put her hormones into overdrive.

Being around him for any length of time would definitely break her.

As soon as Jenna left with the nurse, Birdie went to stand closer to Titus. She took his hand and patted it. "Are you really feeling okay?"

"Sure. A little headache, but that's probably just because I need to get all the garbage I inhaled out of my system."

"A nice run in the forest would do you good."

He smiled. "It would. That's exactly what I'm going to do when I get out of here."

"With Jenna, of course."

He sighed. "Thanks for reminding me."

Birdie laughed. "Oh, Titus. Stop that. She's a beautiful woman. Accomplished. Smart. Wicked sense of humor. A body like—"

"Aunt Birdie." He narrowed his eyes. "Can you stop selling her to me?"

"Do you really not like her?"

"She's a pain in the—"

"Language." But Birdie smiled. "Why does she bother you? Because you're so much alike?"

"We are not."

"No? I think you are. And I know you both pretty well."

"Then you should know how annoying she is. She's stubborn and opinionated and, frankly, a little full of herself."

Birdie rolled her lips in like she was trying not to laugh. "You know who that sounds like?"

"Don't say me."

"I was going to say Bridget. And you love your sister."

He opened his mouth to respond, then closed it. Bridget *was* all those things. "That's different."

"How?"

"She's a werewolf. You know how we are."

Birdie's eyes tapered into her *don't start with me* look. "And Jenna is a valkyrie. A legendary Norse warrior tasked with combing battlefields for dying soldiers worthy of being taken to Valhalla. The woman has a magical sword embedded in her back. You think that doesn't entitle her to be a little full of herself? To know her own mind?"

"Okay, okay. You're right. But I still think she's annoying."

Birdie's sly smile was back again. "Of course you do. Sometimes that's how chemistry works."

A nurse came in, interrupting the conversation. But Titus refused to buy what his aunt was trying to sell. Any strange thoughts or feelings he was having about Jenna were all caused by the spells they were under. Nothing more.

Time would prove that out.

Jenna had been back in her hospital room for about thirty minutes when Titus pushed the door open and came halfway in. She put her magazine down. He was in track pants and a T-shirt. There was something infinitely appealing about seeing him like that. Casual. Sporty. "Hey."

"All done with your testing?"

She nodded. "You too?"

"Yep. Just waiting for those test results so I can be discharged, probably like you are."

"I am."

He pointed toward her. "Can I come in?"

"Sure."

He walked through the door, leaving it open. "Heard anything from Alice?"

She let out a long, slow breath. "No. You?"

"Not a word." He stopped at the end of her bed. "Which means we need to get to work figuring this out."

She stared at him, jaw set in frustration because she hated the situation they were in but also because she hated how handsome he was. And hated how she was losing the fight against the magic spell they were under. "I assume you mean the living arrangements?"

He nodded. "Unless we both want to be in constant pain, I don't see that we have a choice but to bunk together. I mean, not *together* together, but—"

"I know what you mean, Merrow." She shifted her gaze to the window for a moment. Why did he have to be so unintentionally charming at times? Like now. It wasn't helping. She got herself under control and made eye contact again. "How big is your house? And where do you live?"

"I live in Wolf Creek."

"Of course you do." Most of the wolf shifters in town lived there because that community was up in the hills and gave them instant access to the forest that surrounded Nocturne Falls. It was a very nice place. Out of her financial reach as a deputy. Not that she wanted to live with a bunch of wolves. On a rainy day, that whole area had to smell like wet dog.

"Hey, it's where my kind lives. What about that bothers you?"

She shook her head, instantly sorry she'd snapped. "Nothing. I'm sorry. It's really nice up there. I'm just on edge, I guess."

"We both are." He blinked like he couldn't believe she'd apologized.

She couldn't either. And she seemed to be doing

that a lot around him. This stupid love magic was changing her. He seemed unaffected, oddly enough. "Yeah."

"I have a decent guest room with its own bathroom. It's all yours. But it would be a little farther to work for you."

She laughed softly, suddenly amused by the whole thing. "I don't think work matters, because I can't go on patrol unless you're with me."

"Oh. Right. And there are days that I'll have to be at the station, with the inspector there." He put his hand on the back of his neck. "This is going to take some getting used to."

"Hopefully, it'll be over before we get used to it."

He nodded. "That would be optimal."

"So I guess we'll go by my place, and I'll pack what I need, then we'll go to yours?" Had she left any bras hanging up to dry? She genuinely couldn't remember. Her mind seemed to have a big blank spot in it. Maybe she'd hit her head when she'd gotten knocked out and fallen? Or was this the short-term memory loss kicking in? Whatever. She'd have to check the second bath as soon as she got in the door.

"Sounds good."

Dr. Navarro came in, a tablet tucked under his arm. "Deputy, Chief. Since you're both in here, I'll tell you at the same time. Unfortunately, the tests have been inconclusive. You're both discharged, though, so you're good to go. Please rest as much as possible. If the abdominal pain reoccurs, please don't hesitate to call or come back in."

"Thanks," Jenna said. "Do we have to wait on wheelchairs again?"

Dr. Navarro's sympathetic smile answered her question. "The orderlies will be along shortly." He gave them a wave and left.

Titus put his hands on his hips and huffed out a breath. It was a very wolfy sound. "A wheelchair. Can you believe that?"

His words held the kind of attitude she'd felt earlier. "I know, right? It's regulation, though, and there's no use arguing."

He glanced at her. "Because you tried?"

"I did. Got nowhere."

He sighed. "Waste of time and money. I'm—that is, *we're* both perfectly capable of walking ourselves to the parking lot." He made a face. "Hey."

"What?"

"I just realized we have no vehicle. And no one here to give us a lift."

"You want me to call the station? Have them send a squad car?"

"No, we shouldn't pull them off duty." He reached into his pockets but came up empty-handed. "I don't have my phone either."

"I have mine. Tessa had it. But I know our uniforms have to be cleaned. Maybe your phone needed to be cleaned too?"

His brows rose. "We'd better call a nurse."

Chuck the orderly showed up with a wheelchair. "Your ride has arrived."

"Hi, Chuck." Jenna got up. "Is there a second one behind you? Also, do you have any idea where Titus's phone is? We need to call for a ride."

"I was about to give it to you." He pulled Titus's phone out of his pocket and handed it to him, then hooked his thumb over his shoulder. "Ben has the other wheelchair. Nurse Lawrence took the phones earlier to the nurses' station to disinfect them, but she forgot to bring the chief's back."

"No worries," Titus said.

"Yeah, thanks." Jenna climbed into the wheelchair he was driving and opened up her Ryde app to call for a car.

Titus was still muttering about the whole wheelchair thing even as he sat in the one meant for him.

She was having a hard time not laughing. She completely understood his grumpiness about it, but having been through it once, it was funny watching him. Maybe a little distraction would help.

She held up her phone with the Ryde app on the screen. "A car will be here in six minutes."

He stopped muttering. "Good. I'm ready to get out of here."

The ride down to the exit seemed to take forever, although Jenna remained amused by Titus's grumblings about having to go in a wheelchair.

The ride to her house took about the same amount of time. The driver was chatty, talking about the weather and how nice it was for picnicking, so they were saved the need to make polite conversation, something neither was much in the mood for.

Their driver pulled away as they walked up the steps of her front porch. Jenna went to stick her hand in her pocket, only to realize she didn't have any pockets in her yoga pants. She'd been tucking her phone in the waistband. No pockets meant she also didn't have the keys to her house. They were in her squad car. Which had probably been driven back to the station.

What was wrong with her? Not only was this not like her, but she was making herself look incompetent in front of a man who didn't need any more ammunition against her. She sighed, frustrated with herself. "Today is not my day."

"What's wrong?"

She couldn't bring herself to look at Titus. This was definitely going to get her mocked. "I don't have my keys. They're in the squad car, which I'm sure was driven back to the station. I don't know what I was thinking."

"Well, it has been a long day. Also, the doctor told us to expect some memory loss, remember?"

"I…think I do."

He had the nerve to look amused. "Don't you have a spare for the house hidden around here? One of those fake-rock things?"

She gave him a sharp look. He might be the fire chief, but he was still a civilian to her. "Are you kidding? Do you know how unsafe that is? That's the first thing burglars look for."

He was struggling not to laugh. "Do we have a lot of problems with burglars in Nocturne Falls?

Also, who would be dumb enough to break into your house?"

"No. And true. But still, I can't get into my house."

He was looking over her shoulder. "Don't you have a keypad on your garage door?"

She really was losing it. She sighed. "Yes. We can get in that way." She didn't wait for him, just went straight to the garage and punched in her code to lift the door.

It went up, revealing her tidy garage. She liked things neat. She also didn't like a lot of stuff. An abundance of clutter, especially the useless kind, stressed her out. All those knickknacks and decorative things other people filled their homes with? That wasn't ever going to be her.

What she had in her house and what she decorated with all had a purpose. Or in some rare cases where there was no obvious purpose, they were things she found beautiful or that brought her joy.

Less was definitely more to her.

A new thought struck her. What if Titus was a slob? Or just a really disorganized person? How long could she put up with someone else's mess? Not long. She might be batty in less than a week.

"Wow," Titus said. "This is one of the cleanest garages I've ever seen."

"Thanks." She watched his face closely. "So is your garage a hot mess?"

He shook his head. "I wouldn't say that. But it's not this neat."

That was code for *hot mess*. She just knew it. Trying

not to grind her teeth, she left the garage behind and went into the house. "I'll just be a few minutes. Have a seat if you like. Or help yourself to something to drink."

She went straight to the second bath. There were indeed some unmentionables drying on the little wooden rack she'd set up in the bathtub. At least she'd remembered them. She gathered all of it into her arms and turned for her bedroom down the hall.

And ran smack into Titus.

The tangle of brightly colored lace and silk exploding from Jenna's arms caught Titus off guard. If put on the spot and made to guess what kind of underwear she wore, he would have said white cotton. Or those nude colors a lot of women wore. His ex, Zoe, had always chosen those. Flesh tones. Because they were practical.

Nothing in Jenna's arms looked practical. Unless neon pink, bright blue and candy-apple red were the new nudes. There was even a lime green in there.

He couldn't stop staring. Worse, his mouth was open in surprise, and he couldn't be bothered to close it.

He'd never look at her the same way again. Jury was out on whether or not that was a good thing, given their current bespelled state.

"Do you mind?" She raised her brows. "You're in my way."

"Sorry, I was just…" What had he been about to do? He scratched his head. "Are you having trouble remembering things? I feel like I'm struggling with my short-term memory a bit. You think it's that stuff we were exposed to?"

She nodded, squeezing past him to get to her bedroom door. "Yes. Remember how I forgot my keys? And how you just told *me* the doctor said we'd forget stuff?"

"When?" Then he laughed. "Did I just prove my own point?"

She laughed, too, but more like she was laughing with him than at him. "I think you did. I won't be long. I just need to pack enough for a few days."

"Packing! That's what I was going to ask you." His head still wasn't right after being doused. "Do you need me to get anything together for you?"

"I don't think so—actually, you could go through the fridge and pack up all the perishables to take to your house. I have steaks in there I was going to make tonight. We could have them for dinner."

He nodded. "Okay, I can do that."

"My shopping bags are in the narrow lower cabinet next to the fridge."

"On it." He went into the kitchen but took a look around before getting to work. Her whole house was like her garage. Neat to the point of overkill. But then, she worked a lot. Maybe she just wasn't home enough to make a mess. There were much worse things than being neat.

He pulled out a shopping bag and opened the fridge.

Everything was lined up, label out. Even the half shelf of imported beer. He chuckled. Okay, maybe she was a little obsessive. Everyone had their quirks, right?

He loaded up the bag with everything that seemed important or perishable, then looked around the kitchen for anything else she might need. Was she a coffee drinker? There was a coffeemaker on the counter but no creamer in the fridge. Lots of cops took their coffee black, though.

Just because he was curious, he opened the freezer. More meat, some vegetables, and four containers of ice cream. Rocky road, triple-chocolate smash, chocolate peanut butter, and chocolate chocolate chip.

Someone had a little addiction. Good to know.

He peeked down the hall. She was still in the bedroom.

He opened a few of the kitchen cabinets. All just as neat as everything else he'd found. Plates stacked just so. Food grouped by kinds and arranged the same way as things in the fridge. Labels out. Tidy rows.

"Looking for something?"

He'd been caught. No point in denying the truth. He closed the cabinet and turned around. "Nope, just being nosy. Trying to see what you like and don't like. Since we're going to be living together."

"Don't say 'living together.' That makes this whole thing sound more salacious than it really is."

"Salacious? From the woman who gave me grief because I used the word 'keen'?" He laughed.

She smirked at him, but that was all the fuss she made. Just set down her large duffel bag and glanced at the shopping bag he'd filled. "I'm not a picky eater, if that's what you're trying to figure out. Did you get the steaks?"

He nodded. "And the cheese and lunch meat that was in there, too, plus the veggies that were in the crisper."

"Good. Thanks. Did you get the beer?"

"I have beer."

She made a face at him. "You have Warhammer Stout?"

"No. I have Coors. And I think some Sam Adams."

She snorted. "If I want bottled water, I'll buy some Fiji." She turned. "I'll get a crate from the garage."

She went out and came back in with a plastic milk crate, put it on the table, then started loading it with bottles. When it was full, she shut the fridge. "That'll do it."

He was too amused to keep quiet. "You realize that's *also* beer, right?"

"Warhammer Stout isn't beer. It's the nectar of the gods. Literally, the founder is a berserker, and rumor has it he stole the recipe from Valhalla."

Now Titus was curious.

It must have shown on his face. She laughed. "You can try a bottle."

"Thanks."

She put her hands on her hips. "We'll need to call for a ride again, either to the department or the station, to get one of our vehicles."

"I can do it." He pulled out his phone. "How do I do it?"

She squinted at him. "I'll take that to mean you don't already have the Ryde app on your phone, which means you don't have an account set up." She got her phone out. "I'll take care of it."

She tapped a few buttons, and they were set. "Eleven minutes."

"I assume we're going to the fire station first, since it's closer?"

"Yep. Then you can drive me to the department, and I'll get my car and follow you."

He nodded. "Sounds good. Should we wait outside? I can carry the groceries and beer, since you have your bag."

She gave him another look but said nothing. Probably she wanted to say something about how she was just as strong as he was. Maybe stronger. She was a valkyrie, after all. A very sexy—whoa, where had that come from? He knew where. He just didn't want to admit it.

But it had to be the love spell. There was no other explanation. Was she feeling it too? She wasn't really acting like it.

Was the spell also why he couldn't stop thinking about all those brightly colored underthings he'd seen earlier and why he couldn't stop wondering how many of them had made it into the duffel bag?

Whatever the answer, he had the distinct feeling he was already in trouble.

Jenna didn't want to be impressed with Titus's house, but she was. The Craftsman-style lodge home seemed exactly like the kind of house a rugged, alpha male werewolf would live in.

To be honest, the place looked very much like the sort of house she'd want to live in someday. From the square white columns that broadened into stacked stone foundations, to the crisp white trim and clean lines, the house had a strength about it. A presence that felt solid and unshakable. Like you knew whoever lived here was someone you could depend on.

She supposed that was precisely who the fire chief should be. And maybe Titus was that kind of guy. Most likely. She didn't know him that well. Didn't need to, either, no matter what the love spell was influencing her to do.

What did her house say about her? Probably not much. It was a simple three-bedroom ranch. Neat, well maintained, but it certainly didn't have this kind of charm or personality.

She'd parked her squad car in the driveway beside his fire chief's truck. She got out and stood there for a moment as Titus got out of his truck. "Do you think we should park in the garage? Or is your garage too full of stuff to actually fit cars into?"

His glance held a little moodiness at the question. "My garage might not be as empty as yours, but it's not full of junk either. Why do you want to park in there?"

Her brows bent. Did he really not get it? "You don't think having my car parked in your driveway is going to cause tongues to wag?"

"Is that another dog joke?"

"No. I'm just saying word's going to spread fast that I'm staying here." She'd never been one to give much attention to rumors or care what anyone said about her, but something about this situation made the impending gossip seem unfair.

"For one thing," he started, "we're together out of medical necessity. Or…magical necessity. Because of magic gone awry. If anyone can understand that, it's the citizens of Nocturne Falls. For another, for all anyone knows, that could be my brother's car. He does stop by every once in a while. He lives just down the street."

"Right, but does he often stay overnight?" Mostly, Jenna wanted to tell Tessa before she found out through the grapevine and assumed something else was going on.

"No. I guess I see your point. If you really want to park in the garage, I suppose I can make room."

"I don't want to put you out. Any more than I have. I just need to call Tessa and tell her what's going on. Everyone else can get bent." She hoisted her duffel over her shoulder, grabbed her purse, and headed for the front porch.

He snorted. "There you go. That's the right attitude."

She walked up onto his porch. There was an actual swing. A really pretty one too. Looked custom made. If she had one of those, she'd sit in it all the time. "Hey, that's cool."

"You like that?" Titus asked as if he didn't believe her. Or wasn't sure if she was making a joke or not. He joined her at the front door, his keys jangling in his hand.

She realized she was smiling. "Yeah, it's really nice. You must use it all the time."

He shook his head. "Nope. Not at all."

"Really? Why not? I'd be out here every—"

"Let me get the door unlocked." He set the crate of beer down, then shifted the bag of groceries to his other arm so he could slide the key in. A second later, he swung the door wide. "After you."

He'd cut her off so quickly about the swing, she knew better than to ask again. But why? Since when was a porch swing a touchy subject? Maybe he'd tell her after a Warhammer Stout. That brew had a way of loosening up those who weren't used to its punch.

"Thanks." She walked into the house, unsurprised

that it was equally as beautiful on the inside. And thankfully, pretty uncluttered.

Sure, he had more stuff than she did, but it all worked well in the space. The whole Craftsman cabin look of shelves filled with books, throw pillows spread about, and rag rugs gave off a very cozy vibe. Here and there were small objects that looked like they held significance. Like the red and yellow crudely crafted mug that sat on the fireplace mantel. It had to have been made by a child. Unless Titus had terrible taste in pottery.

"Kitchen's this way." He walked past her and through the dining room.

She followed, taking in the house as they went. It wasn't a large house, but it was considerably bigger than hers. More open, really. And, well, just bigger. At the back was a wall of sliders that looked out over a huge rear deck and the forest that lay beyond.

That alone made it easy to see why he liked living here. All that green. So inviting. And how nice not to have neighbors behind you. Her backyard butted up to the Stewarts. Nice people but sometimes noisier than she liked.

They went into the kitchen, and he flipped the light on, which wasn't really necessary because of all the natural light already filling the space.

The kitchen continued the heavy presence of wood in the house with beautiful caramel-colored cabinets topped with polished tan-and-black granite. The wrought-iron handles and pulls on the cabinets pulled the whole thing together.

It was a man's kitchen for sure, but she liked it. More interesting than her plain white with brushed-nickel hardware.

She especially liked that his fridge was covered with kids' drawings and school pictures. It was unexpected and disturbingly heartwarming. He was clearly a proud uncle, and there was something undeniably sweet about that. Which sucked in a way. She didn't want to like this guy. Not more than a usual level of like.

But she had to give him props for the space he lived in. "This kitchen is beautiful. Like something out of a magazine. Your whole house is, really."

"Thanks." He put the beer and groceries on the long center island that divided the cooking area from the dining room across from it. "There's room for some of your beer in the refrigerator, but I usually keep drinks in the garage fridge."

"I can put them out there, no problem. So did you decorate the house yourself?"

He tilted his head back and forth as he started putting her groceries in his fridge. "My sister, Bridget, helped. So did my mom a little. But I had final say on everything. That was our deal."

"Well, the three of you did a fantastic job."

He nodded. "My mom and Bridget are really good at that kind of stuff. Bridget designed Howler's, you know."

"I didn't know that. I love that place."

"I know. I see you in there sometimes."

"Mostly on Thursdays every couple of weeks."

That was usually the night she hung out with the other deputies after work. "I see you too. But I guess you go there a lot since your sister owns it."

He laughed, but there was a self-deprecating undertone. "Every night, pretty much."

Her brows went up. "Really?"

He laughed again, harder this time and without any edge. "Don't worry, we can stay in. I realize eating out every night isn't normal."

"Hey, it's normal for you, so that's cool. I just don't have the budget to eat out every night."

"Bridget doesn't charge me."

"Because you're her brother. I'm not family. I wouldn't expect or want her to feed me for free."

"Right, good point." He put the last of her supplies into the fridge.

She folded the reusable grocery bag now that it was empty. "I suppose that means you're not much on cooking, then."

"I'll have you know I'm an excellent cook."

"And yet you eat out every night?" She tilted her head in disbelief.

He shrugged. "I cook a lot at the firehouse. And it's hard to go from cooking for a crowd to cooking for one. Plus, it's easier to eat at Howler's."

"That makes sense, I guess." She hoisted the crate of beer. "Which way to the garage?"

He started forward. "I'll get the door."

His gentlemanly tendencies weren't helping her not like him. "I can get it. Really. Just point me. If I'm going to be here until this spell is removed, and we're trying not to let it get the best of us, you might as well just treat me like one of the guys."

He took one more step forward, which put him in her personal space. "What's wrong with treating you like the woman you are? I don't want to treat you like one of the guys. Because you *aren't*."

"I…" He was so close words failed her. She could smell that fresh forest scent again. She shook her head, finding her voice. "You're letting the spell get to you."

"No, I'm being the man my mother raised me to be." He took the crate out of her hands. "Come on, I'll show you to the garage."

He walked ahead, leaving her no choice but to follow. And to admire his mother for the fine job she'd done.

Jenna might have also admired the way his track pants fit his lean lower half, but she'd never admit to that in a court of law. She could do only so much to prevent the spell from working on her. As long as she could keep the effects to herself, she'd be fine.

She hoped. And said a little prayer to Freya that it would be so.

Halfway down the hall, he opened a door but paused, turning to nod at a door across the hall. "That's the powder room. Guest room is the next door down, and it has its own bath."

"That's nice."

He nodded. "Pandora suggested it when I built the house."

"You built this house?"

He laughed. "No, I mean when I had the house built."

Inwardly, she sighed with relief. She had a soft spot for men who were handy like that. Finding out he'd built this place might have given her weak knees, as odd as that might be. "Oh, right."

"Anyway, this is the garage." He pushed the door wider with his hip and went down the steps.

She was right behind him when he flipped on the switch, and she understood why they couldn't park in the garage.

He was using it as a woodworking shop.

The smell of lumber filled the space with a rich aroma. She blinked twice. "This is all yours? I mean, you're making all this stuff?"

He nodded. "The rocking chair is for Aunt Birdie's birthday. The rocking horse is for Hannah Rose."

Oh, this was as bad as thinking he'd built the house. Maybe worse. He was handy. Not just ordinary handy, but the kind who made beautiful things. *Useful* things. She walked toward a small, gorgeous stand. She wasn't sure what it would hold, a vase maybe? But the color and shine of the wood, combined with the scrolling pattern carved into it, made it hard to ignore. "This is really cool. Who's it for?"

He set the crate down, opened the fridge, and started adding her bottles to one of the shelves. "Agnes Miller. She owns the Bell, Book & Candle."

"I know the shop, of course, but I don't think I've ever met her. What kind of wood is this? I've never seen anything like it."

"Katalox. I'd never worked with it before, but it's what she requested. It's very hard and very dense. Heavy too. Not easy stuff. But it's what she wanted."

"It's really cool. It's a stand, right? What's it for?"

"To hold her crystal ball. In fact, I need to deliver it tomorrow since it's done."

That got Jenna's mind working. "Is Agnes a witch, then? I think I knew that."

He closed the refrigerator. "She is. And a pretty good one."

"Maybe we could talk to her about our problem."

"That might be stepping on Alice's toes a bit."

"Titus. We have been hexed. The more help we can get, the better. We can tell Agnes that Alice is working on it too. Never hurts to get a second opinion."

He looked unconvinced. "I don't know if that's true where Alice is concerned. She can be…particular."

"What if we haven't heard anything from her by tomorrow when you go to see Agnes?"

"Fine. Then we can talk to her about what's going on." He shook his head. "Is this what you do to the perps you catch? Wear them down?"

She grinned. "Please, that was nothing."

His expression went serious. "Listen, I have a favor to ask."

He wanted something from her? She couldn't imagine what it was. "Sure. I mean, we're in this together. We have to get along. What's up?"

"I really need to run tonight."

"Okay, so run. Oh. Yeah. I'd have to go with you." She shrugged. "I can run. You think I can't keep up? I need to keep in shape for the 10K anyway. I'm the department's anchor, you know."

"I'm aware. But I'm not talking about that kind of run." He rubbed the back of his neck. "And it's not that I don't think you can keep up."

"You mean, like, a wolf run."

"Yes."

"So? I can run through the woods just as well as on the street. What's the problem?"

He frowned and looked altogether uncomfortable.

"Oh, for Odin's eye, just spit it out."

"You're not a wolf, and I've never run with anyone who wasn't." He let go of his neck. "I don't want to sound…selfish, but I either run with the pack or alone. And running with the pack isn't like running with someone else. It's hard to explain."

Not to her it wasn't. She crossed her arms. "You want me to keep my distance and let you do your wolfy thing." She lifted one shoulder like it was no big deal, which it wasn't. They both had to do whatever was necessary to keep the spell from getting the better of them.

"That doesn't bother you?"

"No. Why should it? You're a werewolf. I'm a valkyrie. We each have our things, right?"

He nodded. "Right. Thank you." He turned like he was going back into the house, then stopped. "In the interest of full disclosure, because I feel like the only way we're going to get through this is by being honest, the spell is definitely affecting me. But I'm doing everything I can not to let it change how I act toward you."

She exhaled, suddenly aware she'd been holding her breath. "Same here. Thank you for saying that. I know we rarely see eye to eye on things, but as long as we're civil, we'll get through this without killing each other."

The golden hint of wolfen glow lit his eyes. "I promise, what's on my mind isn't murder."

She straightened at the feral tone of his voice. "Titus. You can't say things like that to me. Being under this spell is hard enough without comments like that. I do have feelings, you know."

Feelings she was struggling to control. Maybe she should kiss him and get it over with. Prove to herself that the spell was causing all these thoughts, that there was nothing truly physical or chemical happening between them. Because a love spell might make her want to kiss him, but it couldn't create chemistry where there was none.

It was just magic. Plain and simple.

But what if it wasn't? What if this magic had unleashed something that had already been inside her?

That was ridiculous. But just in case, she shelved the kiss idea. Now wasn't the right time anyway. His eyes were already glowing.

And she had a pretty good idea of what that meant.

"What kind of feelings?" It wasn't a question he should have asked, but his body was betraying him, his control was thin at best, and the woman in front of him radiated the kind of feminine strength that filled him with desire even when he wasn't under a magic spell.

She shook her head, causing a few wisps of hair to swing free from her ponytail. "We shouldn't have this conversation."

"Why not? You think ignoring what's going on between us is going to make it easier to bear?"

"Yep. Sure. Let's go with that."

"You're lying to yourself if you really believe that." Had her lower lip always been that full? "I thought valkyries were all about honor and truth."

Her eyes narrowed at those words, the muscles in her jaw working. "Don't push me, wolf. We are not friends. We never have been. We only barely managed to be polite to each other when your brother forced us to work together on the race. Anything I feel for you is because of this spell. That's it."

He rolled his shoulders like he was bored. "Still lying. Sad. I always thought your kind were such noble—"

"Fine." She launched toward him, covering his mouth with hers in a move so fast she went from standing in front of him to pressed against him in a split second.

After a moment of shock, he closed his eyes. He wasn't going to protest, if that's what she was expecting. His hands found her hips easily. Like they'd been there a thousand times before. Like they'd be there again.

Her kiss was insistent. And maybe a little angry. She was trying to prove to him that there was nothing between them. He got that.

But once again, she was lying.

Desire had a scent, at least to his sensitive nose, and she was sending it out in waves. She wanted him, plain and simple.

The spell had created tiny little ignition points of need inside him. Now, the heady perfume radiating from her caused all those sparks to flare like Fourth of July fireworks, setting him ablaze.

A deep growl built in his throat, and he decided to show her just how much of a liar she was. He kissed her back. She was warm and willing and the most perfect combination of hard muscle and soft woman. He lost himself in the moment. In her.

His fingers dug into her hips, pulling her closer.

A rumble spilled out of her, deep and throaty and needful. It spoke to his wolf. The beast lifted his head and took notice.

The woman who'd been off-limits was now well within bounds.

But Jenna was no woman he'd ever experienced before. Although he didn't really remember any other woman besides Zoe. It had been too long.

This was a damn fine way to break that dry spell.

The thought made a laugh bubble up, breaking the kiss.

Jenna pulled back, flushed and looking like she'd just ridden through battle. He liked that look. It was wild and a little reckless but undeniably strong.

She heaved out a breath. "Why are you smiling?"

"Why aren't you? That was pretty amazing."

She shook her head. "It was just a kiss. To prove that there's nothing between us. You can turn off that glow in your eyes now and settle down."

"My wolf does what it wants."

She made an amused face. "Right. Your *wolf*. Well, then, get him a rawhide and tell him to chill."

"The creature inside me is a wild animal. Not a domesticated house pet. If you think that side of me is so easy to control, you're wrong."

Her expression said she wasn't taking this seriously, but she'd learn. If she was around him long enough.

He took a deep breath, which didn't help, because all he could smell was lemons and sunshine and desire.

"You're also wrong if you think that kiss proved your point. If anything, it proved the opposite. We definitely have chemistry. Sorry if that's a problem for you, but if we're going to deal with this spell, better to be honest about what's happening rather than to pretend nothing's changed."

"You want honest?" She squared her shoulders. "I'm not interested in you."

Sure. She was so uninterested, she'd kissed him. "Tell yourself whatever you need to. Doesn't matter to me. But don't confuse what you want, or don't want, with the truth. We're attracted to each other. Admitting that will help us get through this."

She lifted her chin ever so slightly. Her cheeks were still flushed and her bottom lip slightly swollen from the kiss he couldn't stop thinking about. "I'm *not* attracted to you."

He rolled his eyes. "All right, valkyrie. You go with that." He turned and walked back toward the house.

"I'm not," she repeated. Then a second later, she followed him. "Just show me the guest room, and I'll get out of your hair."

"Just so long as you're not more than a hundred feet away." He went inside, holding the door for her only as long as it took for her to get a hand on it.

He could practically feel how confused she was. He believed very much that she didn't want to be attracted to him. But she was. He knew that. Everything about that kiss, that *amazing* kiss, had said otherwise. So did her scent. The flush of her cheeks. The size of her pupils. The thump of her pulse.

She was struggling with what she was feeling. Obviously, he wasn't her idea of the perfect mate.

Truth was, she wasn't his either. But he also knew life didn't always turn out the way you expected it to. Zoe was proof of that.

He grabbed Jenna's duffel bag from the kitchen, then went back down the hall to the guest room. She kept up behind him.

Did valkyries even have mates? They must. Her sister, Tessa, married Sebastian Ellingham, so that was proof right there that valkyries had relationships. Was Sebastian Jenna's idea of the ideal man?

If that was the case, no wonder she wasn't interested in him. Titus didn't come close to having the kind of wealth and power that Sebastian had. He never would either. Didn't want it. His life was just fine the way it was. He had a job he was good at, a great family, great friends.

He tried to ignore the obvious missing link but couldn't.

He had no family of his own. He'd failed there. Zoe had chosen her parents over him. He didn't blame her for it. They needed her. Needed someone to take care of them. And she'd stepped up.

It was admirable, really.

But losing her had left him broken.

He pushed the guest room door open. "Here you go."

Jenna took the duffel bag from him and went in, looking around. "It's very nice. Thank you."

"You're welcome."

She turned, looking very much like she had something more to say. "What, uh, time do you want to run?"

"After dinner. Right around dark."

She nodded. "Okay."

There was more. He could feel it. He leaned against the doorframe, waiting.

She swallowed. "I'm sorry about the thing in the garage."

Well, that was a little vague. And he wasn't in the mood to let her off easy. "You mean you're sorry about kissing me?"

She closed her eyes for a moment. "Yeah. That. I really thought it would prove something."

"Oh, it did."

She sighed. "Can we just have a truce and get through this? I was wrong to kiss you, okay? I'm sorry."

"You have nothing to apologize for. I'm not mad about the kiss." Mad he wasn't getting another one, maybe.

"Well…thanks."

He straightened. Whatever she needed to get through this. "It's been a long day. Why don't you get settled in? If you want, after I shower I can fire up the grill and cook those steaks. If you're ready to eat."

"I am. That sounds good."

"About an hour, then." He walked away, down the hall to his room, doing his best to focus on another woman. Alice Bishop.

He had no idea how long it would take her to free them from this spell, but it was time for a phone call and an update. Because at the rate he and Jenna were going, they were either going to end up in bed together or kill each other.

Or both.

Jenna closed the bedroom door and exhaled. Why on earth had she kissed him? To shut him up? To prove there was no attraction? Because she'd really, really wanted to?

Maybe all three. She sat on the bed and lay back, closing her eyes. If those were her reasons, she'd failed. She hadn't shut him up. She hadn't proved there was no attraction. And she still really, really wanted to kiss him again.

They'd been under this spell for less than a day, and she was already losing her mind. And her ability to ignore Titus. He was becoming more irresistible by the hour, which was fueling her bad mood and her crankiness.

It wasn't a good combination. An irritable valkyrie could do impulsive things. Which clearly, she was prone to.

Maybe she could distract herself from thinking about the whole situation for long enough to relax. Unlikely, but worth a try. She pulled her phone out to call Birdie and found a text from her mom.

An old friend of yours from the service called, trying to track you down. Ingvar Swenson? Said she's coming to Nocturne Falls for some R&R. I told her where you work and gave her your number. I hope that was okay?

Memories, most of them very good, filled Jenna's head and made her smile. She and Ingvar had done their time in the ranks together and become close friends. It was a shame they'd fallen out of touch as life had taken over. Jenna typed in her response. *Of course that was okay! I haven't talked to Ingvar in ages. Thanks for letting me know. Love you.*

With that sent, she dialed Birdie's personal cell number.

"Hey, Jenna. How are you?"

"I'm okay. I know you're off work for the day, so I won't keep you. I just wanted to check in, see what had come of Deputy May talking to Pandora, or if anything was found at the house that might lead us to who planted that bomb?"

"Hold up. How are you feeling? Are you still at the hospital?"

"Pretty much like myself. And no, I'm at—" She almost said, *Titus's house.* Birdie would know that soon enough, but Jenna wasn't ready to share.

"Titus's house?"

Jenna rolled her eyes. How did the woman know everything? "Yes, but please don't say anything to anyone about that yet."

"You have my word. Glad to hear you're out of the hospital, though. Nothing new to share on the case yet, unfortunately. Pandora doesn't have any exes or possible stalkers that she can think of. House is owned by the Lemmons. They're selling because they're moving to Illinois to be near their grand-children. Nothing unusual going on with them either. Not that I can see. Still digging through their financials to check for anything strange."

"Okay." Birdie was nothing if not thorough. "No prints at the scene?"

"None so far that couldn't be identified and explained."

Jenna sighed.

Birdie clucked her tongue. "I know, it's frustrating. I promise I'll call the minute there's something new."

That lifted Jenna's mood a bit. "Thank you. I appreciate that."

"You got it. Now you better call your sister and let her know where you are."

"I was just about to do that. Have a good night."

"You, too, honey."

Jenna said goodbye, hung up, then dialed Tessa's number.

It took four rings for her sister to answer, and then she was out of breath. "Hello?"

"Did I catch you at a bad time?"

"No, no. Sebastian and I were just doing a little fencing. Are you still in the hospital? Home? What's going on? Do you need me to pick you up?"

"Slow down. I'm not at the hospital anymore, so I don't need you to pick me up."

"You're home? That's good."

"No, not home." Jenna took a breath. "I'm at Titus Merrow's. And will be until this spell is removed."

"Say what now?"

"The spell is multilayered and has a binding aspect. If Titus and I get more than thirty yards away from each other, we end up in tremendous pain. Like the pain I was in when you pulled out of the parking lot."

"A spell caused that? That's not good. It was nice of him to offer up his house. Yours would have been kind of small for all that man." Tessa snickered.

Jenna rolled her eyes. "Comments like that don't help."

"How's the love spell part going?"

"It's…going."

"That's not really an answer. Are you attracted to him? Outside of the spell, I mean. I know he gets on your nerves, but he's also your kind of guy."

"Back up. Why would you think he's my kind of guy?"

"First of all, *Real American Firemen* is your favorite reality TV show."

"It's *Real American Firefighters*, and I don't see what that has to do with any of this." So what if she'd downloaded every episode and watched each one multiple times?

"Did you get knocked on the head too?" Tessa laughed. "Come on! He's handsome, outdoorsy, good with his hands. He's a first responder, like you, so you have all that in common. He comes from a strong family. He's a supernatural like us. What's not to like?"

"You said it yourself. He gets on my nerves."

"Why is that?"

"Because he argues with everything I say."

"So you said you wanted to stay at your house, and he refused?"

"I don't mean that. I mean, like, whenever we've had to work together. The race, for example." Except that he hadn't argued with her on how to handle the gas leak.

"I think you're being obstinate. You are pretty stubborn."

Jenna sat up. "Whose side are you on?"

Tessa laughed. "The side of love."

"Oh, shut up. It's not happening."

Tessa let out a frustrated sigh. "I know you had your heart broken, but—"

Jenna stiffened. "This conversation is over. You know where I am and why I'm not home or at work. That's all I really called to tell you."

"Jenna, you have to know that Titus is not Eric."

Just the mention of that name made Jenna's vision go red around the edges. "I don't want to talk about him."

"Well, you should. You're obviously not over what he did to you."

Jenna's jaw went so tight she swore she heard something pop. "You know what he did to me. How he betrayed me. And with…*her*. That's not something that just goes away."

"I know, but—*oh*, I think I know now why you don't like Titus."

Jenna shook her head. "I don't want to talk about—"

"Yep, it all makes sense. It's because he has a broken engagement in his past, too, isn't it?"

A shudder went through Jenna, and painful memories washed over her, leaving her as numb and hurt as if they'd just happened yesterday. "Please," she whispered. "I don't want to talk about it."

"Okay," Tessa said, her voice softened by sympathy. "I'm sorry. But just know that there are good men out there. Sebastian is proof of that. And a good man can erase the damage of a bad one."

"Yeah. Thanks." But Jenna's head was elsewhere. Lost in the past and the pain that had been dealt to her. "I need to go."

"Call if you need anything."

"I will." Jenna hung up and tossed the phone on the bed, then stood and walked to the window. The forest beyond was deep and inviting. A run sounded pretty good right now. Maybe it would clear Eric from her head.

At least temporarily. Because she wasn't sure anything could remove him forever. Not after his lies and the way he'd humiliated her. Any man who could betray the woman he supposedly loved was not the kind of man she could ever be interested in.

And that included Titus. She didn't know the details of his past, just that he'd had a fiancée and that the relationship had dissolved. It was possible the woman had left him, she knew that, but it was a rare story that didn't have two sides.

So much as she might truly be attracted to him, she refused to allow herself to fall for another man who would break her heart.

She'd be celibate the rest of her life before that happened.

She sighed and tipped her head back. She hadn't let Eric into her head in a long time. Not like this. She'd really thought she was over him, but Tessa was right. Jenna was lumping Titus into the same category as her ex because of his past. She was allowing the results of her broken engagement to Eric to influence her perception of Titus.

It wasn't a fair thing to do. But protecting her heart was more important. Maybe she was protecting her pride a little too. She never again wanted to be as vulnerable as she had been with Eric. That's what love did. Made you vulnerable. And when love went wrong, it left you humiliated. She didn't need it.

She had her job. Her family. Her friends.

She didn't need love to be happy. Was she happy? What did that mean, anyway?

She was…content. And that was fine. That was safe.

But just thinking that way made her die a little inside. She was a valkyrie. *Safe* shouldn't be what she settled for.

And yet the pain of Eric's betrayal still lingered, making her accept safe as good enough.

Eric hadn't just broken her heart. He'd broken her spirit.

There was nothing okay about that.

After a quick call to Alice, Titus took a long, hot shower, then put on jeans and a Howler's T-shirt and went barefoot onto the back deck to fire up the grill. He stretched, enjoying the sunshine and breezes of the early summer evening. The fresh, earthy scent of the forest behind his house filled the air, along with the subtle buzz of insects.

Life was good, other than the current crazy spells he was under. And even then, there were worse people to be stuck in those spells with. For all her bluster and attitude, Jenna was beautiful and smart and never dull.

There were definitely worse choices.

He leaned on the railing and inhaled, filling his lungs with the clean air. Nocturne Falls was a great place to live. Especially up here in the hills. He couldn't imagine living anywhere else, really.

Tonight's run would be new and different with Jenna along. He hoped she would be able to enjoy herself. He needed this run. Needed to let his wolf burn off some energy.

He cranked up the grill, then went back inside to season the steaks. Bridget might wonder where he was when he didn't show up at Howler's, but then again, she knew what had happened today. She might just figure he went home to rest.

He sent her a quick text anyway. *Eating at home tonight.* Then he put his phone away and got to work on the steaks, sprinkling them with sea salt and freshly ground black pepper.

Jenna walked in wearing dragon-scale-print leggings and an NFSD T-shirt. Her hair was in a messy knot on top of her head, nothing like the perfect bun she wore for work. This was casual Jenna. Not a side of her he'd seen before.

He approved very much. "Hey."

"Hey. You have the grill going?"

"I do." He studied her. She looked…defeated somehow. Was the spell getting to her? "I put salt and pepper on the steaks. You good with that?"

"Yep. That's how I do them at home. Simple." She took a seat at the island, her lips pursed like she was struggling to find words. After a moment, she said, "Can we move past what happened earlier? Maybe start over and just be civil? And agree to keep it that way?"

He got out plates and utensils. They weren't going to need them for a while, but the activity kept him busy so he wouldn't have to look at her. "Sure. That's fine with me."

"Thank you. I need to say, too, that I mean it about keeping it civil. No matter what this spell does, I don't plan on giving in. It's not you. It's me."

He laughed without much humor as he put the plates and utensils on the counter. "That line usually comes at the end of a relationship, not the beginning."

"Well, I'd like our relationship to stay the same."

He finally turned to face her. "I wouldn't. Our relationship is…antagonistic. You said 'civil.' That'd be better than what we have now, so if that's what you really mean, then let's do that. I'd prefer it. We need to be able to work together."

"I know. The race."

"Also to figure out who set that bomb." He hadn't said a word about the creepy, shadow figure he'd seen, mostly because he was pretty certain it had been a hallucination. Also because he hadn't wanted to look like an idiot for telling her about something that had just been a figment of his imagination.

"No disrespect, but that's really more my job."

"I realize that, and I'm not looking to step on your toes. But I'm the only other eyewitness. And I'm trained to be observant. I can help, you know."

She nodded. "I know. I suppose that would be all right."

"I won't get in the way of your investigation."

She shrugged. "Not sure how much investigation I'll be doing from your office at the fire station. Not saying I won't work on it as much as I can, just that not being able to go into the field makes it harder."

"I'm not always at my desk, you know. I'm the chief.

I can go where I need to. And you need to investigate, so we'll make that happen."

"Except you said you have the inspector coming this week."

"I do, and I'll need to be there for his visit, but I'll be able to find a few hours here and there whenever you need to get out. There may be one day I can't leave, but it won't be the entire week."

"Okay. I really would like to move forward on this investigation."

"I'd like you to as well." He leaned on the counter. "Any idea who might have done this?"

"Not a clue. I talked to Birdie. She said they didn't find any useful evidence at the scene. And Pandora doesn't have anyone in her past she thinks would do something like this. Even the homeowners seem clean. I guess I need to see if Alice has turned up anything new."

"She hasn't. I called before I took my shower."

Jenna huffed out a breath. "That's disappointing."

"It is." He chose his next words carefully. She needed to know about what he'd seen, even if it was just a hallucination. "Did you see anything weird up in the attic? Besides the box with the bomb in it. Maybe right before you passed out."

Her eyes narrowed. "Like what?"

He shook his head. "Probably just a hallucination brought on by the stuff in the bomb, but I thought I saw movement in the shadows."

Her head came up a little. "You mean you think whoever set the bomb was still there?"

"Not exactly. Well, maybe. I don't know. It literally seemed like the shadows moving."

She didn't answer for a second. Maybe she was trying to remember. "I didn't see anything like that."

He wanted to tell her that it had reached for her. That his snarl had stopped it. But he didn't know if the memory was real or the wild imaginings of his bespelled brain, so he let it go. "Like I said, probably just a hallucination."

"Probably. Pentothal can cause them, you know."

He glanced toward the deck. Twilight's purple cast was a little way off yet. "Grill has got to be hot enough by now. You should come outside with me. The air is really nice this time of night."

"Sure." She got to her feet.

He picked up the platter of steaks and led the way, opening the slider wide. He went straight for the grill, lifted the lid, and laid the steaks on the rack. They sizzled and gave off the most tantalizing aroma as he turned the heat back.

When he looked for Jenna, she was standing a few feet away at the railing, eyes closed, looking very much like she was enjoying the evening air.

She was so pretty, it was impossible not to stare. "Nice, isn't it?"

She looked at him, her expression much more serene than it had been in the house. "It's amazing. You're lucky to live here."

"I think that every day." He stayed where he was, despite the urge to join her. "Do you spend much time at your sister's?"

"No." Jenna stared out at the forest. "I work a lot. And I don't want to intrude on her and Sebastian. I'd be a third wheel, you know?"

He nodded. "I do know. I feel that way with Hank and Ivy sometimes, although it's a little different because of the kids. If Bridget and Birdie are there, then it's not a big deal at all. But yeah, I get it."

"I suppose you do."

He shoved his hands in his pockets. "So, uh, you dating anyone?"

She looked at him as if a second nose had sprouted from his forehead. "No. And why are you asking me?"

"Just trying to make conversation. But also trying to figure out if there's going to be an angry boyfriend pounding on my door, wanting to know what's up." And maybe to find out if he had competition.

"You don't have to worry about that. What about you?"

He grinned. "Why? Want to know who you have to beat out?"

She rolled her eyes, but there was amusement there. "No. Just figure turnabout is fair play."

"Nope. No girlfriend. No dates, really. Although Birdie is constantly trying to fix me up. Bridget gets in on it, too, sometimes."

Jenna snorted softly. "I feel for you. Birdie is relentless."

"That she is." He came to stand at the railing but kept a few feet between them. "You know she's probably already plotting on how to get us together."

"I'm sure." Jenna's smile faded by half. "There's no way Birdie's behind this whole love spell, right? I mean, that would just be crazy."

"No, she'd never do something that could potentially harm anyone."

Jenna laughed. "Right. Even your aunt wouldn't go that far." She tipped her head. "Hey, you want me to call her and tell her it's not going to happen between us? Get her off your back?"

"It won't help."

"It might."

He raised a brow. "You've met Birdie, right?"

Jenna laughed, an incredibly sweet sound. "Yeah, okay, point taken."

He went back to the grill to flip the steaks. "How do you like yours?"

"Medium is good. You probably like rare, huh?"

He gave her some side-eye. "I order medium rare."

"I forgot your sister cooks all your meals."

"Yes, so funny." Steaks turned, he closed the lid. "Bridget doesn't do the cooking at Howler's, you know."

"I know." Jenna's expression was all kinds of sly. "But I amuse myself."

"Clearly." He nodded at her. She was in bare feet like he was. Her toenails were the same electric blue as the underwear he couldn't stop thinking about. "Is that what you're wearing to run?"

"Yes. With sneakers. No good?"

"It's fine. Just curious."

"How often do you wolf out and race around the woods?"

"I do not *wolf out*. And I try for once a week. At least."

"And on the full moon?"

"We run as a pack." That was only a few days from now. They'd be able to be separated by then, wouldn't they? Because the pack might not appreciate having a guest. Something he realized he might have to consider.

She ran her hand along the railing. "That must be nice. To have a pack."

"Do valkyries have anything like that?"

"Not really. We tend to be a little more solitary. Not always, of course, but we're generally all right with being alone. Doesn't mean we don't have friends or like people. In fact, an old friend of mine is supposed to be coming into town. Another valkyrie." She jerked her thumb toward the house. "You want me to set the table?"

He pointed behind her to the little table for two on the deck. "I thought we could eat out here."

"That would be nice. I'll go get the plates." She started into the house, then paused. "You want a Warhammer Stout?"

"I do, but maybe not before I run. After, definitely."

"Okay. I'll wait, too, then." She went inside.

He smiled. If this was civil, it wasn't bad. And it could only get better from here.

Being around Titus was getting harder. Being nice to him wasn't helping with the love spell either. It kept lulling her into a state of thinking that they were friends, and that was going to get her into trouble. Friends could quickly turn into more, and more would be dangerous.

A lot of fun, for sure, but ultimately, heartbreaking. And she'd already told herself she wouldn't get involved with another man who couldn't keep a promise.

Oath breakers were not for her.

She took the plates and silverware back outside to the small table. It was wood and beautifully finished. She set everything down, looking at it more closely. "Did you make this?"

"Yes. And the chairs."

"It's really nice." Such a useful little set. Why did he have to be so handy? And why did she have to find that so…sexy?

"Thanks. You want to bring me the plates? Steaks are ready."

She picked the plates up, then stood there, looking at him. "Are we only having steak?"

He blinked as if her question took a moment to register. "I don't like vegetables. If God meant us to eat vegetables, they'd grow out of the ground."

"They do."

He grinned. "It's a joke, Blythe."

She shook her head. "Did you bring the veggies from my crisper?"

"I think I scooped up everything that was in there."

"Then how about I fix a salad while the steaks rest?"

"Sure, get crazy."

She handed him the plates and went back into the kitchen. She found her stash of veggies on a shelf in his fridge. She took a moment to organize the whole thing, then in a few minutes had whipped up a simple addition to their meal. Fortunately, he had a bottle of blue cheese dressing in his fridge. Probably used it for chicken wings, if anything.

He was at the table with the steaks when she brought the salad out in a wooden bowl she'd found. "Did you make this bowl too?"

"Yep. In high school shop class."

"So you've been crafty for a while, then." She set it on the table, then took her seat.

He gave her a very direct look. "You could say that."

She let that go by without a retort. She figured not saying anything might be better. Which was kind of the opposite of what she'd usually do, but this was new ground.

They ate, keeping the talk light. The steaks were good, the salad was…salad, and before long, they were cleaning up.

She gave him a quick smile. "Thanks for cooking."

"Seemed fair since you provided the steaks. And the salad."

"Which you actually ate some of."

"Only to be polite." He laughed. "Kidding. It was good. Bridget makes me eat salad sometimes. You dry if I wash?"

"You don't have a dishwasher?"

"I do, but I don't think I've ever used it."

She snorted. "Come on, I'll teach you. Not that you need to run it for such a small amount of dishes, but with two of us here, you will soon enough."

They carried everything inside, and he pointed out the appliance in question. "There you go. I think the buttons are on the inside."

She opened it and saw the controls on the top of the door. Then she peered inside the unit. The manufacturer's energy tag was still hanging from the top rack. She yanked it off and looked at him. "You really haven't used this before."

"Told you."

"How long have you lived here?"

"Three years."

That was interesting. She'd assumed he'd lived here longer. "That's not what I would have guessed."

He shrugged. "It's nice to be close to family."

But why had it taken him three years to move up here? He'd been the fire chief for longer than that.

Then it hit her. A new house closer to his brother. A porch swing he never used. He hadn't built this house for himself.

He'd built it for his fiancée.

And just like that, Jenna had sympathy for him. She didn't want to feel that way toward him, but there it was.

The longer she was here, the more she grew to like him. To see him as a friend and not a foe.

A hundred feet of distance had never been so close.

Titus was as ready to run as a shifter could be. He itched with the need, especially because he'd come to a hard realization in the kitchen. Being around Jenna so much meant conversation. It was impossible to avoid if they were going to be civil, which he definitely wanted them to be.

But conversation required revealing small parts of himself.

That was a dangerous path. He wasn't used to talking to anyone about things from his past. Hank and Bridget understood that there were topics better left unspoken. He preferred it that way.

But Jenna didn't know that unwritten rule. And he was quickly discovering that even harmless conversations had a way of moving into personal territory without warning.

First, she'd asked about the porch swing. Then they'd verged dangerously close when they'd hit upon the subject of dating. Sooner or later, Jenna would probably come right out and ask about Zoe.

Women did that. He knew from Bridget and Birdie just how much they loved to talk about past relationships. If he let them, they'd bring up Zoe at least once a week. Maybe more.

He wanted nothing to do with that. No part of dredging up old history. Old pain. Old reminders about how wrong things had gone.

He was already on edge about that failed relationship, and he worried that if Jenna brought it up, he'd get mad. Not intentionally, but it was definitely a sore spot for him, and he knew it made him snap. He didn't want to get angry around her, not when they were getting along. It was nice.

He wasn't even really trying. Just being himself.

Was she trying? Was it hard for her to be nice to him? He hoped not.

But if he snapped, that could change things. Even if he apologized. Should he just tell her now about what happened with Zoe? A preemptive strike, as it were? That way, he could give her the short, easy version, and maybe, hopefully, that would be enough.

But then again, if he brought it up, she might think his past was suddenly on the table as a viable topic. He wanted to shut that down, not open it up.

He thought about calling Birdie for advice, but the second she realized he and Jenna were engaging in civil communication, she'd be all over them like the Velcro matchmaker.

Birdie would be setting up dates for them at the romantic restaurants in town before he could say no.

Complete with strolling violinists, if that was an option.

He closed his eyes and sighed. Calling Birdie was out.

Bridget wouldn't be much better.

That left Hank.

Titus snorted. He already knew what his brother would say. *If you don't want to talk about it, don't.*

Yeah, that wasn't going to help either.

Unsure which tactic to take, he decided to let things be for now. He'd be in wolf form during the run, so he'd be unable to speak to Jenna anyway, solving the problem temporarily.

"Jenna?"

The guest room door opened, and she came out, sneakers on. She looked adorably sporty. "You ready to run?"

"Yep." He took a few steps backward toward the deck. "This way."

"Lead on."

He turned and went through the house, out onto the deck, then down the stairs to the backyard. The sky was dusky purple and getting darker by the minute. A bright, nearly full moon added a good amount of light, but his eyes didn't need much.

The rich, loamy scent of the forest filled his nose as he inhaled. His wolf, already anticipating the impending run, panted with eagerness. Titus glanced over at Jenna. "Ready?"

She nodded.

"If you can't keep up…well, I guess I'll figure that

out by the ache in my gut. If that happens, I'll slow down."

"It won't happen. I'll keep up."

"All right, then." He rolled his shoulders. "Here we go."

He opened himself up to the change, putting his wolf in charge. The shift was instant, and a moment later he was down on all fours, the earth warm and alive under his paws, the breeze ruffling his fur.

He glanced at Jenna.

The look in her eyes was different. Curious. Her fingers extended toward him ever so slightly. She wanted to touch him.

He whuffed softly, then bent with his front legs stretched out.

She chewed on her bottom lip. "I just want to see what you feel like. Is that okay? If I touch you?"

He whuffed again, keeping his head down.

"If you bite me, I will not forgive you." She sighed. "You can understand me, right?"

He nodded.

Tentatively, her hand came closer. Then her fingers coasted over the curve of his head.

A little breath of surprise escaped her. "Oh wow. You're softer than I expected. And this is weird, isn't it?"

His laugh came out like a sneeze.

She jumped back, then looked embarrassed at her reaction. Her hands clenched and went to her sides. "We should just run."

With a woof, he straightened, gave her one more look, then charged into the forest. His wolf was in command. He was a creature of instinct and drive. The joy of being able to run and have such freedom took over.

He howled, a short, exuberant burst of sound. Behind him, Jenna's footfalls were quick and steady.

Good, he thought. Because he'd only just begun to run.

Titus in wolf form was stunningly beautiful. His fur was a sleek mix of black, silver, and gray. And incredibly soft. He was an enormous beast. Breathtaking, really, to be in such proximity to such a stunning animal.

She'd be lying if she said it wasn't a little bit intimidating. And there was very little that set her back on her heels.

That hadn't stopped her from asking to touch him, though. Maybe she shouldn't have, but she couldn't resist. Maybe that was the love spell; maybe it was just the rarity of being so close to such a magnificent creature. She wasn't sure.

Seeing him in the attic, while she'd been under the influence of that magic bomb, was nothing compared to seeing him surrounded by forest and bathed in moonlight.

The best word to describe him seemed to be *majestic*.

But Jenna should have asked him more questions before he'd shifted. Like, could he understand her? She thought he could. He seemed to have nodded when she'd asked about touching him. Plus she hadn't lost a hand, so that was a good sign. Did he remember who she was? She also thought that was a yes. Was there any chance he'd think she was a foe since she wasn't also a wolf? She prayed that was a no.

She ran a couple of yards behind him, giving him room but keeping pace even as she watched her footing as best she could in the dim light. The last thing she needed was a misstep and a twisted ankle. If only he wasn't so fast, but then, he had the advantage of four legs and a lower center of gravity.

He had a home field advantage too. He knew these woods, ran them all the time. Probably spent hours out here in his human form too. But running through this forest, either with his pack or alone, gave him a sure-footed confidence that she didn't have.

Valkyries tended to have more of an affinity for cats thanks to Freya and her giant felines, but there was an elite group of berserkers who were actually known as wolf soldiers. She'd known a few. One in particular came to mind. She shook the memory off.

Now was not a time for gloomy thoughts. This run was to help release some tension, to get the blood flowing, and to enjoy nature. Fresh air and all that. Sure, it wasn't four-wheeling through the mud, but it was still fun.

She'd never run through the woods at night.

While following a wolf. Who was also a very sexy man with great kissing skills.

There was something kind of primal about that. Not the kissing. The wolf part. It brought out the warrior in her. Made her feel like she was preparing for battle. Even *Helgrind* crackled with anticipation.

Titus pulled ahead by a few yards as he picked up speed. She dug deeper and closed the gap he'd created.

A second later, she wondered if he was trying to put more space between them. She slowed a little, giving him room. They had a hundred feet after all. Why not let him have as much space as she could give?

She dropped back farther, leaping over a fallen log he'd jumped seconds ago. The gap widened.

Was there any chance the spell had worn off? She wasn't eager to test it out here, but the thought was valid. How long could magic last against supernaturals, anyway?

They ran on, miles and time passing without regard. Jenna didn't care where they were or what the hour was. If Titus needed this to be happy, then she needed it too. He'd be easier to be around if he was in a good mood.

Even more so if she was the one who'd helped that mood happen.

Ahead of her, Titus slowed to a trot.

Jenna adjusted her speed to match his, hearing the sound of running water. She wasn't as familiar with the woods as he was, but she knew this area.

Most locals did. They were near the falls.

Once she topped a small rise, the river was visible through the trees. She could hear the falls but not see them. They were farther up.

Titus stopped, looking back at her. He made eye contact, gave a short jerk of his head, then continued on to the bank. He went down to the edge of the water to drink.

She leaned against a tree, letting him do his thing. The tops of the trees swayed a bit, but in the thick of the forest, there wasn't much breeze. The real heat of summer was still a couple of months off, though, and the air tonight had enough coolness to it to be utterly enjoyable.

She closed her eyes for a moment and took a deep breath. The forest smelled so clean and crisp. She could see why Titus liked this. Of course, getting to run through the woods as a wolf had to be so much better than running through it as a human.

Something rustled in the woods behind her. She turned, keeping the tree at her back, and scanned the dark for any sign of what had made the noise. There were lots of nocturnal creatures. Could be anything. A rabbit, a possum, a skunk. She really hoped it wasn't a skunk.

She glanced back at Titus. If it was a rabbit, would he go after it? She grimaced and was about to join him at the riverbank when she heard more rustling.

Once again, she peered into the forest, trying to see what had made the sound.

This time, the shadows moved.

She stood transfixed, watching as a hulking, man-shaped form emerged from the darkness. It was as if the shadows had given birth.

The form came closer, and bright, blazing eyes blinked at her. They looked like flames in the darkness. Arms reached toward her.

She sucked in a breath and stared at the thing in shock for a second, before snapping out of it. Questions ran through her head as she moved to unsheathe her sword. What in Loki's name was this abomination doing here? Why was it here? Was it after her?

Then the guttural snarl of a wolf broke the silence.

Titus was in front of her, the fur standing up in a ridge down his back, teeth bared, jaws snapping. Truly a formidable sight.

The shadow creature hesitated, then growled.

Titus lunged forward, and the creature vanished like smoke in a strong wind.

A second later, Titus the man stood next to her. She spoke to him while her gaze stayed fixed on the woods. "Thank you."

"You could have handled that yourself."

That was kind of him to say. She wasn't entirely sure that was true, but she nodded all the same.

He shrugged. "Wouldn't have been right of me not to jump in."

She exhaled, still wordless in shock. She clenched her hands to stop them from shaking. Why here? Why now?

He looked at her, and she finally made eye contact with him as he spoke. "Have you ever seen anything like that before?"

She had, but not in a very long time, and she didn't want to talk about it here. Not when it could come back. "Can we go home? Now?"

He nodded. "Are you okay to run, or do you want to head into town and find a ride?"

"No, we can run." She just didn't plan to stop until she was back inside Titus's house.

The run back wasn't as much fun, but Titus had gotten the energy burn that he'd needed on the way to the river. Even if he hadn't, he'd still be fine with going straight home, because Jenna seemed so shaken up.

That alone was enough to cause him concern. She hadn't seemed this out of sorts even after the magic bomb had gone off.

Obviously that meant whatever the creature was they'd seen in the forest, the same one he'd seen in the attic, that was the reason for her alarm. Did that also mean she knew what it was? That she'd seen it before?

He'd asked her if she'd seen anything in the attic, and she'd said no. But maybe she had seen something and had chalked it up as a hallucination like he had.

As they approached his property line, he came to a stop and shifted back to his human form.

Jenna slowed but kept going toward the house.

"Hey," he called out, glad to have a voice again. "Are you okay?"

She didn't look at him, didn't stop moving, just shook her head. "Not sure." She put her hand on the railing that led up to his deck, finally turning. "I'm going to bed."

He jogged to join her. "Jenna, we need to talk about what just happened."

She stood there, staring blankly. Gaze distant. Like she was lost in thoughts she wasn't ready to share.

He tried a different approach. "How about we have a couple of Warhammers and unwind from that run with a soak in the hot tub? The relaxation might do you good."

She blinked. "You have a hot tub?"

He nodded. "Other side of the deck where it wraps around. Right outside my bedroom."

At the word *bedroom*, her eyes narrowed slightly.

He held his hands up. "No funny business. Just a soak. Really. I take one almost every night." She really looked like she could use a little relaxation.

After a moment, she nodded. "Sounds good, actually, but I didn't bring a bathing suit."

"You have gym shorts and a sports bra?" He wasn't going to guess what she had on under her T-shirt.

She hesitated. "Yeah, I have those."

"Good enough. I'll get the beers and meet you out there."

"Okay." She went up the stairs. "But just a soak."

"Just a soak." He followed but gave her some space by falling back until she was down the hall and opening the door to the guest room. Then he went into his bedroom, through the French doors out to the deck, and pulled the cover off the hot tub. He turned the jets on. The temperature was already good. He kept it cranked up so that he could use it at a moment's notice. With his schedule, that worked best.

He went back in to change into trunks, grabbed two big towels from the linen closet, then hit the garage fridge for two of her special beers.

By the time he got back to the hot tub, she was coming out of the house through the main sliders. Her hair was still knotted on top of her head, but she was in running shorts and a sports bra. The exposed section of her taut belly was impossible not to look at. He'd known she was in good shape, but man. Good wasn't the right word.

Her gaze raked over him, but she averted her eyes quickly. Trying not to look? The fact that she'd checked him out stirred feelings he was powerless to squelch.

Maybe sharing a hot tub with her while under a love spell wasn't such a hot idea. No pun intended.

But here they were.

He dropped the towels on one of the deck chairs, then held a beer out to her.

She took it, clinked the bottom of the bottle against his, then wrenched the top off and took a long sip. She closed her eyes as she swallowed. "That's better."

He set his beer on the edge of the tub and climbed in. The heat was perfect, sinking into his muscles and instantly relaxing him. He sighed with pleasure as he settled onto the molded seat. "Come on in, feels great."

She sat on the edge, swung her legs around, and slid in. "Oh! Hotter than I expected."

"Too hot?" He cranked the cap off his beer and tried it. Not bad. A lot more complex than the stuff he usually drank. He could see it growing on him. "I can turn it down."

"No." She exhaled and slipped farther into the water, finding a seat of her own while holding her beer above the churning surface. She found a spot for the bottle on the edge, then tipped her head back. The sky was filled with stars now that it was completely dark. "This is really nice."

"It is. I like the Warhammer too. The flavor's a lot more layered than the beer I usually drink. It's good."

She smiled. "I'm glad."

They settled into a comfortable silence, enjoying the moment despite having not yet discussed the evening's earlier event.

Then one of her feet brushed his leg, sending a current of sensation through him that had nothing to do with the bubbles or the water or the heat. It made him think about those electric blue toenails. It made him want to kiss her. Even so, he ignored it and held still. She hadn't meant to do that, he was pretty sure.

To keep himself from drifting into the clutches of the love spell, he went right to the thing most likely to kill that mood. The elephant in the room. "That dark, shadowy thing in the woods? I've seen it before."

She stopped staring at the sky to look at him, new tension bracketing her mouth. "You have?"

The skepticism in her voice was interesting. Why would she doubt him? "Yes. At the house. In the attic."

Her eyes widened. "That's what you saw?"

He nodded. "After the bomb went off. When we were lying on the attic floor. You were already passed out. It came for you. Out of the shadows. Reached for you like it did in the woods."

Fear entered her gaze. She sat up taller, causing the water to slosh. "Why are you only telling me about this now?"

"I thought it was a hallucination. And I did sort of bring it up. I asked you if you'd seen anything when we were in the attic. You said no."

She frowned. "I didn't. But I certainly didn't think you meant a wraith."

He frowned back. "A wraith? You've seen one before?"

She sighed, took a long, long drink from her beer, then looked at him. "I have."

He took a pull off his bottle, set it back on the edge, and waited for her to elaborate.

After quite a few seconds, she spoke again. "They're dangerous creatures with a lot to lose. They're a little on the slow side, but they fight hard."

"What is a wraith, exactly? How do you know so much about them?"

"A wraith in my world is the trapped soul of an undesirable who died but refused to be transported to their final resting place."

"Undesirable?"

"In every sense of the word. There's a reason they don't want to go to that final resting place, if you get my drift."

"I do. But what do you mean 'refused to be transported'? Isn't transporting souls kind of what valkyries do?"

She nodded. "That's why I know so much about them. When I was in service, I was part of a task force assigned to hunting down wraiths and delivering them to where they belong. Didn't happen all the time, but when one showed up, we were called in. We went in teams of two. A valkyrie and a seer. That's what it took to eliminate one. Not a single wraith ever wanted to go either."

"I can imagine. If they knew they were headed where I think they were."

"They were. And they knew." She picked up her bottle, holding it just above the surface of the bubbling water. "Battlefields are a prime breeding ground for them. Men who took advantage of whatever war they were in the middle of to further their own ends. Men who deserved death for one reason or another, but were too stubborn or too awful or too evil to allow death to take them. Men who considered war a game. A way to release their already murderous natures." She grimaced. "We hunted them down, captured them, and disposed of their black souls."

His lip curled in disgust. "That sounds like a terrible job."

She took another drink and put her bottle down. "Valkyries in service don't spend their time hosting tea parties and attending fashion shows. We work amongst the dead and dying. It wasn't the worst assignment I've ever had." She dipped down until her chin was half in the water. "But yes, some jobs are worse than others."

"How do you not have PTSD?"

She looked up through her lashes at him. "Who says I don't?" She went back to staring at the water. "I have nightmares sometimes. But for the most part, we're built to handle the things we see. And we generally do handle it."

"But seeing that wraith set something off in you."

She nodded. "Like I said, they're dangerous. They can't be killed because they're already dead. Also, a blade goes right through them without doing any damage. It's like trying to stab smoke. At least in the early stages."

He sat up. "So how do you kill a thing that's already dead and can't be hurt?"

"Two ways. One, you bring along a seer who knows the right incantation to hold the wraith in place and make it solid, or you wait for it to get strong enough that it becomes solid again on its own. That method generally leaves you with a much bigger threat that you do not want to go up against."

"Well, how long before it goes from a little threat to a great big one?"

"Not sure. It's different with every one."

"Why was it reaching for you? What does it want from you?"

"It's complicated." She was quiet a moment.

"Why? What else aren't you telling me?"

Her silence lasted awhile longer. "Sometimes valkyries create the wraiths. It's not intentional, but on the battlefield, things happen. Hard choices are made. Sometimes, the soul becomes a wraith before we can transport it to its final end."

That seemed a heavy burden to bear. "Do you think this is one of those? One that's come after you?"

Her gaze turned sharp. "What makes you say that?"

"You brought it up." He shrugged. Was that anger in her eyes? Or fear? The latter was such an unlikely emotion from her, and yet the topic seemed to bring it out in her. Maybe that hard gleam was a mix of both. "Just seems like a possibility after what you said."

"It's not," she snapped.

"Hey," he said softly. "If it is, it's not like you're to blame. No one, and I mean no one, would say it's your fault that some undead baddie has tracked you down."

She stared off into the night. "Yeah, right."

"Jenna. *Jenna*."

She finally looked at him. "What?"

"Anyone says a word to that effect, and they will answer to me."

The brackets around her eyes softened, but her mouth was still a hard line. "Why would you do that?

It's not your job to—never mind, I know why. The spell is messing with your head, making you pay attention to ideas you'd dismiss otherwise."

"So it's wrong that I'd want to be your friend in this situation? What's so crazy about one first responder wanting to help out another first responder?"

She stopped looking at him again.

That wasn't going to shut him up. "I like you. And that's not the spell talking either. Sure, I think you're all kinds of annoying at times, but so is my sister, and I'm crazy about her."

Jenna snorted. "You just want me to kiss you again."

"I'd be lying if I said you were wrong."

That got her attention. "Titus, don't."

He let out a long sigh. "Do you ever have any fun, or is your whole life just you being hard on yourself?"

"I have fun."

"Really? When?"

"Tonight's run was fun."

"When did you last have fun on your own?"

She frowned at him. "I have fun," she said again.

He wasn't convinced. He wasn't done talking either. There had to be a way to break through the walls she kept up. "Wouldn't it be easier for us to deal with this spell if we were a team and not two opponents? We're facing the same battle. Why not join forces?"

"We're in this together whether we like it or not."

"Exactly. So let's be a team."

She gave him a hard look. "Meaning?"

"Stop treating me like the enemy, for one thing."

She took a breath before answering. "I'll try."

"Gee, thanks." He looked off toward the woods. "What is it about me that you dislike so much?"

She tipped her bottle back, finishing it. "You really want to know?"

He glanced at her. "Yeah, I do."

"You're sure? Because if you want me to be truthful, you can't get mad at the answer."

He could. But he wouldn't. Not for the sake of them moving forward in a meaningful way. "I won't. Promise."

She pointed the empty bottle at him. "You're an oath breaker. And I don't want anything to do with someone like that."

Jenna knew the slight buzz from the Warhammer was partially to blame for her sudden impulse to tell Titus what she really thought of him. But hey, he'd asked.

He stared at her in confusion. "What are you talking about?"

"You broke your engagement." She shrugged and put the empty bottle down. Something inside her gave way to the anger she still felt toward Eric. Maybe all the magic influencing her was causing it, but there was no stopping what she wanted to say. "I know you had a fiancée and I know she left you and I know there are two sides to every story, so whatever the reason that arrangement dissolved, you still had a part in it. Which means you share the blame."

An angry wolfen glow lit his eyes. "You don't know anything about my engagement."

"I know what I need to know." He was getting mad. And mad seemed like a good way to shut down the effects of the love spell.

"No, you don't."

She rested her arms along the edge of the tub and leaned back. "So tell me."

He swallowed, some of the angry light in his eyes fading until, a moment later, it was gone completely. But something new had taken its place. Sadness? Regret? Disappointment?

That wasn't the response Jenna had expected. A pang of sympathy went through her. What had happened to Titus to make him feel that way? And why on earth had she asked? If she felt sympathetic toward him now, how was she going to feel after listening to his story?

She'd made him mad enough. There was no point in pushing this further. She held her finger up. "You know what? I changed my mind. You don't have to tell me."

"No, you asked. And you assumed. So I'm going to tell you, because you clearly have some false ideas about me." His jaw was tense, making his words come out sharp. They matched the angry light that had crept back into his eyes.

She pulled her arms back into the water and tucked her hands under her legs. "Okay."

"Zoe was...perfect in every way. She's a schoolteacher. Great with kids. And they love her right back. She's wolf, like me. And just a beautiful person, inside and out. She's everything I wanted in a partner." He hesitated, obviously a little lost in memories.

A moment later, he started again. "But it wasn't meant to be. Her parents are older, and then her father fell and broke his hip. She's an only child and felt obligated to move home and take care of them. So she went back to Oregon and her parents. I certainly can't fault her for doing the right thing by them. In fact, her willingness to give up everything for them is an example of the person she is. The person I fell in love with."

"Why didn't you move with her?"

He shook his head. "I was already chief. I'd built this house for us. My brother and sister lived here, my parents not far away. My life is here."

"But if you really loved her…"

He looked miserable. So much so, she felt bad about bringing up the subject. A vein in his forehead pulsed. "I guess I didn't love her enough to give up everything I worked for. To leave my family behind for hers." His words grew angrier as he spoke. "I'm as responsible for our breakup as she is. Or maybe you're right, and it's all my fault since I wasn't willing to move."

"So you're admitting you were selfish?"

"Selfish?" The glow in his eyes was almost blinding, and his voice had a growl that hadn't been there before. "You want the truth? Yes, her parents needed her, but she was already planning to leave because she hated my job. Thought it was too dangerous. Couldn't stand the idea of worrying about whether or not I'd come home after every shift. So I let her go. Happy? Feel better now that you've gotten that out of me?"

Jenna sat there, mouth open, realizing how wrong she'd been about everything. About him especially.

He abruptly stood and climbed out of the hot tub, sending water splashing. Without another word, he went into the house, leaving her sitting alone.

She watched him go, the guilt at what she'd just done sinking in. Why on earth had she pushed him? It wasn't his fault his engagement had been broken. She'd projected her own heartache onto him. Her own anger and disappointment. She was a terrible person.

Tessa was right. Titus wasn't Eric. It wasn't Titus's fault that Eric had betrayed her and treated her heart like it was disposable.

Her throat ached, and her stomach felt worse. Neither one had anything to do with the spell they were under either.

She got out of the hot tub, dried herself off with the towel he'd kindly provided for her, and thought about how best to apologize. If he'd even talk to her.

And if he wouldn't, well, she'd earned that.

She wrapped the towel around her body, went in through the sliders and down the hall to his door. She knocked softly. "Titus? I'm sorry. Please, can we talk?"

A whiny, grinding noise started up in the garage.

She tugged the towel a little tighter and headed in that direction. She opened the garage door.

Titus was in jeans, T-shirt, and safety goggles, sanding down a big hunk of wood, his back to her. Little bits of sawdust floated through the air, along with the scent of the wood he was working on.

She waited until he stopped sanding and she could be heard. "Titus?"

He straightened and slowly turned. He put the sander down and pushed the goggles onto his forehead. He didn't say a word. Just stared at her, the weight of accusation heavy in his gaze.

But she already knew what she'd done. She hung her head. "I'm really sorry. For a lot of things. For saying you were to blame for your relationship ending. For saying you were selfish. For trying to make you mad on purpose. For making assumptions about you that I shouldn't have. I was wrong about all of that. I don't know why I…" She sighed. "That's a lie. I know why." She couldn't bring herself to confess more. That part of her past hurt too much.

"You care to elaborate on that?"

She shook her head, unable to look at him as the knot returned to her throat. "I'm really sorry I was such a jerk to you. You've been nothing but nice to me. You didn't deserve that."

"Apology accepted."

"Thank you." She really needed to go to bed. This day had been enough already.

"Why were you trying to make me mad?"

"So the love spell wouldn't work." With nothing left to say, she turned, and her hand went to the knob. Was it any wonder she didn't have anyone in her life? Who would want to be around her? Eric certainly hadn't considered her worthy of his loyalty or respect.

"Jenna?"

Her name on his lips wasn't what stopped her from leaving. It was the sympathetic tone in his voice. A tone she didn't deserve. Not even with her apology.

"What did he do to you?"

The question almost undid her. As it was, a momentary wash of numbness went through her. She wanted to snap back at him, tell him that no one did anything to her. But the lie would be obvious.

More than that, Titus deserved her honest response. And her respect. After all, they'd said they'd be civil to each other, and so far, she was failing at that.

Besides, lying to herself that she was fine wasn't helping one bit. It was time to come clean. With Titus. And with herself.

She turned back around and sat on the step. "He broke my heart. Then ruined my life. And I'm still not over it."

"Of course you're not." Titus came over and sat next to her. Close enough that she could feel the heat emanating off him. It was nice being close to someone who was warm. And handsome. And forgiving. "Who was he?"

"Eric Peerson." Just saying his full name took something out of her. She inhaled, but her breath caught and sounded more like the beginning of a sob. She hated how weak that made her seem. How affected by that stupid, stupid man. How pathetic she felt considering she was a valkyrie.

"Who was he?"

"My commanding officer. And the man…I thought I was going to marry."

Titus sucked in a breath. "That doesn't sound good at all."

She shook her head. There was sawdust on his jeans. Was the spell making her notice such things about him? "It wasn't." She expected Titus to ask next what Eric had done. That's what people always did. Asked for details about the really painful stuff.

But a long, quiet moment passed before he spoke, and that wasn't what he said at all.

"If you ever want to talk about it, I'm here. You can yell, cry, scream, rant, whatever you need. I know firsthand how much someone you care about can turn your world upside down."

She looked at him. Just a sideways glance through a few tendrils of loose hair, but it was enough to see how sincere he was. "I bet you do."

He genuinely cared. Wasn't mad—anymore— about what she'd said to him in the hot tub. Wasn't holding a grudge. He just wanted her to know he was available if she needed someone to listen to her.

She saw him with new eyes. *Really* saw him for the kind and caring man he was. She'd been utterly and completely wrong about him. And all because she'd let her past color her view of him.

That understanding was such a revelation that it caught her off guard and sent a shiver through her, which was exacerbated by the wet clothes she still wore.

Without hesitation, he put his arm around her and pulled her close. She leaned in. "I'm really sorry," she whispered.

"I forgive you. I promise."

"Thank you. But I'm also really sorry things didn't work out between you and Zoe."

A moment of silence passed. "Thanks. I was sorry, too, for a long time. Still am, most days. But I think it's time I got past that." He squeezed her shoulder where his hand was resting. "I'm sorry about what Eric did to you."

"Thanks."

"Did you kill him?"

His startling question caused a laugh to bubble out of her from deep down inside and burst out with such force that her whole body rocked back. "What? No! But he probably deserved it."

Titus grinned. "Don't you kill anyone who crosses you?"

The mischief in his eyes told her he was joking. She decided to go along with it. "I do, actually. Does that frighten you?"

"Me? Frightened? I think the real question here is…" Magic danced over his features, transforming them just slightly so that when he smiled at her, his eyes glowed and his canines were wolf-sized. "Aren't you afraid of the big, bad wolf?"

She let out a playful shriek and jumped off the steps. "Don't you dare bite me." But even as the words left her mouth, the idea didn't seem that bad.

He stood and came down the steps toward her with the kind of slow, predatory stride that sent another shiver through her. "You do smell awfully good. The only problem is, I don't know if you're Little Red Riding Hood or the huntswoman."

"My sword's not drawn yet." Freya help her, she wanted him. It was definitely the spell. The magic was thick in her blood and clouding her brain. But deep inside, she knew that wasn't the only reason.

His grin widened. "Can I see it?"

"My sword?"

He nodded. "You've seen me as a wolf. Only seems fair."

To her, what seemed fair was kissing him again. She squeezed her eyes shut at the idea but didn't force it away like she had the last time. Maybe showing him her sword would distract her brain. Fill it with thoughts of battle and fighting and kissing— nope, that wasn't helping. She smiled back at him, eyes wide. "Sure."

She untucked the towel still wrapped around her body and dropped it to the floor beside her so that he could see her back. Then she turned around. "Watch now. You should be able to see it despite the straps of my sports bra."

She thought about her sword, about the magic that hid it from all non-valkyrie and non-berserker eyes and then about opening that magic so he could see it too.

A ripple of sensation went down her spine where *Helgrind* resided like a magical tattoo, waiting for her touch to bring her to life. "Can you see it?"

"Wow," he breathed. "I can. It just came into view. Pretty cool how you can do that."

"Generally, our swords aren't visible unless you're a valkyrie or berserker. Or a vampire. Basically, if you're not a valkyrie or a berserker, you have to be dead to see our weapons. Pretty sure that's all tied into how souls on the battlefield recognize us."

"That's pretty interesting. Cool that you can show it to me, though. It's the most realistic ink I've ever seen. I swear the metal is actually gleaming in the light as you move."

"It is. Because it's not ink." She glanced over her shoulder at him, loving the curiosity in his eyes. "It's...hard to explain. Better I just show you, I guess."

Just talking about the weapon made it vibrate with anticipation, its bladesong dancing through Jenna with a happy trill.

"How old were you when you got it?"

"I was born with it. We all are."

He pondered that a moment. "Then you didn't have a choice in being a valkyrie. Just like I didn't have a choice in being a werewolf."

She nodded. "In that, we are alike."

"We're alike in a lot of ways."

So she'd been told. She just smiled. "Do you want to see it, then?"

He nodded. "I do."

She reached back and felt the hilt solidify in her hand. An electric current zipped over her skin.

The sensation wasn't something she'd felt in a while. It was *Helgrind*'s anticipation at being unsheathed.

On the job, her service weapon was the only thing she used. Wasn't like she could go around brandishing a sword, despite her proficiency with the blade. Sad, really, that *Helgrind* didn't get to come out for more than practice.

Jenna liked that Titus seemed so interested. "Step back a little."

He did as she asked, still looking very eager.

She tightened her grip on the hilt. Then pulled the sword free.

Titus had never known the hiss of metal could have such a sweet, melodious sound to it, but that's exactly what he heard as Jenna unsheathed her sword.

It was bigger than he'd expected, gleaming bright with an almost blue-white light that made it seem like a living thing. Set in the pommel was a blue-green stone that seemed to have a beam of light deep within its smooth-polished heart. Other than that, the sword was unadorned. But it didn't need anything more.

"Wow," he breathed again. "It's a work of art. What's the stone in the handle?"

"Just glass," she said.

"It's beautiful all the same. But I guess that makes sense, considering who owns it."

A look of disbelief filled Jenna's eyes for a moment. "You think my sword is beautiful because…"

"You're beautiful. Yes. I do." He was done resisting the spell, done pretending he didn't like her.

That he wasn't attracted to her. Done with anything close to lying. Especially after learning that she'd been hurt by someone she'd cared for. It wasn't his job to heal that wound for her, but he certainly wasn't going to add to it.

And if he could give her some happiness by being kinder, by being truthful, then that was an easy thing for him to do.

Plus, she was standing in front of him, holding a deadly weapon. Now was the perfect time to start being complimentary, if ever there was one.

"Oh," she said softly. "We, um, that is, valkyries generally are naturally attractive, so that's really just genes—"

"Can I hold it?" He'd rather change the subject than hear her discount his compliment.

She smiled. "No. I mean, you can try, but the sword won't let you."

His brow wrinkled. "The sword won't let me."

"Nope. *Helgrind* is pretty picky about who lays hands on her. Basically just me."

"*Helgrind*?"

Jenna nodded. "Means hell gate."

His eyes widened just a little. "That seems appropriately intimidating. But how do you know *Helgrind* won't like me? Maybe she wants me to hold her."

She laughed and held the sword out, freeing her hand from the hilt so that she was only holding it between her thumb and forefinger. "Be my guest."

"Really?"

"Sure."

He wrapped his hand around the hilt. The metal thrummed with its own energy. "I can feel the magic in it."

She nodded, looking very pleased. "It's really something, isn't it?"

"It is."

"Got it? I'm going to let go."

He tightened his grip. "I have it."

She was almost laughing now. "You sure?"

He got the sense she was playing with him. "Yes."

"Okay." She took her hand away.

The sword vanished.

"Hey." He looked around. "Where is it? What kind of trick is that?"

She turned to show him her back. The sword once again ran from the edge of her hairline down her spine, disappearing beneath the waistband of her gym shorts. When she twisted to face him, her eyes were alive with amusement. "Told you."

"So the sword only exists if your hand is on it?"

"No." She reached back and brought the blade out again, then walked over to his workbench and laid it down. "It can exist without me. It's absolutely real on its own."

"I see that."

She stepped away. "Go ahead, pick it up."

"Pretty sure I know how this turns out." The moment his fingers made contact, the sword disappeared again. "Let me guess. It's returned to you?"

She nodded. "That's how valkyrie and berserker swords work. Trust me, it's a good thing."

"I believe you. It's pretty cool. Like the best possible safety a weapon could have. Thank you for sharing that with me." He wiggled his eyebrows. "I feel special."

Her gaze narrowed. "Are you making fun of me?"

"No. I really do feel special. I'm guessing you haven't shown that sword to many people. Have you?"

She shook her head. "Sorry for assuming the worst."

Against every instinct telling him not to, he reached out and took her hand. "You don't have to think that about me anymore. I promise. I'm going to do everything I can to be friends with you. I want us to be a team and work together."

She looked at his hand holding hers, then up at him. "The only problem is…"

When she didn't immediately finish her sentence, he did it for her, his heart sinking in his chest. "You don't want to be friends with me."

"Right."

He let go of her hand and walked away. She was impossible. Hard-hearted and—

"Titus."

"What?" He snapped, turning to look at the most difficult woman he'd ever met.

Oddly, she looked nervous. Almost reluctant. She sighed and stared at the ground. "I meant that I don't want to be *just* friends with you. I would be okay with trying to be a little more than that. I know that's a complete reversal from what I said earlier and that it's a big ask coming from me, the same woman who just said terrible things to you in your hot tub, but you're such a different man than I thought you were and—"

He stepped into her space and kissed her, hard. He threaded his fingers into her hair, cupping her face in his hands, and pressed his mouth to hers. He wanted to show her he was serious.

She melted against him, the little sigh that escaped her throat caught between them. Her hands went to his waist, then slid under his shirt and higher to his ribs.

Her touch nearly took his breath. How long had it been since he'd felt a woman's touch? Too long.

A little voice told him they were just feeding the spell, strengthening it. He didn't care, even while he understood that he didn't know what was real and what was magic. The separation between the two ceased to matter.

Only she mattered. Only this moment, this kiss.

Temperatures went up. His, hers, the room's. They might as well have been standing on a lava field.

After a few more long moments, she put her hands to his chest and pushed, ending the kiss. They were both panting.

She shook her head. "Are we really doing this? Giving in to the spell?"

"I don't see it that way."

She looked up at him. "How do you see it, then?"

"The spell wouldn't work if there wasn't something there already, right?"

"I don't know. But...maybe." She held his gaze. "I guess we'll know when Alice breaks it."

He nodded. "We should probably go to bed."

Her eyes widened. "Settle down, Merrow. That's too fast for me."

He snorted. "I meant we should go to *sleep*. In our own beds. The inspector arrives tomorrow. And you need to get to work on figuring out how to stop that wraith."

"Oh. Right. Sleep." She laughed, cheeks going pink. "Do you usually have breakfast? Or do you go straight to work?"

"I go straight to work, where I make breakfast for my crew."

She was still smiling. "Does the binding spell make me part of the crew?"

He nodded. "Absolutely. Can you be ready to leave by six thirty?"

Her brows went up. "Wow, you do start early. Sure, I can be ready."

"Good. I usually swing by Zombie Donuts on the way in, grab a couple dozen."

She smirked. "That's very nice of you, but buying doughnuts doesn't qualify as making breakfast."

"Oh, the doughnuts are just the appetizer. You'll see." Then he pulled her in and kissed her once more, short and sweet. "Now, we really should go to sleep. Because if I kiss you a third time, sleep will be the last thing on my mind."

Jenna slept. But she also dreamed. Weird, happy, scary, mixed-up dreams that had everything in them from her ex to the wraith to Titus in the hot tub. There was even a cameo by Duncan, Tessa's cat.

Jenna woke needing coffee but feeling okay about things between her and Titus.

Honestly, she was slightly giddy in the weirdest way about suddenly being involved with Titus. Okay, *involved* was probably too big a word for what was happening, but she wasn't about to speak it out loud. Anyway, that feeling had to come from the spell, but it felt real.

Or was it? Could it be real even if it was magic-induced?

She didn't know and didn't have time to dwell on the question longer than it took her to shower, dry her hair, and put a little makeup on. Titus wanted to leave by six thirty, and she was not going to make him late.

Normally, she'd wear her uniform, but since she wasn't going to be at the sheriff's department or on patrol, that didn't seem like the right choice.

Technically, she wasn't going to be officially on duty again until the spell was lifted. She was still free to work on figuring out who'd set that bomb—and how the wraith played into it—but she didn't need to be in uniform to do that.

Because of that, she settled on skinny jeans, then grabbed the first T-shirt on top of the stack she'd brought, along with a cardigan in case the firehouse was chilly. To that, she added a belt and cute flats.

She checked the time. She had twenty minutes before they left. Was that enough time to have some coffee here? She realized she could smell some, which hopefully meant he'd made a pot.

She went out to the kitchen and found him standing by the window, drinking from a cup. "Morning. Is there more of that?"

He nodded without turning. "I made a whole pot."

"Thank Freya," she muttered.

"Mugs are in the cabinet above. You need sugar or creamer?"

"Just sugar, but I can go without if you don't have it."

"Same cabinet." He looked at her. "Didn't you sleep well?"

She got a mug down and found a small white container of sugar packets that looked like they'd come from Howler's. "Tossed and turned a bit. Weird dreams. Lot on my mind, you know."

"I know. Had a bit of that myself."

She added two packets of sugar, then filled the mug with coffee and turned to lean on the counter as she took her first sip. She closed her eyes and let the coffee reach her soul before attempting further communication.

She opened her eyes at the sound of Titus's soft chuckle. "What?"

He shook his head, his expression morphing from pure amusement to the most innocent of faces. "Nothing. How's the coffee?"

"Good. Really strong, which is how I like it."

"Isn't that the standard sheriff's department brew?"

She smiled. "Pretty much. Your brother likes it strong enough to work a shift on its own."

"And then there's Birdie."

"She loves her fancy coffee, doesn't she? Good thing there's lots of that to choose from in town. I think she's got her own account at the Hallowed Bean."

"I think you're right." Titus glanced past her. "Almost time to go."

"It won't take me long to drink this. Unless you have a travel cup I can put it in?"

"Take your time." He winked. "You have three minutes."

"Gee, thanks, Merrow." She rolled her eyes good-naturedly, then took another big sip of her coffee.

"You're welcome, Blythe. I'm going to brush my teeth, then I'll see you in the truck."

She gave him a thumbs-up since she was still drinking. After he left, she took one more big sip, then put the cup in the sink and went to brush her teeth a second time. Coffee breath wasn't conducive to kissing. Which was totally the spell talking.

She rushed through brushing her teeth in an attempt to stop thinking about kissing, a wholly unsuccessful endeavor, then went straight out to the truck.

She had to get it together. She was going to be with him all day!

Titus locked the house before joining her. He smelled so good. That wasn't helping.

As he pulled out of the driveway and headed for the exit, the look of amusement returned to his face. "Nice T-shirt, by the way. You are definitely going to make some friends today."

She glanced down only to realize why he'd been grinning so hard in the kitchen earlier. She'd inadvertently put on the T-shirt Tessa had given her for her last birthday.

The one that proudly proclaimed *I ♥ Real American Firefighters*.

Jenna groaned, but Titus laughed heartily. He'd been holding it in since the kitchen. "Hey, as a real American firefighter, I love that you love us."

She pressed the palm of her hand to her forehead. "I didn't mean to wear this shirt. I just grabbed the first one in my bag," she groused. "I didn't even know I brought it."

"Serendipitous, then, considering where you're spending the day."

She looked unimpressed. "I don't suppose there's any chance we can go back so I can change?"

He shook his head. "Sorry, too late. I have a schedule to keep."

He could just see her squinting at him. "You did that on purpose, didn't you?"

"This is my schedule every morning."

"I mean you didn't say anything in the kitchen so that I wouldn't change."

She wasn't wrong. "How did you not see what shirt you had on?"

She sighed. "I was focused on getting ready on time. And drinking my coffee. I didn't want to make you late."

He gave her points for that. He hadn't needed to prod her once. But she seemed the kind of person who liked to be early anyway. "I appreciate that. Almost as much as I appreciate the shirt."

She crossed her arms and stared straight ahead. "I'm going to hear about this all day, aren't I?"

"If it's a slow day, there's a good chance it'll be the main topic of conversation. Sorry, not sorry." He snorted. "How did you end up with that shirt?"

"Tessa gave it to me for my last birthday."

"Your sister has a wicked sense of humor. As gag gifts go, that ranks right up there."

"Not a gag gift." She gave him a quick side-eye. "It's actually my favorite reality show."

"Really?" So she liked firemen after all. How about that? "I would have figured you for a *Live PD* fan."

She shrugged. "I live that every day. I don't need to watch it on TV. Besides, *Real American Firefighters* isn't…well, they don't just follow the firefighters on calls."

"No," he said, trying hard not to laugh again. "I understand they also show the men working out and washing the trucks. Often shirtless."

"That's not *all* they show."

"Right. Didn't they also show them posing for a calendar once?"

She glared at him.

He snickered as he made the turn toward Zombie Donuts. "Come on, you have to admit it's amazing how often those guys aren't wearing shirts. But then, I suppose that's why the show is so popular with certain viewers."

"Yeah, yeah." She tipped her head. "How exactly do you know so much about this show?"

"You can't be a fireman and not know about it." He pulled into the parking lot and found a space. "I just hope you won't be too disappointed at the firehouse today."

She frowned at him as she unclicked her seat belt. "About what?"

He turned the truck off, barely holding his laughter in. "We'll all have our shirts on."

She rolled her eyes at him and opened her door. "Just for that, you're buying me a muffin."

"I'd be happy to." He got out of the truck. "If it means I get to keep my shirt on."

She snort-laughed. "You're sooo funny."

He shut the door and met her at the front of the truck. "I really am. Come on, let's get some doughnuts."

They went in and got in line. The place was busy, but the line moved fast. In a few minutes, they were at the counter.

One of the workers, Bess, greeted them with a nod. "Good morning, Chief. The usual two dozen?"

"Morning, Bess. Yes, two dozen," Titus answered. "How about one dozen Glazed From The Dead, then mix the other one between Boston Scream, Boo-berry Cake, Dr Prepper, and… What's your doughnut of the day?"

"Today's doughnut is the Reaper. It's a chocolate cake doughnut with a raspberry sugar glaze."

"Sounds great. Throw a few of them in, too, please."

"You got it." She went to work filling the order.

Jenna tipped her head as she looked at all the doughnuts on display. "Those all sound good. Now I'm not sure I want a muffin anymore." She glanced at him. "How about I buy a dozen too? Any chance that'll get me less grief about the T-shirt?"

Her generosity would definitely be appreciated, but nothing was going to stop the guys from ribbing her over that shirt. "Maybe a little, but that shirt isn't an opportunity they're going to pass up."

"Worth a shot." When Bess came back, Jenna smiled at her. "I'll take a dozen, too, please. Three each of Scary Cherry, Death By Chocolate, Cinnamon Ghost Crunch, and Marshmallow Mummy."

Bess got Jenna's dozen together. She and Titus paid, then headed back to the truck. The boxes went on the back seat, but that didn't stop them from filling the cab with their delicious aromas.

By the time they got to the station, Jenna's stomach had growled twice.

"Hungry?" Titus asked.

She put her hand on her stomach. "It's the smell of the doughnuts."

"Well, I'm starting breakfast as soon as we get in,

so it won't be long before you can eat. If you want more than a doughnut, that is." He parked in his reserved spot.

"I do. What are you making?"

"The usual. Bacon, sausage, eggs, pancakes, home fries, and biscuits. Might do a side of sausage gravy since we have company."

Her mouth came open. "You don't really make all that food."

"I do. I have a whole station of big eaters to feed." He got out of the truck and took his boxes off the back seat.

She did the same. "Are they all supernaturals?"

He shook his head. "It's a mix on every shift. Probably like the sheriff's department is. But those who aren't supernaturals seem to eat just as much."

"No wonder you cook such a spread. You want help?"

"I never turn it down." Being in the kitchen with her would be interesting. Hopefully in a good way.

They headed toward the building and went in through the regular door, since the big garage doors at the back and front weren't open yet. They allowed the trucks to pull straight in and straight out, cutting down on response times.

A little conversation and the smell of coffee greeted them. As they walked farther in, Titus made an announcement to all within earshot. "Fair warning. Guest on the premises."

Jenna looked at him. "Did they really need a warning?"

"Sure. What if one of them was shirtless?"

She sighed with playful exasperation. "If I could drive back to your house and change, I would."

"Not a chance I'm letting that happen." He headed into the station's big communal kitchen. "Men, this is Deputy Jenna Blythe. Some of you probably know her already. She's going to be with us for a little bit."

Jenna followed him and was greeted by six curious faces. Two she knew pretty well from seeing them at Howler's. The first was Sam Kincaid, who was also Bridget's boyfriend. The second was Liam Murphy. She knew him because they'd been in the same CPR recertification class. Sam was a werewolf. Liam had a little bit of leprechaun in him, which made him extra good at finding things and unbelievably lucky.

She knew two others in passing—Frank Childers and Skip Mulvaney. They were old-timers, good guys, both human, although Skip was married to a woman named Jeanie, who was a crossing guard and a weather witch. The remaining two she didn't know at all.

She gave a little wave. "Hey."

Titus introduced the two unfamiliar faces first. "This is Brenden Nguyen and Kurt Amsler."

Each nodded as Titus said his name.

Brenden spoke. "Are you Tessa Blythe's sister?"

"I am. You know Tessa?"

"Not really, but my sister goes to Harmswood, and I know Tessa's the dean of library studies over there."

Jenna smiled. She was proud of her sister. "She is."

Kurt came over to get the doughnuts, taking the

boxes from Titus and Jenna. He gave her a longer-than-usual look, then glanced at Titus. "Three dozen today? Does that mean you have bad news?"

Titus shook his head. "Third dozen is from the deputy."

"Hey, thanks," Frank said. "We always run out of doughnuts too fast."

"Not today," Jenna said.

Titus hung his keys on a pegboard by the door. "If you have time to lean, you have time to clean. Trucks need washing. Floors need mopping. Toilets need scrubbing. Let's get the doors open. Don't make me find work for you to do. Breakfast in thirty."

Liam raised his hand, his smirk hard to ignore. "Chief, one question."

"Yes?" Titus said.

Liam glanced at Jenna. "Are we allowed to keep our shirts on?"

Titus laughed while Jenna rolled her eyes. "Until *Real American Firefighters* starts filming here, shirts will remain on. Now get moving."

And just like that, the men scattered with a chorus of "Yes, Chief," and "On it, Chief."

Jenna snorted. "It's good to be the boss."

"Takes a lot to keep this place running right." He went over to a rack on the wall and took down two aprons. He threw one to her. "Put this on. We have work of our own to do, Deputy."

"You Merrows are all alike. So bossy." But she put it on all the same. Maybe happy to hide her T-shirt for a little while.

"You can always leave." Grinning, he tied his, then headed for the big stainless-steel fridge that looked like an industrial version. He yanked the door open and started collecting ingredients.

"You need help?"

"Sure. Take these." He handed her two dozen eggs and a big package each of sausages and bacon. He came out with two gallons of milk in one hand and a gallon of orange juice in the other. "You can put those on the counter."

"What else can I do?"

"Bowls are in the big cabinet against the wall. We need three big ones. Get the set of measuring cups, plus the big Pyrex one with the handle. And the cookie sheets."

While she did that, he got the rest of the ingredients together.

Before long, things were cooking, and delicious smells were filling the space. While he poured pancake batter onto the griddle and fried the bacon, she made more coffee, checked on the biscuits, and turned the sausages. They took turns stirring the eggs and watching the home fries.

Jam, butter, and syrup made it to the big table, along with stacks of plates, utensils, juice glasses, and coffee mugs.

Finally, Titus added a few more pancakes to a big stack, then nodded at her. "Go ahead and ring the bell."

"Bell?" She looked around. "That one by the door?"

"Yep."

She went over and gave the clapper a few good rings. The peal rang out over the station, and within a few seconds, the men started returning.

They filled in around the table and began loading their plates with food.

She took her seat beside Titus and helped herself to a pancake and some bacon, the two things closest to her.

The phone rang.

Kurt jumped up. "I got it."

He answered the old-fashioned black phone on the wall. "Nocturne Falls Fire Department. Yes, she's right here." He looked at Jenna. "It's for you, Deputy. It's Birdie, down at the sheriff's department. She says it's important."

"Thanks." Jenna got up and immediately pulled her phone out of her back pocket. She'd had it on silent and had missed two calls, both from Birdie. "Rats," she muttered.

She went to the phone on the wall, taking the receiver from Kurt. "Hi, Birdie. Sorry I missed your calls. I was helping Titus make breakfast for the guys at the station."

"How nice! Well, I'm sorry to interrupt your domestic bliss, but a woman just came in here looking for you. She says she's only in town for a few days and thought you worked here and wanted to get in touch with you. She says she's an old friend and that you go all the way back to something called battle camp? Said you served together?"

Jenna's memories of those days came flooding back. They were good times. Battle camp had provided some of her favorite moments growing up.

Her time in service had been harder, but the friendships she'd formed had helped. "Was it Ingvar Swenson?"

"Yes, how did you know? Beautiful girl, although—"

Jenna interrupted to answer the first question. "Ingvar is an old friend. She contacted my mom, trying to find me a day or so ago. I can't believe she's here. I haven't seen her in ages. Did she leave a number?"

"She did. But, Deputy, I have to say, even if she is a friend of yours, she gave off a slightly creepy vibe."

Jenna laughed. "That's Ingvar. She's a seer. They tend to be a little different. Seers are kind of the ancient Norse version of a witch. They also do some healing work." Now that Ingvar was in town, she might be able to help figure out the spell that had been cast over her and Titus. "Let me guess. Was it the raven's claw necklace or the tuft of cat fur in her hair that got your attention first?"

"Ugh." Birdie sniffed. "Is that what that fuzzy headband was? I thought I smelled cat. I'll text you her number, although she said she already had yours. She was just hoping to surprise you."

"Thanks. Did you tell her what's going on? Or where I am?"

"Nope. Not a word. I just said you were out in the field working on a case. I figured that would cover it without being a complete lie."

"That's perfect, thank you. I guess I'll talk to you later."

"Hey! How's it going with my nephew? Must be all right if you helped him cook for the house today."

"It's…going." Jenna was hesitant to say too much, knowing what a frenzy Birdie could get spun up into. Also, because he was only about ten feet away. Engaged in conversation with his guys but still close enough to hear her if he wanted to. "We've agreed this whole thing will go a lot easier if we work as a team. So that's where we're at."

"A team, huh?"

Jenna could practically hear Birdie's smile. "Anything new on the evidence gathered at the attic scene? Prints? Anything like that?"

"Partial thumb and fingerprints were recovered off of a piece of the box, but they haven't turned up any matches yet."

"What about from Alice? Anything new there?"

"Nope. Sorry, Jenna. You'll be the first to know, I promise."

"Could you have a copy of the case file sent over to the firehouse? I don't have a laptop, just my phone, so a hard copy would be great."

"You got it. I'll get it there within the hour."

"That would be awesome. Thanks."

"On it." Birdie hung up.

Jenna put the receiver back on the cradle and stood there for a minute. She hadn't seen Ingvar in ages. They'd been thick as thieves once but had drifted apart after their service had ended. It happened. Not because they'd made a conscious decision to stop being friends. They'd never do that.

But Jenna had moved to Nocturne Falls and taken the job with the sheriff's department. And Ingvar had gotten an apprenticeship with a well-known seer and had disappeared into her own intense studies.

Life had happened to both of them. It would be good to reconnect and catch up. Jenna had a feeling it would be as easy between them as it always had been, which would be nice. Having someone to talk to about Titus and the spell would be great. Someone, unlike Tessa or Birdie, who could keep a calm head about the whole thing and not start making wedding plans.

"Everything all right?"

She blinked, looking at Titus. Handsome, handsome Titus. "Yep, everything's fine. Nothing new from Birdie on the case. Well, they found some partial prints but haven't identified them yet."

"That's a bummer. You seemed happy. I thought maybe there was some good news."

How much catching up could she and Ingvar do with Titus around? He wasn't going to want to go for a girls' night out. "There was, but it didn't have anything to do with the case. Just an old friend in town who stopped by the department to see me."

"A boyfriend?"

She narrowed her eyes. "No." Was he jealous? "A female friend. Someone I was in service with. All valkyries and berserkers have to do mandatory fieldwork for four years. A few get exempted. A few stay in longer. Some even make it their career. Ingvar and I both did an additional two, so we were in for six."

"She's a valkyrie, too, then?"

Jenna nodded. "And a seer. Her last two years were in seer school, actually. Once she got out, she continued her studies independently."

His brows bent. "A seer as in she can see the future?"

"In our world, a seer is more than that. They often do healing, sometimes guide battles, do a little magic. And yes, sometimes they can see or read the future. I don't know what she can do now. She's been studying for years. Unless something's changed in her life, I imagine she's gotten really good. She probably can see the future. Maybe even influence it. Legend says the best seers can."

His face brightened. "Hey, then can she see how we get out of this? And help us with the wraith?"

"I plan to ask her about it, but I don't know what she's capable of. For all I know, she's decided to focus on herbal medicine. I should also warn you that she's quirky. And probably not as easygoing as I am."

He snorted. "You're easygoing?"

"For a valkyrie, I am. Let's just say some of us are strung a little tighter."

"Yeah, well, you and your BFF enjoy your time together." He hooked a thumb over his shoulder. "I'll be elsewhere."

"You know that's not really possible."

"We can be a hundred feet apart. That seems like a good plan for your reunion." His smirk said he was only half joking. "In the meantime, there isn't going to be any breakfast left if you don't come back to the table soon."

She glanced over his shoulder. The plates of food had dwindled fast. Were these firemen or locusts? She stepped around Titus to point at the guys at the table. "Hey, I will take that dozen doughnuts back if you guys don't leave me another pancake and at least two strips of bacon."

Titus laughed. "And here I was worried how you'd fit in."

They went back to their seats and finished their breakfast. When it was over, Frank, Brenden, and Sam went to work on cleanup, leaving Titus and Jenna free. The other guys disappeared into different parts of the station.

Titus had his hands on his hips. "I'm headed to my office. I have about an hour's worth of work to get done. A hundred feet won't get you full roam of the firehouse, but it'll get you to the meeting room next door if you want some private space."

She folded her arms and looked up at him. "Is that your way of telling me you don't want me in your office?"

"No. I just thought you'd be bored in there. I have some paperwork to do. It's not going to be very exciting. Unless you find field reports and acquisition forms thrilling stuff."

"Not really." Being near him was exciting enough, thanks to the spell. "I have some things I can do. Birdie's sending over the case file on the bomb. But maybe later, after your paperwork, we could have a look at the race details? Make sure nothing's fallen through the cracks?"

"That would be great. We really should make sure we're all set for race day. It's only five days off. Maybe we could do that after we run by Bell, Book & Candle? We could pick up pizzas at Salvatore's for lunch."

"Sure. Sounds like a plan. One more thing…"

"Yes?"

"Would you be up for Howler's this evening? I was thinking I could set up dinner with Ingvar there tonight, and you could have your usual spot at the bar. We could both be there in such a way that no one would be the wiser that anything's going on."

"I can do that. In fact, let me know what time, and I'll have Bridget reserve a booth for you guys near the end of the bar where I usually sit."

"Thank you." He really was a good guy. She was glad they were giving each other a chance and trying out this teamwork thing. Which also meant there might be more kissing. Nope, not an appropriate thought for the middle of the fire station. Thank you, stupid magic spell.

If Ingvar could do anything to help with this, Jenna would be eternally grateful. Being friendly with Titus was great, but it was unsettling to know that something she couldn't control was influencing her thoughts and feelings.

She'd much rather know those thoughts and feelings were hers and hers alone.

Kurt came back into the kitchen with a large envelope that had the sheriff's department seal on it. "Deputy Blythe? This just came for you."

"Thanks." She took it from him, sticking it under her arm. Birdie never failed to deliver. Literally and figuratively.

"I guess that's our cue to get to work." Titus showed her to the conference room, which was actually one door away from his office, separated by a storage closet. It was perfect. She settled in and immediately texted the number Birdie had sent her.

Ingvar, it's Jenna. Just heard you were in town and looking for me. Can't wait to see you! Can you do dinner tonight?

She sat back to wait, wondering how much Ingvar had changed. What she was doing these days?

Ingvar's response came quickly. *Hey, great to hear back. Where are you now? I could come there.*

Jenna glanced toward Titus's office. As much as she wanted to see Ingvar, the firehouse didn't seem like the right place for that. She and Ingvar were going to want to hang out and talk. Titus had work to do, too, and she didn't want to be in the way of it.

Not to mention, she was dying to dig into this file to see if she could come up with anything new that might help them.

She texted back, *Tonight is better. Just so much going on. Let's meet for dinner in town. Place called Howler's right on Main. Seven OK?*

Sounds great. If anything changes, let me know. Can't wait to see you!

Same here. See you tonight! Jenna smiled at the screen. That was something to look forward to.

Until then, maybe she could make some headway on the case. She opened the envelope Birdie had sent. Besides the case file, there was a legal pad and two sharpened pencils inside. Jenna grinned. Birdie was on the case.

She spread out all the scene photographs and notes to give herself an overview of everything that had been gathered. Then she read through the notes, focusing on the interview Deputy May had done with Pandora.

On a whim, she picked up her phone and called the real estate agent.

She answered before the second ring. "Pandora Williams, how can I get you home?"

"Hi, Pandora. Deputy Jenna Blythe here."

"Hi, Jenna. Are you calling in an official capacity?"

"I am. I know you already answered some questions about the incident yesterday at one of your listings, but do you have time for a few more?"

"Sure. How are you doing, by the way? I know there was magic in that bomb. I did a walk-through with Deputy Cruz to make sure there wasn't any other damage to the home, and I could just sense it."

"There was. Alice is working on figuring out just exactly what kind of magic. And I'm doing fine. The physical effects weren't really lasting."

"That's not what I heard." She laughed. "Sorry, you know how word spreads in this town, and being a witch and all, anyway, it's been all the buzz in the coven."

Jenna paused for a breath. She shouldn't be surprised. "What do you know?"

"That you and Titus Merrow were both the victims of a love spell that apparently had a binding agent in it." Pandora's voice went from amused to serious. "Word has it that you can't get too far away from each other without experiencing some pain."

Jenna sighed. "That would be accurate."

"You don't sound thrilled."

"It has its ups and downs, I'll say that. But it would be great to have our freedom back."

"I'm sure. Well, the good news is Alice is calling a special meeting of the coven tonight to share her findings and put us all to work on a solution."

"That is good news."

"No kidding! I mean, I don't need to remind you what happens when the moon turns full."

Jenna paused. "Um, I think you do, because I don't know what you're talking about."

"Oh. Did you not speak to Alice yet today? She just sent out an email letting us know time is of the essence because if the full moon rises before this spell is broken, the effects become permanent."

16

Titus hung up his phone but sat staring at it, letting what he'd just heard sink in.

His door burst open, and Jenna stood there, looking like she'd been slapped. "We're in trouble."

He nodded. "Yeah, we are."

She frowned. "Wait. Why do you think we're in trouble?"

"Because Alice just called me and—"

"This spell becomes permanent on the full moon? Yeah, I know."

"No, that's not what she—hang on, what?"

Jenna came in, closed the door, and sat in the chair across from his desk. "I just got off the phone with Pandora. Which reminds me, I never did ask her about the Lemmons."

"What do you need lemons for?"

"Not the fruit. The people who own the house. Listen, Pandora said Alice is calling a special coven meeting to try to help us, which is great, but Pandora

156

also said she heard it's urgent because this spell becomes permanent when the full moon rises. That's not what Alice told you?"

"No. She said she'd like samples of our blood and a few strands of our hair to help her diagnose a solution to the spell. She thinks if she can't break it, she might be able to counterspell it. Enough to free us." He shoved a hand through his hair. "The full-moon thing is not good."

"No, it's not," Jenna said. "Maybe she didn't tell you because she didn't want to freak us out. That's only a few days away, right?"

"Yes." He rocked back in his chair. "Three days, actually."

"And the race is two days after that."

"It's going to be hard to run that if we can't be apart." He sat forward. "We need to get Alice these blood and hair samples immediately."

Jenna stood. "Let's go."

He got up. "Just need to grab my keys. We'll deliver the stand to Agnes at Bell, Book & Candle after we leave the Ellingham estate. Meet you at the truck? It's unlocked."

She nodded and headed in that direction.

He went toward the kitchen to get his keys off the rack. His head was spinning. It was one thing to be temporarily under this love spell, but to have it be permanent? To spend the rest of his life never being able to be more than a hundred feet away from another person? Even if you loved that person, that would be an incredibly limiting way to live.

Especially when those two people were first responders, like he and Jenna were. How would Jenna ever chase down another suspect? Or hunt for a lost child? Or drive street patrols?

How would he run into a burning building to rescue those trapped inside? How could he do school visits to talk to kids about fire safety? Or teach CPR at the senior center?

Both of their lives would be severely impacted. They had to work this out. *Alice* had to work this out.

He snatched his keys off the rack and went straight to his truck. Jenna was already inside, staring through the windshield like she was having a lot of the same thoughts he'd just had. He climbed in and put his seat belt on. "I know. It's not good."

"It's not good at all," she muttered. She looked at him, the slightest bit of panic tightening the skin around her eyes. "This isn't personal, but I do not want to be tethered to you the rest of my life. Not with only a hundred feet of line between us."

"I agree." He started the engine and threw the truck into reverse to back out. "For the next three days, our new job is the same one. Get free of this spell."

He drove with a heavier foot than usual, but he figured he could get away with it with a cop in the truck.

They didn't get pulled over, thankfully, and they made it to Elenora Ellingham's estate in about three minutes less than it usually took.

They got out and headed up to the big front doors.

"Nice driving," Jenna said.

He looked at her. "Are you being sarcastic?"

"No. That was genuinely nice driving." She grinned. "It's a good thing I was with you, though. Otherwise, I would have had to give you a ticket."

"Yeah, well, I know people at the department, so…"

She snickered.

He laughed. This was nice. But not nice enough to give up a lifetime of freedom for. He rang the bell.

Alice answered so quickly he wondered if she'd been waiting on the other side. "Chief. Deputy. Please come in."

They followed her through the house. She was a small, prim woman, at least compared with Jenna, who had the kind of athletic build and blazing good looks perfect for a woman with a magical sword tattooed on her back.

But there was no mistaking the power Alice wielded. He couldn't point to one thing, but taken as a whole—the glint in her eyes, the straightness of her posture, the set of her jaw—everything about her pointed to a force to be reckoned with. And she was.

After all, she was the woman who'd created the magic that made Nocturne Falls a safe place for the supernaturals who lived here.

She led them to her quarters. As they went through the double doors, Titus realized her quarters were one whole wing of the estate. He'd always known Elenora treated Alice well. He just hadn't known how well. The furnishings weren't as grand or opulent, but Titus imagined Alice wouldn't have wanted them that way.

Instead, her space was much simpler. It almost felt like they'd entered a different building. This was definitely Alice's style.

Crisp lines, quiet fabrics, with a lot of walnut, cherry, and stone. There was a serenity to it that he liked very much. He looked around for photos or touches of memorabilia but found very little. That also seemed to match Alice's style. She was a very private person.

No one knew much about her beyond her brush with death at the Salem witch trials, where Elenora saved her. Alice seemed intent on keeping it that way. The power she wielded had earned her great respect in town, but she was also feared because of it. Outside of Elenora, no one really knew Alice Bishop.

They went straight through and into a room that felt very private and very personal. He didn't know what witches called the space they practiced their magic in, but to him this was Alice's inner sanctum.

A thick woven rug covered most of the slate flooring, and Gothic arched windows let in natural light. At one end, a mammoth fieldstone fireplace took up a good span of the wall. Close by was a comfortable chair and small table.

The remaining walls held shelves stuffed with books and the trappings of her craft, which seemed to be more books, bottles, and boxes. There were a few ceramic and glass jars, as well.

What he focused on, however, was Alice's large, simple, wood worktable. It sat in front of one of the tall, arched windows so that it was bathed in light. Clusters of beeswax candles flickered on each corner, perfuming the air with the sweet scent of honey.

Old books lay scattered over the scarred and stained top, most of them open. The words he saw looked like Latin. Here and there, a few drawings broke up the chunks of text. Magic books, no doubt.

But that wasn't what interested him most.

He touched the edge of the table. "I think I made this."

Alice nodded as she came to a stop beside it. "You did. I bought it at one of the first charity auctions the firehouse ever had." She patted it lovingly. "It's served me well."

"I'm glad to hear that." He'd had no idea who'd ended up with the table all those years ago. And to think it'd been Alice, of all people. He liked that, actually.

She faced them both. "Thank you for coming so quickly. Of course, it benefits you to get my help, but it also benefits the town to have you both returned to full service. Such is the role of first responders."

"Thanks for working on this." Jenna glanced at Titus, a question in her eyes.

Did she want him to ask about the metaphorical ticking clock they'd recently discovered? He went with that. If only to get confirmation for himself and Jenna. "Is it true that the spell becomes permanent when the full moon rises?"

Alice flicked her eyes at him. Mad? Amused? Indifferent? The woman was so hard to read. "Nothing stays secret in this town, does it?"

"Not for long," he answered. "But that's a detail we deserve to know."

"I agree. However, I was hoping not to have to tell you at all. I'm sure you also know I've convened a coven meeting for this evening, specifically to discuss your spell."

They both nodded.

"I apologize for not telling you about the full moon, but I truly think that after tonight's meeting, it will no longer be an issue. I hope that will be the case, anyway."

"Us too," Jenna said. She pushed up the sleeve of her cardigan. "How much blood do you need?"

Alice smiled. "Not that much. A few drops from a fingertip will suffice. As will a few strands of your hair."

"I'm ready," Jenna said. She reached back and pulled a few pins out of her hair as well as an elastic, then shook her head.

Titus had never seen her hair down. Or how much of it there was. It fell to the middle of her back in sun-streaked blond waves.

Suddenly, he had an image of her, sword in hand, hair blowing in the wind, the smoke of the battlefield billowing around her. The warrior. The valkyrie.

The woman he was rapidly falling in love with.

He shook himself and looked away. It was just the spell, he knew that. But why did it feel so real?

Jenna ran her hands through her hair and pulled out a few loose strands. She held them up. "Is this enough?"

"Yes." Alice took the strands and laid them on a square of muslin. "Titus?"

He did the same thing Jenna had, running his hands through his hair. He came up with a few strands. "Mine are a lot shorter."

"Doesn't matter," Alice said. She added them to the muslin.

She went to a shelf and took down a few things, coming back with a couple of empty glass vials and a narrow metal case. She put all of it on the table, then uncorked both vials. Next, she opened the case and took out a long, thin gold pin.

"Your finger, Deputy."

Jenna held out her hand.

Alice pricked a finger, then squeezed several drops into one of the vials. When she had enough, she corked it, then ran the end of the needle through one of several beeswax candles burning on the table. She wiped the end on a different piece of muslin before gesturing to Titus. "Chief?"

He took a few steps forward, hand out.

She repeated the process, pricking his finger, then squeezing blood into a vial. This time when she cleaned the pin in the flame, she put it back in the case.

"How long before you can tell us something?" Jenna asked.

"One moment," Alice answered.

Jenna gave Titus a skeptical look. "So fast? I didn't know magic could work that quickly."

Titus didn't either, but then, he'd never been so close to magic like this.

Alice lit a new candle, different from the ones already on the table. It was a thick, squat, black beeswax stump with a red center. She looked at Jenna. "I'm going to test your blood first to see how deeply the spell has sunk into you. Once I know that, I can adjust the counterspell. I will know how strong to make it."

"I see. How do you test our blood?"

"Watch." Alice gathered a few more things. Long, thin metal rods. They were dark, so maybe iron. Then two small boxes, one with a crystalline substance in it. Salt? Sugar? Something else? The second held a waxy yellow powder that smelled of eggs. Sulfur. The same thing he'd smelled at the house where they'd encountered the magic bomb.

Maybe she had to use the same ingredients to do the test? He didn't know. Witchcraft was a foreign language to him.

She dipped one of the rods in Jenna's blood first, then sprinkled a little of the white and yellow powders on the end. She ran it through the black candle's flame. It sparked white and blue before turning the flame a brilliant green.

Alice set the rod aside. "The spell is surrounding you, Deputy. It's influencing everything in your world. But that's what I expected. That's how a spell works."

"So that's...good news?"

"As good as can be expected."

Jenna sighed as Alice prepared the second rod with Titus's blood.

When she ran it through the flame, it sparked white and blue, but this time when the flame turned green, it wasn't nearly as bright. As they watched, it darkened until it went black.

Titus had never seen a black flame before. "What does that mean?"

Alice stared at the flame for a moment longer before setting the rod aside. She looked at Titus. "It means...I cannot remove the spell from you."

Jenna put her hands flat on the table, unwilling to accept what she'd heard. "Why not? How can that be?"

Alice shook her head as she peered at the rod now cooling on the table. "Blood. That's how."

Titus rubbed the back of his neck. "I don't understand."

"Neither do I." Jenna twisted her hands together. "Please, Alice, explain what's going on."

Alice straightened the rod so that it lay parallel to the one she'd used for Jenna. "For you, Deputy, the spell has worked as it was built. It's enveloped you in its magic. Like an unbreakable bubble. But for Chief Merrow…"

When she didn't finish, Titus cleared his throat. "It's okay. Just say it."

Alice's brows bent as though she were deep in thought. "This spell isn't surrounding you. It's *in* you.

In your blood. It's become one with you. That makes it impossible to separate you from the spell."

"How is that possible? Why is it different for me than for Jenna?"

Alice's expression changed to one of concern. "There are two possibilities. One is that this spell was built with you in mind, and whoever did it had access to your blood and included some in the spell. If that's true, whoever built this spell is powerful. Or stupid. Or both. Blood magic is not for the uninitiated. It's dangerous even to those who understand it."

"What's the second possibility?"

"That the spell wasn't meant for you but got into your system by another means. But blood was still involved. And that's what complicates things."

He shook his head. "Why would someone target me? For a love spell?"

Jenna leaned her hip against the table. She could imagine all kinds of reasons someone would want to be part of a love spell with him. "We never considered you as the target, but I guess we should have. After all, that sulfur scent could very well have been about getting you there."

"True. But it could have just been to get someone in the house. Not necessarily me."

"Let's say it was," Jenna continued. "Do you have any secret admirers? Have you gotten any anonymous emails, letters, or texts from anyone recently? How about an ex-girlfriend who never really got over you?"

"No. Since Zoe, I've kept a pretty low profile dating-wise."

Jenna wasn't done. Her training as a law enforcement officer wouldn't let her give up that easily. "Have you made any witches mad?"

"Not that I'm aware of."

Alice blew out the black candle before asking the next question on Jenna's mind. "Who would have access to your blood?"

"Not many people," Titus answered. "You know shifter blood has its uses, so as a community we're pretty careful about who we see for our medical checkups and such."

"Wait a second," Jenna said, suddenly curious. "What do you mean shifter blood has its uses?"

Alice spoke before Titus could. "Supernatural blood, be it vampire, shifter, witch, valkyrie, whatever, is a powerful ingredient in certain types of magic. Mostly the worst kind. But that only adds to the price a vial of such blood can bring. Shifter blood is especially potent." She looked at him. "It's wise that you choose your doctors carefully."

"Hold up." Things clicked together in Jenna's mind. "You mentioned something about the spell getting into his system by other means."

Alice nodded. "It's possible, yes."

Jenna glanced at Titus. "You cut your hand on a nail right before the box exploded."

He opened his palm as if remembering. Then he shifted his gaze to Alice. "Would that be enough? A cut on my hand?"

"Did it bleed? Was it open that much?"

"Yes, but I heal fast."

She sighed, closing her eyes briefly. "It may not have been quick enough. I'm sorry. That could definitely do it."

He swore softly, balling his hand into a fist. The wolf shine gleamed in his eyes for a moment, then vanished as he seemed to compose himself. "So that's it, then. You can't remove the spell from me?"

"No," Alice replied.

"What if it's removed from Jenna but not me?"

"She would be free of it. You would still feel the effects for the remainder of your days."

"All my life? You're sure of that?"

Alice hesitated. "There is a very good chance, yes, but it's not definite. It might fade as the years go on. But it might not."

Jenna felt for him. He was clearly unhappy about this new development. She got it. Being temporarily stuck in this love spell was bad enough, but for a lifetime? She reached out and touched his arm to get his attention. "Hey, this is Nocturne Falls. Anything is possible. I'm sure Alice and the coven can figure out a way to free you."

The anger had left his face, but a spark of it remained in his eyes. "And if they can't?"

"Then they can't. Don't forget, the spell is supposed to become permanent for both of us when the full moon rises." She smiled at him. "Better to be stuck in it together, right?"

"No," he barked. "Not better. Who wants to spend a lifetime wondering if their emotions are real? Worse, knowing the person they care for only cares for them in return because they're magic-bound to do so. What kind of way is that to live?"

Jenna's heart ached, and instantly she understood. Did she feel for him because of the spell? Or because she genuinely cared? She had no idea.

He looked at Alice. "Is it just the love spell or the binding spell too?"

"Both," was her quiet response.

He shook his head. "There has to be a way out of this. What do you need? How do we unlock this prison?"

Alice frowned. "Chief Merrow, the magic used on you two was death magic, I've figured out that much."

He snorted. "Death magic for a love spell?"

She nodded. "It might seem ironic, but death magic is the most ironclad of them all. It's as dangerous to cast as it is to break. Maybe more so."

"Alice Bishop is afraid?" His eyes narrowed. "That doesn't sound like you."

"I'm not afraid for myself. The danger would be to you and the deputy. Breaking a death magic spell takes time and knowledge and great power. That's why I was going to try to create a counterspell first. To buy us all some time."

"So do that. Give us a counterspell."

"That won't work for you now that it's in your blood."

Titus went quiet for a moment, his gaze on the floor. When he lifted his head, he looked as though he'd come to peace with something. He gave Jenna a little half smile before turning to Alice. "You can still create a counterspell for Jenna?"

Alice nodded. "Yes, but that would mean—"

"I know what it means," Titus said. "Do it."

"No," Jenna said. She stepped closer to him so that she could put her hands on his chest. "That's not fair to you."

"Keeping the spell isn't fair to either of us. At least this way, you could be free."

"You're being chivalrous but also stupid. I'm not letting you do this alone."

He put his hands over hers. They were big and warm, and the gesture touched her in a way she didn't expect. "Jenna, you don't want to be tied to me for the rest of your life. You don't even like me. Let Alice and the coven do their best to free you."

"No." She slid her hands free of his to cup his jaw. "I like you just fine." She liked him a lot more than fine, truth be told.

He snorted. "That's the spell talking."

"So what if it is? I don't care. I'm not letting you do this alone. You think life would be hard never knowing if your emotions are real or not? If the person you love actually loves you back? How much harder would it be if you had to watch the only person you could ever love fall for someone else? *Marry* someone else? And all while you were bound to stay within a hundred feet of them?"

His jaw tightened as he took in her words.

She didn't give him a chance to answer with more macho, I-can-handle-it nonsense. "I'll tell you what kind of life that would be. The worst kind. One that was a daily misery."

He swallowed but said nothing.

"We're not doing that, Titus." She shook her head slowly while looking deep into his eyes. "Because we're in this together."

A few breaths went by without him saying anything. "You really want to do that?"

With her hands still on his face, she leaned in and brushed her lips across his. "I really do."

"Okay." He took her hands, kissed her palms, then looked at Alice. "Whatever you can do for us, do it. But please, there has to be a way to fix this. You said time, knowledge, and power. How can we give you more of those?"

Alice took a deep breath. "I have the power. The time cannot be changed. But the knowledge…that might be something you can help with."

They turned toward her and in unison said, "How?"

"If you can find the witch or sorcerer who crafted this spell, that could give me some insight as to how to break it."

Jenna tipped her head. "Don't you have any magical way of finding that out?"

"I do, but it would take longer than we have. I doubt I'd have my result until after the full moon."

"Understood." Jenna looked at Titus. "I know you have the inspector coming, but I really need to dig into this investigation if we have any chance of figuring this out in time."

He nodded. "We'll make it work. This takes precedence."

"In the meantime," Alice said, "I will have every available witch in the coven working on this."

"Thank you." Jenna smiled. "Are you sure there isn't anything else we can do to help?"

Alice thought for a moment. "There is one thing, but I don't think you're going to like it."

"Anything," Titus said.

She looked at him with a curious glint in her eye. "Stop fighting the spell. One of the elements I found in it was a strengthening agent, which means the more you fight it, the harder it works."

A thousand things went through Jenna's head. All of them to do with Titus. "Are you telling us to give in to…what we've been feeling?"

Alice nodded, the corners of her mouth turning up in a cheeky smile. "Would that be so bad? You're both young, attractive individuals. Both consenting. I'm not telling you to go on a murdering spree through town here. Just stop fighting the attraction. All that does is strengthen the spell. You may find that if you give in a little, things mellow out."

Jenna looked at Titus, and he looked at her. She shrugged. "I'm game if you are."

He slipped his hand in hers. "It's worth a shot."

Having that much contact with him sent a ripple of pleasure through her, and for a moment, she wanted to push back at that pleasure in an attempt to keep the spell at bay. But that wasn't what they were supposed to do.

Instead, she allowed herself to feel the satisfaction of his touch and gave his hand a little squeeze in return. "You'll let us know the minute you figure anything out?"

Alice nodded. "I will." She started pulling books and bowls and ingredients from the shelves.

Titus tugged Jenna toward the door. "We'll see ourselves out. Thank you again."

Alice mumbled something as she stared up at one spot on her bookcase.

They left and went straight to the truck, where he finally let go of her hand. He started the engine, and they left the estate, headed for town.

"You're really okay with this?" he asked. "You're not going to hurt my feelings if you change your mind and want to be free."

She sat back a little, studying his profile and seeing traces of his wolf here and there. "Would you do that to me?"

He glanced over. "No."

"Then there you go." She smiled and looked out the window. "We're in this together, Merrow. And that's it."

His phone chimed with an incoming text at the same time hers did. She pulled it out of her pocket. "It's from Alice. She says she forgot to tell us there is one other way to break the spell."

"What's that?"

"If the creator dies."

18

"That's kind of harsh," Titus said. The outcome at Alice's had been both disappointing and encouraging. He might be stuck in this spell, but he wasn't alone. Jenna's refusal to leave him had only made him fall harder for her.

And he'd decided, in light of what Alice had told them, that from now on, he was just going to lean into those feelings.

Jenna nodded. "So is the spell. But yeah, what are the odds that would happen? I'm not about to have blood on my hands for this. These spells are just annoying and inconvenient. Not fatal. Thankfully."

"I'm with you on that."

She put her phone away. "Are we still headed for Bell, Book & Candle?"

"Yes. Then Salvatore's to pick up pizzas for lunch. Which reminds me, would you mind calling that in?"

She got her phone out again. "Sure. What's the order?"

"Two meat lovers, two pepperoni, one extra cheese. All larges." He grinned at her. "Feel free to get something for yourself."

She laughed. "Seriously? Never mind, I saw them plow through breakfast. Hey, can we get one of their white pizzas? Those are really good."

"I've never tried it, but if you like it, then I'm in."

"Yeah?" Her smile grew. She made the call to Salvatore's and ordered all the pies. When she hung up, she gave him a curious look. "So was agreeing to try the white pizza you giving in to the spell? Or are you the kind of person who likes to try new things?"

He couldn't resist throwing the question back at her. "Is this you asking, or is the spell making you ask?"

She let out a little snort-laugh that made him laugh too. "It's me asking. So? Answer the question."

"I like to try new things." He turned onto Main Street.

"Is that why you eat dinner at Howler's every night?"

"Point taken. Since we're going there tonight so you can meet your friend, how about tomorrow night we go to Big Daddy Bones? You told me I should go there anyway."

"Okay. If we're not knee-deep in investigating this spell."

"We still need to eat." He parked in the closest spot to the bookstore. "Come on, I'll introduce you to Agnes."

He got out, got the crystal ball stand out of the back seat, then joined Jenna on the sidewalk. He held the shop door for her as they went in.

It took Agnes all of three seconds to greet him. "Titus! How are you?"

"I'm good. How are you?"

She approached him, arms wide, and embraced him in a hug. "I'm better now. Is that my stand?"

"It is." He handed it over.

She took it, but her eyes, bright blue even behind her round, black frames, flicked over to Jenna. "Who is this gorgeous creature you've brought with you?"

"This is my friend Deputy Jenna Blythe."

"Blythe?" Agnes tapped a finger on her hot pink lips. "Are you related to Tessa Blythe? You must be. You look like sisters."

"We are," Jenna said. "She must shop here a lot."

"Oh, yes, I love Tessa. She's in here all the time."

Jenna smiled. "She does love bookstores. And books. And reading."

Agnes took a step back, then pointed at Jenna's T-shirt. "And I love your taste in television. Come with me. I have something to show you."

Jenna glanced at Titus, but he just shrugged. Agnes was a force to be reckoned with. If she said *come*, you went.

They both did, following her into a different part of the store.

Where she promptly pointed out a display of *Real American Firefighters* merchandise. "Have you seen this stuff?"

Jenna's lips pursed. "I, uh, I'm not really that much of a fan. I just—"

Titus leaned in. "Quit lying, Blythe. You know you want one of everything."

"I do not." She stuck her tongue out at him.

Titus snickered. "She'll take the coffee mug. And a sticker. Do you want the body pillow too?"

Agnes laughed. "Why would she need the body pillow when she's got you?"

In two seconds flat, Jenna flushed.

Titus realized that wasn't ground either of them was ready to cover. He stepped in front of her and changed the subject, giving her a moment to regain her composure. "Make sure you don't get that stand wet, Agnes. But if you do, dry it off immediately. And keep it out of direct sunlight."

She seemed to understand the *Real American Firefighters* topic was over. "It won't get wet or be in sunlight. Let me go grab my checkbook, and I'll give you what I owe you."

"I'll be right here."

Agnes left, and he checked on Jenna. "She definitely says what she thinks, doesn't she?"

Jenna nodded. "Yeah. You think everyone's thinking that?"

"No. But what if they are? Is there something wrong with being involved with me? I thought we were past all that."

"There's nothing wrong with being involved with you, and we are past that. I guess I'm just not used to my personal life being discussed like the weather."

She picked up a coffee mug that said *Real American Firefighters—Bigger, Hotter, Better*. "Maybe that's because I haven't had a personal life."

"I suppose that alone might make people talk. But the fact that neither of us has been dating and now we're together…that's going to cause some discussion."

"Yeah. I just need to get used to it, huh?"

"Until it dies down. Or you could embrace it."

Her eyes narrowed, and after a moment, she nodded. "Hard to tease someone about something when they embrace it."

"That's right."

A slow smile spread across her face, and she turned toward the display.

Agnes came back, check in hand, taking all his attention. "Here you go. Thank you so much."

Titus accepted the check. "You're welcome. Let me know if you need anything else."

"I will."

Jenna reappeared at his side, arms full of *Real American Firefighters* merchandise. "Found a few things."

Agnes nodded. "I see that. I think that qualifies you for a volume discount."

Agnes rang her up, Jenna paid, and they were on their way to Salvatore's.

The pies were ready. Titus put them on the firehouse's account, then Jenna helped him load them into the back seat, and they were off again.

"Oh man," she said. "It smells so good in here. I didn't think I was hungry after that breakfast, but now I want to eat all of it."

"You can't go wrong with Salvatore's." He turned toward the firehouse, which took them toward Pandora Williams's real estate office.

"Hey," Jenna said. "That reminds me that I never got the information I needed from her. I ended our call after she mentioned the spell could become permanent."

"Pandora?"

"Yes. I wanted to ask her for more info about the owners of the home. The Lemmons." Her eyes followed the business as they went past. "I'm not leaving any stone unturned."

"You want me to go back?"

"No. Let's get the pizzas to the station while they're hot, let the guys eat. I can call her. I don't need to see her in person to get the info I'm after."

"Okay."

She left her *Real American Firefighters* stuff in the truck and helped him unload the pizzas and carry them in, but only got a few steps inside before Liam took the boxes from her.

"I got these, Deputy. Although I guess this is one of those things I should do shirtless, huh?" He laughed at his own joke.

She gave him an appraising glance. "I don't know, Liam. Best leave that to the professionals."

"Nice burn, Deputy," Kurt said. "We might have to make you an honorary firewoman."

Hands on her hips and a glint in her eye, she shook her head. "Thanks, but I'm not ready for a demotion at this point in my life."

"Ouch," Titus said, laughing as he came out of the kitchen. "What have we unleashed?" He pointed behind him. "Go eat, but don't touch the white pie. That's Jenna's."

Kurt looked at her. "Aren't you eating with us?"

"I have a call to make. Then I'll be in."

Titus stayed while Liam and Kurt disappeared to eat. "You going to use the conference room?"

She nodded. "Yes. I'll be in to eat as soon as I'm done."

"Okay. See you in there." He went to the kitchen, expecting her to be a while, but she came in only a few minutes later. "Everything all right?"

"It's all good. Pandora was with a customer, but said she'd pull the Lemmons file and email me the info." She took the seat next to him, the same one she'd had at breakfast. "Let's eat some pizza."

Pandora's file arrived half an hour after lunch, but it took Jenna only a few minutes of reading to see that the Lemmons were pretty ordinary folks. Humans, from what she could tell. She sent a quick text to Pandora, who confirmed that, yes, they were.

It was unlikely that the human couple, who were in their late sixties and moving to Illinois to be close to their grandchildren, had hired a witch to build a magical bomb to entrap someone in a love spell.

Jenna was back at square one. Could Titus have been the focus of the bomb? It didn't seem that way. There were no obvious admirers in his life who were capable enough to pull something like that off. And how would anyone have known Titus would be the firefighter to respond? They couldn't have. Not really.

Was she the focus of the love spell? That seemed even less likely.

So what about the wraith? Titus said he'd seen it in the attic, though that didn't mean it was connected to the bomb. Wraiths had no capability for magic and no way of contacting anyone capable of doing something like that on their behalf.

Alice had said the bomb used death magic. Jenna couldn't imagine anything more like catnip to a wraith than death magic.

Could the wraith really be after her? The hard truth was…yes. The fact that it had shown up in the attic meant it had probably been in town for a few days. Watching. Waiting. Looking for the right chance to come after her.

The dark recesses of the attic were a pretty perfect place for a wraith to materialize. Just like the woods in early evening had been.

But that didn't help her figure out who'd created that bomb.

She put her head in her hands and sighed. This was the frustrating part of any investigation, that feeling that she'd hit a brick wall and didn't know which way to go next.

Maybe if she went back out to the house and had

another look around, that would spark something. Give her a new direction or a fresh idea.

Knowing how important it was to find out soon who'd created this spell only increased the pressure she was feeling. She got up from the table and went next door to Titus's office.

He looked up as she knocked. "How's it going?"

"Not great. I was thinking if I could go back to the house, take another look around…"

"Seems like a good idea. Do you need to call Pandora to let you in?"

"No, I have the number for the lockbox she put on the house. I can get the key out of there."

He stood. "Then let's go."

"What about the inspector?"

"I called and told him this isn't a good week and the inspection would have to wait. We have to figure out this spell."

"Thank you."

Thirty minutes later, they'd been around and through the house without finding anything new or noteworthy.

She and Titus now stood in the attic, having one final look around.

"Still smells like sulfur up here," he said.

She nodded. "Did you notice Alice used that when she did the blood tests?"

"I did. What does that mean?"

Jenna shrugged as she searched the shadows with the flashlight on her phone. "Just that it must be a common ingredient in magic. Enough so that it might not have been added to the spell used on us for the purpose of making us think there was a gas leak. That might have just been a side effect. Then again, how was anyone supposed to get in range of that bomb if they weren't in here investigating?"

"Are you saying you think it could have been aimed at the first person to happen upon it?"

"No, I don't think that was the case. First of all, that's a lot of work and setup to make a random person fall in love with you." She turned her phone's light off and faced him. "That part of it makes me think they were aiming for Pandora. She was the one most likely to be in the house."

He crossed his arms and leaned against one of the trusses. "But?"

"This house is on my regular patrol route. My routine isn't hard to figure out. Look at it this way: If the smell of gas was intentional, that means they were trying for a fireman. But that's random. So if the smell wasn't on purpose, then they must have been trying for me."

He seemed to think about that. "So it was supposed to go off while you were here alone."

"I'm starting to think that. But who would target me? And why?"

"I'd say for that sword of yours, but after seeing how impossible it is for anyone else to get their hands on it, that can't be the reason. Although…"

"Although what?"

"Is it common knowledge that a valkyrie's sword can't be held by anyone but her?"

Jenna thought that over. "I mean, maybe? If you did some research, I suppose you could find that out. But not everyone knows we carry our weapons on our bodies like we do."

"So then, let's say you are the target. If that's true, and someone was going to make an attempt at your sword, that narrows down the suspect list a bit."

She nodded. "They'd not only have to know I'm a valkyrie but also about my weapon." She took a sharp breath. "Or maybe they know that when we die, our swords separate from our bodies. Same with berserkers. It's how our souls are carried to Valhalla. In our blades. It's why the walls of Valhalla are covered in swords."

"Okay, that's pretty interesting. Who would know that?"

She narrowed her eyes. "Besides you now? A few people would know some of those things, but probably not all of them. And none of those people would qualify as viable suspects." She ticked them off. "Your brother, Birdie, Tessa, Sebastian. I suppose all of the Ellinghams, really. Maybe someone at Harmswood that Tessa works with?"

"Yeah, none of those people are suspects." He sighed. "This seems like an impossible—" His eyes widened, and he stood up straight. "Behind you, Jenna. The wraith is back."

"Holy Loki." Jenna whirled, whipping out her sword in one smooth motion. The wraith was indeed behind her, looking more solid than the last time they'd seen it in the forest. In fact, it looked more human. And slightly, terribly familiar. But that couldn't be. Could it?

She brought her sword to bear in its direction. "There is nothing here for you, wraith."

Those burning ember eyes stared into her, but the wraith came no closer, just hovered in the attic's dark recesses.

Something was different about those eyes now. Something that felt like a memory.

She shook that thought off, refusing to believe the impossible. "Go! Back to the dark realm you emerged from."

But the creature still didn't move.

She wasn't about to stand here all day, waiting for it to do something. She lunged, sending the sword into the creature's amorphous belly. "Be gone!"

The creature dissolved, only to reappear a few feet away. This time, it opened its mouth, a dark gaping hole, and growled something at her.

"Did it just say 'Blythe'?" Titus asked.

Before Jenna could answer, the wraith reached for her. For her sword.

Titus stepped slightly in front of her and let out a hair-curling snarl.

The wraith shrank back.

Titus kept his gaze trained on the wraith. "Looks a lot more solid this time."

"It does. That's not good. Means it's getting stronger." Although its soul could be collected when it was solid.

"So what do we do?"

The wraith moved to the side, swiped at her again, this time connecting with the tip of her sword. *Helgrind* sang out with a metallic hiss.

Jenna jumped around Titus and jabbed, driving the wraith back. "There's only one thing I know to do. I'm going to have to trap it, collect its soul, and get it out of the mortal realm."

"How do we do that?"

"We don't. I do. But I need the help of a seer." She glanced at him. "Fortunately, I happen to be having dinner with one tonight."

"Great. What are *we* going to do about the wraith right now?"

"Didn't you scare it off last time while you were a wolf?"

"I did. Guess it's worth a shot."

In seconds, Titus shifted from man to beast.

The wraith seemed transfixed. Until Titus snarled again, teeth bared, fur raised along his spine.

Then the wraith shuddered and vanished, this time curling out in shadowy wisps into the darkness until nothing remained. Jenna exhaled in relief.

They stayed in battle readiness for a few moments, then Titus shifted back to his human form. "You need to get ahold of your seer friend and meet with her sooner."

"Agreed. But let's get out of this attic first." She didn't want to risk the wraith coming back while they were still there.

"I'm with you on that one."

They descended the narrow attic pulldown stairs, closed up the house, and got back in Titus's truck. Jenna got her phone out and sent Ingvar a text.

Any chance you could meet sooner? My day just opened up.

She looked at Titus. "Text sent. We can go back to the station."

"Great." But he still didn't move the truck. "You know, we never said anything to Alice about the wraith."

"No, we didn't." She stared at her phone.

"Why do I get the sense you don't want to? Is there something you're not telling me?"

"Maybe." Definitely. But there were things she wasn't cleared to share.

He twisted in his seat to face her as best he could. "Did that thing say your name? Does it know who you are? Jenna, this isn't the time to keep secrets."

She sighed. "I realize that."

"And?"

Could she really keep this information from him when they were in this together? No. Not in good conscience. "There is a chance the wraith knows me. And that I know him."

"Him? Explain."

Her phone chimed with an incoming text. Ingvar had answered. *Sure! You want to meet at the same place? Get dinner early? I can be there in an hour.*

Jenna held up her phone. "Ingvar can meet at Howler's in an hour. You good with that?"

"Yes. Now, please, answer my question."

Jenna typed fast. *Sounds good. See you there!*

Then she looked at Titus and trusted that he would keep her secrets. "Leif Guddersen. He was in the class ahead of me at battle camp. Very powerful berserker, but also very full of himself. At first, he was the kind of guy everyone wanted to be best friends with. Big man on campus, you know?"

Titus nodded. "I know the type."

"But as we entered service, it became clear he thought a lot of his abilities. And what they should bring him."

She shook her head, remembering. "He wasn't content to fight the battles he was assigned to. He wanted personal glory beyond the promise of Valhalla. He wanted fame and fortune and the spoils of battle he had no right to. He got this attitude that he was owed something just for being him."

"Sounds like a great guy."

Jenna slanted her eyes at Titus. "He was a problem, to be sure. A thorn in the side of the gods. A berserker gone bad is not a good look for them. And despite warnings, he persisted in seeking to make a name for himself by whatever means necessary. They couldn't let it go. My time in service was nearly up. I guess maybe because of that, I drew the short straw, as it were. I was assigned to take care of him."

Titus's brows went up. "I can guess what 'take care of him' meant. But why you?"

She nodded. "I was the ranking officer in my division. I was a couple months away from leaving the service. And I was… That is, I am…" She glanced at him. He would keep her secrets, wouldn't he?

"What?"

She had no choice but to tell him the full truth. "This isn't information I'm authorized to speak about, so you need to take this to your grave. Not even Tessa knows this, although she may suspect. I don't think my parents know either. Ingvar knows, but we were in the same unit and actually worked as a team for a while. Still, she wouldn't tell anyone."

"And you're sharing it with me?"

"I am. Partly because you deserve to know what's going on here. We're in this together. But also partly because that chapter of my life is behind me. Doesn't mean I still won't get in trouble for speaking about these things. I never thought I'd have to talk about it again, really. But now it seems impossible to explain what I think is going on without telling you everything."

"I won't say a word." There was nothing but sincerity in his eyes.

She took a breath, the confession weighing heavy on her. "I'm also a fell maiden. A kind of special ops valkyrie. We're a small group specifically chosen by Freya to wield life or death on the battlefield. Not just collect souls but decide whether or not a soul should be collected or given a second chance. That was one of the main reasons I was chosen to deal with Leif. And that green stone in my sword?"

"The one you told me is glass?"

"It's not glass."

"I figured that much. So what is it?"

"It's a resurrection stone. It's meant to allow me to save the life of a worthy soldier on the battlefield, but if Leif could take possession of it, his body would become corporeal again. He'd essentially regain his life."

A curse slipped from Titus's mouth before he could stop it. "No wonder he's hunting you down. He reached for your sword in the attic."

"I'm sure it's what he wants. The very fact that he's become a wraith proves he refuses to take his mortal rest."

"How did he find you?"

She looked at Titus. "He knows I'm the one who took his life. I'm sure it just took him this long to gain enough strength to hunt me down here."

"And he's gaining strength because…"

"He's close to his target. That's empowering him."

"The resurrection stone?"

She nodded. "And me."

"But how can he get the stone if it's in your sword? How can he even lay hands on your sword after what you showed me?"

"He's a berserker. Valkyries and berserkers can handle each other's swords for a short amount of time. Say, long enough to hand a weapon back to a comrade. Or take the fallen one's soul back to Valhalla."

"So he just has to grab your sword, rip the stone out, and he's alive again?"

"It's not quite that simple. He has to own my sword."

"And he does that how?"

"By killing me with it."

Titus sat in stunned silence. "He has to kill you with your own blade."

She nodded.

"Wonderful."

She faced him a little more. "Look, Ingvar can help me. I think. So long as she didn't shift her studies to creating natural dyes from plants or healing with herbs. If she stuck to the track she was on—practicing magic, working with runes, and reading the future— she should be able to help me get rid of Leif. Even if she is working on another aspect of study, she should still remember the ritual required to eliminate a wraith. She performed it plenty of times."

"I hope you're right." He put his hands on the wheel. "Do you think we should get her hooked up with Alice and the coven?"

Jenna nodded. "I'm absolutely going to toss that out there. She may not need their help. And really, her magic isn't the coven's kind of magic. But our seers can be incredibly powerful, and as this wraith is so connected to me, she should be able to deal with him pretty quickly."

"I really hope you're right." He pulled out of the driveway.

"Me too."

Titus sat at the bar at Howler's with a ginger ale in front of him. He'd picked a seat that allowed him to stare into the mirror behind the bar and perfectly see the booth Jenna was in. He wouldn't be able to hear her. Not clearly, anyway. There were too many other conversations going on in the restaurant for him to make out distinct words. But if she needed him, all she'd have to do was get his attention and he'd be there.

That was also why he wasn't drinking. He needed to have his faculties about him. If Ingvar really could help them with the wraith, there was no telling what she'd need from them. The last thing he wanted to do was slow things down because he'd had a beer.

Jenna was in the booth alone since Ingvar hadn't shown up yet, but they'd arrived early. Two waters and two menus sat on the table. Every once in a while, he'd catch her looking at him in the mirror. She'd smile, but it was tentative and strained.

He understood. He felt the same way, although he knew it was worse for her. She was in danger through no fault of her own. Being hunted for following orders. That was enough to set anyone on edge.

Jenna's head came up. She smiled and slid out of the booth.

He looked toward the door.

A tall, thin woman in a long black and burgundy dress flowed toward Jenna. She had black hair and dark eyes but a bright smile that helped offset her smoky makeup and the piles of strange jewelry she had on.

Everything she wore seemed to be made of bones or feathers or fur or decorated with skulls or carved with runes.

And there was an undeniable presence of power about her. In Nocturne Falls, people would easily assume she was a witch.

Jenna confirmed this was Ingvar by greeting her with a hug. The woman hugged her back. They seemed genuinely happy to see each other.

Good, Titus thought. Because Jenna was about to need her friend's help.

The two sat and fell into deep conversation. Their server came over, but Jenna sent her away with a kind smile and a few words that Titus understood was a request for more time.

He watched them, sipping his ginger ale and occasionally giving Bridget a shake of his head to let her know he didn't need anything.

Ingvar had the same proud bearing as Jenna. He took that to be a valkyrie thing. She wasn't traditionally beautiful, but her strong features were captivating. At the very least, there was something interesting about her. It was hard not to look at her, actually.

At the moment, her brow was furrowed as she listened to Jenna's story. Ingvar was nodding and seemingly listening with great intent. She reached across the table to take Jenna's hands.

Titus took that as a good sign. A gesture of *I'm here to help*.

Her gaze flicked to him suddenly. Jenna's did too. Then she waved him over.

He picked up his ginger ale and went to them.

Jenna reached for him, taking his hand as he joined them. "Ingvar, this is Titus."

Ingvar smiled at him. Then she blinked hard, and a cloud seemed to settle in her gaze. Another blink, and the cloud was gone. "You're…a wolf," she said softly. "It's my pleasure to meet you."

"You too." He glanced at Jenna. "Did you tell her?"

She shook her head. "Nope. Seers just pick up on things."

He'd have thought, after years of living in this town, that he'd be used to people with extra abilities, but it was still a little unsettling to have a stranger suss out what he was within seconds of meeting. He let it go and smiled back. "Again, it's a pleasure to meet you, Ingvar. Jenna speaks very highly of you."

Jenna slid over and patted the seat. "Sit down. Ingvar thinks she can help. Not just with the wraith but with the spells that we're under."

He sat beside her, putting his ginger ale on the table. "That's fantastic."

"I'm glad you think that." Up close, Ingvar's strong features made her look worldly wise. Considering what she was about to help them with, that seemed like a plus. She also looked a little world-weary, which probably wasn't as good. Or maybe she was tired from traveling.

But then what did he know? Maybe she always had dark circles under her eyes and a gauntness about her.

She shook her head. "But you may change your mind when I tell you what needs to be done."

He leaned forward. "I might, but do we have any choice?"

She frowned sympathetically. "No, not if you want to protect Jenna, and for the sake of my dear friend, I pray the sacrifice is not in vain."

"Sacrifice?" Jenna wasn't as much worried for herself or Titus, but for Ingvar. The truth was her friend looked a little frayed at the seams. Jenna hated to even think such a thing, but there was no better way to describe Ingvar's current appearance.

The seer nodded. "You have to offer yourself as bait. You know that. And we're not on a battlefield where we can work in the open and set our trap wherever it suits us. There's a lot more here to protect. We have to draw him to us, to a place that will keep all the unsuspecting safe. And there's no better way to draw the wraith out than with the thing he most desires. You and your sword."

Jenna sighed. "Yeah, I pretty much suspected that would be the case."

Titus frowned. "I don't like you being in harm's way."

"I'm in harm's way now," she said. "What's to stop him from materializing right here in the middle of Howler's?"

Titus looked around like that was a possibility he hadn't considered. "You think he would?"

Ingvar's dark brows bent. "A wraith has one singular focus. To regain the life they believe was stolen from them. Nothing else matters. A public place isn't going to deter him. Neither is killing anyone who gets in his way." She leaned in. "And as he grows stronger, as he's already doing, according to Jenna, he will get even harder to stop."

Titus shook his head. "But he'll eventually become solid enough to kill, right? So he won't be *impossible* to stop then."

Ingvar lowered her head slightly. "I've seen a berserker kill fifteen men with a blade through his shoulder and an eye swollen shut from the blow of a mace. I saw another doused in burning oil, then shrug off his blistering skin and fight on as if nothing had happened. These are not ordinary men. They are supernatural warriors. Imagine a being like that wandering the streets of your town in search of Jenna."

Titus grimaced, but Jenna spoke before he could respond. "No, we have to find him soon, while I can still subdue him. The time to do this is now. But…"

Ingvar looked at her. "But what?"

Jenna didn't want to hurt her friend's feelings, but this was a conversation that needed to be had. "You came here for rest and relaxation. You told me that much. Now you're in the middle of this, and I'm asking you to use your skills to help me. How taxing is that going to be for you? Because, to be honest, you look like you could use the rest."

Ingvar's smile was gentle. "I could, it's true. This last year of studies has been exceptionally hard. Far more trying than I would have imagined. But I would rather die than sit idly by while you fight this battle alone." She reached out and took Jenna's hand. "We've always fought side by side. Why should this time be any different?"

Jenna squeezed her hand. "When this is over, you're coming to stay with me at my house. For as long as you want."

Something flickered in Ingvar's eyes, a brief moment of unreadable emotion. Then she smiled. "That sounds perfect."

Titus cleared his throat softly. "What do you need us to do?"

Ingvar looked at him. "Nothing. That is, your help is not needed for this, wolf."

His eyes narrowed. "I want to help. Besides, Jenna and I can't be more than a hundred feet apart, so if I'm going to be there, you might as well put me to use."

Jenna smiled. "He's right. We might as well include him."

Ingvar seemed unconvinced. "Jenna told me Leif seems afraid of you, that you've scared him off twice now while in your animal form. I believe that's because he was a wolf warrior. It's very possible he thinks you've come to chase him from the mortal realm."

"A wolf warrior?" Titus asked.

Jenna nodded. "Most berserkers recognize the bear as their sacred animal, but there were others who chose the boar or the wolf. Leif's alignment as a wolf warrior would absolutely explain why he fears you. To him, you're the symbol of loyalty, stout-heartedness, devotion to the cause. Everything he should be, but also everything he turned his back on to follow the path of personal glory."

Titus nodded. "Okay, I understand that. How about if I don't shift?"

Ingvar sipped her water. "I suppose that would be all right. Also, you'd need to stay as far away as you can. We can't risk scaring him off. Once he knows what we're doing, we won't get a second chance."

Titus frowned, clearly unhappy with that option. "Fine."

He didn't sound *fine* with it to Jenna, but she let it go. He'd be there, that was going to have to be enough. She smiled at Ingvar, trying to cut through the tension a little. "I can get Tessa to be there too. Can't hurt to have another valkyrie when we're dealing with a wraith."

"No." Ingvar shook her head, causing her feather earrings to tremble. "Leif wants you and you alone. Even I'm going to stay hidden until things are set in place. I don't think you understand what a fine line we're walking here. If we scare him off, he'll be wise to our plan. He'll only end up biding his time until he's strong enough to take your sword without much effort."

Jenna let out a frustrated sigh. "So it's just going to be me against him? I don't like those odds."

Titus growled softly. "Neither do I."

Ingvar glared at both of them, anger flashing in her eyes. "You think I do? You have to trust me. Trust the runes I will cast for your protection. I haven't spent years in study, trading my health for knowledge, to let my friend be hurt."

This time, Jenna took Ingvar's hand. "I'm sorry. I didn't mean to imply I think you aren't capable or that I don't trust you. I just know how powerful a wraith can be. Facing one alone is not going to be a picnic."

Ingvar's anger turned to sincerity. "But you won't be alone. I'm going to pour everything I have into the runes I cast for you. This is how we've always done it. A valkyrie and a seer."

Jenna nodded. "I know. But this is the first time a wraith has wanted to kill me."

Ingvar bent her head slightly. "Odin's protection will be with you."

Titus made a little growl. "I'd rather she have my protection."

Ingvar's glance held some bitterness. "You may not believe in or understand our ways, wolf, but that doesn't mean they aren't powerful."

He sighed. "I didn't mean to imply—listen, I've lived in this town long enough to know that all kinds of magic can work in all kinds of situations. That's not what I have a problem with here. It's leaving Jenna vulnerable when it doesn't have to be that way."

Ingvar's expression softened slightly. "And I'm telling you that for us to have the best chance at taking this wraith down, it does."

Jenna put her hand on his arm. "You're only going to be a hundred feet away. Less than that, probably. If I need you, you can be there in seconds."

"And what if seconds make all the difference? Do you know everything that wraith is capable of?"

She hesitated, because the truth was hard to put into words. "No one does, really. Each wraith is a little different. Stronger in some areas, capable of different things."

"If you're trying to make me feel better, it's not working." He raked a hand through his hair, clearly frustrated. "I'll do whatever you want me to do. But that doesn't mean I'm going to like it."

"Understood." She squeezed his arm. "Thank you."

He nodded. She got the sense that while he understood they were done talking about this in front of Ingvar, the conversation would be continued when they were alone. That was fine with her. He was allowed not to like how this was going, but the wraith came from her world. Getting rid of it would take magic from her world.

Titus would just have to find a way to be all right with that.

He shifted his gaze to Ingvar. "How do you think it is that the wraith came to build and set that magic bomb? Can a wraith work that kind of magic? Do berserkers have that level of skill?"

"No," Jenna said. She should have told him that.

Ingvar frowned. "Not even remotely. He must have found someone in the dark realm to help him.

A witch who took pity on him. Or more likely, one he promised great riches to once he was made mortal again. Who knows? Maybe he even promised her power. Or something else she wanted."

"Great," Titus said. "Someone else to worry about."

"No," Ingvar said. "I don't think so. That deal would be between Leif and whoever he got to help him. It's not something we have to be concerned about."

"Good," Jenna said. She smiled broadly, eager to move things forward, and picked up a menu. "Should we order while we keep talking? It is dinnertime, and they have great food here."

Ingvar shook her head. "I should go. I have a lot of preparation ahead of me."

Jenna put the menu down. "But we haven't discussed what's going to happen. Or where. Or when."

Ingvar took a breath. She looked very tired. Jenna's heart went out to her. Was she really capable of helping them with this? "As for how, we'll do it the same way we always did when we were in service. As for where… Where did you see the wraith last?"

"In the attic of the house that's for sale," Titus answered. "Same place the bomb went off."

Ingvar pondered that. "Where else?"

"In the forest," Jenna offered. "Behind where Titus lives."

Ingvar nodded. "That's better. Open space, without the remnants of human energy. I can work there. Harvest the forces of nature to do my work. Tomorrow evening. I can be ready by then. Text me the address, and I will come to you. Now, I must rest for the work ahead."

Jenna didn't like the sound of that. "You could take some food with you. A veggie burger or a salad—"

Ingvar smiled. "I'll eat later. I need to rest first. I'll talk to you soon." She glanced at Titus, giving him a nod. "Until tomorrow."

He nodded back. "Tomorrow."

She left, and Jenna sighed as she walked away. "I know you don't like this."

"No, I don't. But then, with the way I feel about you, did you expect me to?"

She gave him a weak but understanding smile. "Hopefully by tomorrow night, you won't feel that way anymore."

He looked so conflicted. "You really think Ingvar can do what Alice can't?"

"I think Alice could absolutely do it, if she had more time. But Ingvar's been training in the ways of the seer for years now. And while dealing with the wraith isn't going to be easy, she's done it before. We've done it together. There aren't two people more suited to do this."

He nodded. "I suppose that's true. Do you think we should get Alice involved? Maybe to back you guys up?"

Jenna tipped her head and did her best to keep her tone light and amused. "Did you hear any of the conversation that just took place? What part of adding another person seems like a good idea to you?"

He sighed. "It was just a thought." He sighed. "You really trust Ingvar?"

"With my life." She smiled at him. "It's going to be okay. Ingvar is really good at what she does. As seers go, she's Alice-level good. I promise. I'm not exactly a slouch either."

He looked at her, deep into her eyes. Slowly, as she stared back, his took on the wolfy gleam she'd come to recognize as an increase in his emotions.

He leaned in and kissed her. Just a brush of his lips against hers. "Okay."

She was shocked by what had just happened. "You, uh, just kissed me. In public. In Howler's. There's no way your sister didn't see that."

His eyes rounded slightly, then he shrugged. "So what? Alice told us to stop fighting the spell."

"Yeah, but when the spell is gone, we're going to be left with a whole lot of friends and family who think we're a thing."

"Is that so bad?"

"Them thinking we're together?"

"No, I meant us being a thing." He was smiling now, looking very pleased with himself.

"But we aren't going to be a thing."

"We could be."

Did he really mean that? Of course he didn't.

It was just the spell talking. Once that was gone, he'd be back to the Titus she'd always known. The one who wanted nothing to do with her or any other woman. The one who thought she was totally annoying. "Titus, I don't think we should make plans for a future we can't see clearly."

His smile faded, replaced by…sympathy? Is that what was in his eyes? "Jenna, are you still that afraid of being hurt?"

His words went deep. "Maybe I am. But can you blame me? Your words, actions, and feelings are spell-driven right now. So are mine. That's no way to lay the groundwork for any kind of relationship. Not when the instant it goes away, we could be left with…nothing."

"That's not going to happen."

She turned away from him, but there was no way to escape him while sitting in the booth. "Titus, I have come to like you, but—"

"You think you might not when the spell is dissolved? I'm still going to be the guy I am right now. That's not going to change."

He was silent for a moment, and when he spoke again, his voice was lower, softer, and filled with the kind of earnest emotion that tugged at her heart. "Things have been good between us. I thought something was genuinely developing. I didn't realize you were just pretending."

She closed her eyes as she put her head into her hands and rubbed her temples. "I'm not *pretending*. I'm as much a victim of the spell as you are.

Can we just have some dinner and let this go? Seeing Ingvar has brought up some memories." Memories of Eric and how shattered he'd left her. Made it hard for her to want to have much to do with love right now.

When Titus didn't respond, she looked up.

He was gone.

Her stomach felt fine, so he hadn't put much distance between them. She just couldn't see him. She jumped up and scanned the restaurant.

Behind the bar, Bridget waved to catch Jenna's attention. Once she had it, she pointed toward the street.

Jenna dropped some money on the table for the server's time and headed out.

Titus was leaning by the door, looking for all the world like an immovable statue. A very handsome one. A very kissable one.

She stood next to him, shoulders squared, unwilling to back down. "I know you're mad."

"I'm not mad. I'm confused. And fed up."

"I'm sorry. I'm confused and fed up too. I didn't mean to take it out on you. But I don't think it's fair for us to get too deeply involved when it's all going to go away when that spell is removed." He wasn't Eric. She knew that. And yet, memories of him had renewed her reluctance to get involved.

He finally turned his head to look at her. "Why would feelings that have already developed suddenly go away? You're borrowing pain. I'd much rather borrow joy."

She frowned at him.

He straightened. "What's the worst that could happen if you took a chance on us?"

"I'd get hurt. Again."

"And what's the best that could happen?"

She knew what he was getting at. "My life would change."

He smiled. "For the better, right?"

She nodded reluctantly. It was such a hard thing to imagine.

"So why not take a chance, valkyrie? Especially when the outcome could be more rewarding than anything you've ever done before?"

Titus studied Jenna's beautiful face as she grappled with how to answer his question. He already knew the truth, but there was no way she'd admit it to him. She probably wouldn't even admit it to herself.

She exhaled. "I'm scared."

A feather could have knocked him over. The words he'd never imagined she'd say had just come out of her mouth. "Hey, it scares me too. The very idea of getting back into a relationship that could tear me apart again…"

He blew out a breath, then laughed. The sound was shaky. "It's hard to willingly put yourself in a place that could end up bringing you pain. Especially when you're like us. Used to winning and being on top. We're not the kind of people who lie down and let the world walk over us."

"No, we're not." She watched a couple of kids in Halloween costumes skip by with their parents. "But it's not just getting hurt. It's…" She seemed to be searching for the right words. "If things go badly between us, yes, I'd lose you as a friend."

She thought of him as a friend. If that wasn't progress, he didn't know what was. "There's every chance that won't happen. Especially if we don't want it to."

She frowned and looked up through her eyelashes at him. "Titus, be real. Have you ever stayed friends with an ex? Especially one who broke your heart?"

He hadn't talked to Zoe since the day she'd left Georgia. "Point taken."

"And it's not like we could avoid each other all that well. This is a small town, and we're both first responders. We're at the same events a lot. We show up at the same calls." She gestured toward Howler's. "We eat at the same places. For crying out loud, I work for your brother and see your aunt on a daily basis."

"All true." He stepped a little closer. Her blue eyes were lit up like diamonds. She was so perfectly beautiful it made his heart hurt. "So there's risk involved. I'll give you that. What good thing in life doesn't involve some risk? But how about this: What if it's all worth it?"

She stared at him, her internal struggle visible in her gaze. "I know," she said quietly. "Then all of my fears were pointless and I kept myself from having something good."

He took her hands in his. "Focus on the reward. The reward is huge. I mean, you get me."

She laughed, which was exactly the response he'd hoped for. "You're so full of yourself, Merrow. It's one of the things I love about you."

The words she'd just spoken seemed to register a second after they'd come out of her mouth. Her lips parted in a soft gasp. "I didn't mean…"

"Yes, you did." He brushed a strand of hair off her forehead. "You love me. Just like I love you. It's probably all the spell's doing right now, and that's okay. We'll soon see if it's real or not. But Alice told us to stop fighting it. How about for what might be our last night under the influence, we give in and let go and see what happens?"

"You're asking a lot."

"One night. That's not so much."

Her brows arched with the skepticism he'd come to expect. "What exactly are you proposing with this *one night*?"

"Oh, I'm talking about the big D." Grinning, he tugged her back toward Howler's. "A date. You know, dinner, maybe some ice cream after, along with a stroll through town enjoying the evening air, doing a little window-shopping. Holding hands. What couples all over the world do when they're out together."

She was smiling now. "We do need to eat."

"See? Fun *and* practical. Come on, Blythe, you know you want to. We can even sit on the same side of the booth again." He'd liked that. Being close to her was nice.

She gave in, no longer resisting his attempt to move her. "All right. I'm in. But how about we don't eat at the restaurant your sister owns? Not that I don't like Howler's, but it's sort of home-court advantage for you. Plus, you know Bridget will probably be texting Birdie updates every five minutes. That's if Birdie doesn't show up before our drinks arrive."

He stopped in his tracks. "Yeah, that's true." And neither of them needed the added pressure of being watched by his family. "So where do you want to go?"

Her mouth pursed coyly. "Somewhere else."

She wanted him to make the decisions. His idea, his plan. And if it all went south, he'd have to take the blame. Fine. But tonight was going to be great. He'd show her just how perfect things could be for them as a couple. "We aren't dressed for anything fancy. How about barbecue, then? Big Daddy Bones. You said I should try it."

"I did. Okay, let's go."

Twilight was fast approaching, dinner was in full swing, and the place was packed, meaning there would be a wait even for the outdoor seating, which was primarily what the restaurant had. But the smoky goodness permeating the air made both of their stomachs growl.

Jenna put her hand on her belly. "I don't know if I can wait. I'm starving all of a sudden. I really want barbecue, but forty-five minutes seems like an eternity."

"I'm right there with you." He would have been

happy to go to Howler's, but Jenna wanted barbecue, and he wanted to make her happy.

A thought came to him.

"I have an idea." He grabbed her hand. "Come on."

She followed. "If you can get us dinner without the forty-five minute wait, you're my hero."

That was all the motivation Titus needed. He took them straight to the takeout window. There weren't many people in line, since seating was reserved for table service. Customers getting food at the window weren't eating it on the premises.

She nudged him. "I don't want to rain on your parade, but barbecue is messy enough to eat sitting down. Standing up to eat it seems like a disaster waiting to happen."

He winked at her. "We're not going to eat standing up."

Their turn to order came up, and hunger drove their decisions. They ended up with two sampler platters, an extra rack of dry-rub ribs, baked beans, green beans, coleslaw, cornbread, banana pudding for dessert, and drinks.

Titus paid, then turned to her. "Can you wait here for the food to come up? I'll just be a few minutes. I need to go do something."

She gave him a curious look but nodded. "Sure."

He went out to his truck in the parking lot, keeping an eye on the time as he worked. He really hoped she liked his efforts, but the possibility existed she might think he'd lost it.

When he got back, their order was just being called. They each took a bag.

"Okay." She looked at him. "Where are we sitting?"

"You'll see. Right this way."

He led her to the back of his truck. "What do you think?"

After putting the tailgate down, he'd set up his cooler in the center of the truck bed as a table and draped it with the old plaid blanket he kept on the back seat. With no candle or flowers to use as a centerpiece, he'd gone with the small emergency lantern that was part of the kit he kept with him at all times. He'd used two stadium cushions, left over from his nephew Charlie's last soccer game, for seats.

"You just came up with this?"

He nodded. He'd done it for her. To impress her, sure, but also to show he was willing to go the extra bit for her. To do whatever it took to make her happy.

She smiled, eyes sparkling with delight. "I think it's perfect. It's better than perfect. Well done, Merrow."

He exhaled the breath he'd been holding. "Thanks. I'm glad you like it."

She leaned over and kissed his cheek. "My hero. Now let's eat."

He laughed as he set his bag down and climbed into the truck bed. He reached for her. "Let me help you."

She put her bag next to his, then took his hand. He lifted her straight up until she was standing next to him. A few stars twinkled in the purple sky. He put his arm around her waist and pulled her in for a kiss.

He kept it short and sweet but did nothing to tame the possessive need coursing through him. He wanted Jenna. He thought maybe he'd wanted her for longer than he'd realized. No spell needed.

She leaned against him even after the kiss ended. "You're pretty good at this dating stuff."

"I'm glad you think so. I am really out of practice." He gestured to one of the stadium cushions. "The truck bed isn't the most comfortable thing to sit on. I hope that'll do."

"It'll do. I'm not a delicate flower."

"I like that about you." Zoe probably wouldn't have cared for it. She'd been a little particular about things at times.

Jenna started unpacking the bags, and in minutes, the top of the cooler was covered with takeout containers, lidded drinks, paper napkins, plastic utensils, and packets of wet wipes.

He sat across from her. Even by lantern light, she was beautiful. He lifted his paper cup. "Cheers."

She tapped hers against his. "Thanks for doing all this."

"Thanks for agreeing to do it."

They dug into the food, which was amazing and messy and delicious in the way only good barbecue could be. They shared the ribs and bites of the side dishes, and when there was nothing left but bones, empty containers, and dessert, Titus groaned.

Jenna laughed and nodded. "I feel the same way. Good thing you're not going for a run tonight."

"Right? It would be more of a roll." He glanced at the containers of banana pudding, which remained untouched. "There's no way I can do dessert just yet."

"Me either," she said. "Eating that now might put me in a food coma."

"We could drive out by the lake and look at the stars."

"That sounds romantic." There was a light in her eyes he hadn't seen before. "Or we could swing by I Scream, pick up a couple of pints to go, then stop by my house so I can grab a few more things, then go back to your place and watch the stars from the hot tub. While eating ice cream."

"A woman who's not only willing to be seen in a small amount of clothing after eating a meal that could have fed a couple longshoremen, but who's already planning on something new to eat? You are definitely the woman for me. Done."

They cleaned up, packed up, and got back in the cab.

At I Scream, Jenna indulged in a pint of dark chocolate marshmallow explosion, while Titus got a pint of brown sugar toffee crunch.

From there, Titus drove straight to her house, waiting in the truck while she gathered whatever she needed. The evening was going exactly as he'd thought it would. Which was just about perfect. Sitting in the hot tub with her would be the icing on the cake.

Not that he had room for cake. Or ice cream, but he supposed he'd give it a shot.

He might even try for another of those Warhammer beers of hers.

She was back out in a few minutes, a secret smile on her face, a stuffed beach bag in one hand.

"What's up?"

She shook her head, mouth quirked to one side like there was no way he was getting that secret out of her. "Nothing."

He nodded but knew better. Something was up. He drove to his house with the radio playing the kind of R&B that made the night feel warmer than it really was.

They went inside. He carried the ice cream and the leftover banana pudding. She hoisted the beach bag over her shoulder. At the hall, she turned. "See you in the hot tub in a few?"

"Yep. You in the mood for a Warhammer?"

She grinned. "Maybe two. I can always eat the ice cream for breakfast."

He shook his head. "I'll get a cooler." He changed into his trunks, then grabbed a soft-sided cooler and stuck a cold pack in it before adding four beers.

On his way through the house, he picked up two towels from the linen closet. He walked outside and inhaled, never tired of how fresh the air smelled up here.

He set the cooler beside the tub before pulling the cover off and firing up the jets. With the lights on and the water bubbling, it looked like a portal to another world. In a way, it was.

The sliders opened and closed, and Jenna's lemony scent reached him as the breeze shifted. He closed his eyes for a moment, letting it wash over him.

"Hey."

Her voice was soft and husky and sounded very much like the voice of a woman who was teetering on the edge of decision. Was he that decision?

He looked at her. And his breath caught in his throat.

He had a pretty good idea now what her secret smile had been about. Apparently, one of the things she'd picked up at her house was a bikini. The top was blue with white glittery stars. The bottom was equally glittery red and white stripes. Not that there was much room for either.

He swallowed and, for a moment, thought maybe he should salute. "God bless America."

She laughed. "You like?"

"Uh, yeah." He was staring. Was he not supposed to? Because he wasn't about to fall back on politeness with all this woman in front of him. "It's, uh, very patriotic."

"Thanks." With a catlike smirk, she climbed into the hot tub and slipped into the water.

In that moment, nothing about the two spells dictating his life seemed like bad things. He pulled two bottles from the cooler and offered her one.

She took it and wrenched off the top. "You coming in?"

"Oh yeah." He got in, barely registering the heat of the water, and settled down across from her.

He twisted off the top of his bottle. He raised it to her. "Great idea."

"The hot tub? Or the bikini?"

He laughed. "Both. Both very good ideas."

"I have them every once in a while." Her smirk stayed while she took a sip. "You're kind of far away."

"What do you mean?" Was she really implying she wanted him closer? They should definitely eat barbecue more often.

"This is a date, right? Don't people usually sit closer on dates?"

He didn't need to be asked any more questions to take action. He slid around to her side until his hip bumped hers. "Hi."

She grinned. "Hi." Then clinked her bottle against his. "Thanks for dinner. It was great."

"It was. I'm glad you got me to go there. I need to take a break from Howler's once in a while."

"Couldn't hurt. But free does have its appeal."

He grinned. "That it does."

She settled in against him, tipping her head back to rest on his shoulder while she looked at the sky. "You can really see the stars up here. Better than in town."

"You can." He wasn't even sure if the words coming out of his mouth were making any sense. All he could think about was the beautiful woman cradled next to him. He kissed the top of her head. "I'm crazy about you, Jenna. You know that, right?"

She glanced at him. "I know…the spell is working on both of us. I feel that way about you. I just don't know if it's real."

"Do you want it to be?"

A longing filled her eyes that surprised him. She nodded. "I do. So long as your feelings for me don't change."

"They won't."

Her smile was quick, then gone. "We'll find out tomorrow."

"Are you nervous about that?"

She couldn't make out the thump of Titus's heartbeat over the bubbling water, but she could feel it where her cheek lay against his shoulder. "I am. The same way I'd be if I were headed into battle. It's more anticipation than nerves. Although there's more riding on tomorrow than any battle I've been in."

"And you trust that Ingvar still has the skill necessary to do what needs to be done? Even after being away from that work for years?"

"I do. Although…"

"Although what?"

Jenna didn't want to speak ill of her friend, but maybe getting Titus's opinion would help. "She looked thinner than I remember, but that doesn't really mean anything. And she seemed tired to me too. Did she seem that way to you?"

"Does she always have such dark circles under her eyes?"

"No." Jenna sighed. "She told me she's been studying long hours, working at her craft with the kind of intensity she didn't expect, but I felt worried for her. Still do. Especially now that she's going to use more energy on my behalf."

"You have every right to be concerned, but if she can't do it or isn't up to it, she'd tell you, right?"

Jenna twisted a little to look at him. "Valkyries don't let little things like personal health get in the way of what needs to be done."

He sighed. "So what's the answer? You won't let me call Alice. Do you know of any other seers who could help?"

"Yes, but the answer is Ingvar will do it. Whatever it takes, she'll make it happen. I just have to put my concerns aside."

"And if she doesn't? Or if the wraith realizes we're on to him?"

Jenna thought about that for a moment. "Then we tell Alice and the coven everything we know and get them involved for our next attempt."

"You're assuming we'll get a next attempt. What if tomorrow night goes wrong? Really wrong?" He sat up a little. "Jenna, this wraith wants to kill you with your own sword."

"I realize that. It's not the first time in my life I've come up against an opponent who wants me dead. None of them has succeeded."

"But this is no ordinary opponent. This one started out as a berserker." Titus shook his head. "I don't like this at all."

"I'm not crazy about it, either, but you have to remember that I've faced down wraiths before. Granted, none of them was out to get me personally, but there's a first time for everything, right?"

He didn't seem amused by that. "How do you deal with one on the battlefield, then? Tell me how it goes."

"A seer reads its energy to understand why it hasn't crossed over, then one of us uses that information to talk it into coming along."

"And that works?"

"Yes. Sometimes." Actually, it worked only with the really confused ones.

"That doesn't seem like the way you're dealing with this one."

"We're not. We're going straight to plan B."

"Why is that?"

"Because the wraiths we encounter on the battlefield aren't usually berserkers. That means we're dealing with a warrior who's already prone to entering an impenetrable trancelike state. There's no talking to a berserker in that frame of mind. It's doubtful this wraith has the ability to see beyond his goal of becoming mortal again."

"Great."

She settled in against him, enjoying his nearness. "It's going to be fine. We know how to do this. And remember, the more he strengthens, the more vulnerable he becomes."

"Explain that to me in simpler terms."

She grinned. "Once he becomes solid, I can put a sword through him."

He kissed her temple. "Fortunately, I have no doubt you're very good at that."

"I am."

They sat for a while longer, talking, drinking their beers, and relaxing, but when her second beer bottle was empty, Jenna decided she needed to turn in. She said good night to Titus with a long, slow kiss that almost turned into more.

Finally, wrapped in a towel, she went back inside, changed into sleep clothes, and went to bed. The ice cream could wait. Titus was really all the dessert she'd needed.

The evening had been perfect. Titus had been perfect.

She just hoped that getting romantically involved with him was the right decision, all things considered.

Titus was surprised in the morning to find Jenna in the kitchen and coffee already made when he walked in. "You've been up for a while?"

She nodded and sipped her coffee. "Lots on my mind."

"Tonight?"

"Yes."

There was a spoon in the sink. "Did you already eat your ice cream?"

"I had a few bites."

He came over to get coffee but kissed her forehead before grabbing a cup. "Tonight's going to be all right. Because there is no other option."

"Exactly. No inspector today, huh?"

"No, but part of moving the visit to next week was me promising to get my reports in to him ahead of time. That'll keep me busy for most of the day. Sorry. I'm sure you have things you'd rather do, but I'll be neck-deep in paperwork."

"That makes two of us. Birdie's already texted to ask if she can bring me the paperwork that's been piling up. I said yes. I'll be buried in daily activity logs and reports all day." She shrugged. "Might as well."

"That sounds…" He laughed. "Sorry, that sounds as terrible as my day."

She chuckled. "It is. But it's the perfect thing to do when you can't be out in the field. Besides, it'll help out the deputies picking up my shifts."

"All right, then. Let's get this coffee down and get the day started."

And so they did, making the trip to Zombie Donuts before heading into the station. Jenna helped him cook breakfast again. Birdie showed up about halfway through with two banker's boxes of paperwork for Jenna to do. She stayed long enough to have a short stack of pancakes and inquire about how their *relationship* was going, then she went back to the sheriff's department after Hank called to see what was keeping her.

The day seemed to drag on, but at the same time, it sped by. Five o'clock rolled around, and Jenna found herself on edge with the anticipation of what was to come.

She was quiet on the way back to Titus's. They'd picked up cold-cut subs from Mummy's Diner, but she wasn't sure she could eat.

"You okay?" Titus asked.

"Yes and no." She smiled. "I just want to get this whole thing with the wraith over with."

He nodded. "Me too. There's nothing I'd like better than for life to go back to normal."

When they got home, they ate out on the back deck. Both mostly quiet, both lost in their own thoughts.

Jenna ate half her sub, then wrapped up the other half. "I can't eat any more. Maybe later."

He did the same. "When this is all over, maybe we'll go into town and treat ourselves. Some celebratory hot fudge sundaes. Or the ice cream we bought last night. Whatever seems right."

She smiled. "I'm in. Whichever way we go."

They cleaned up the kitchen, still without much conversation, then went to change. Jenna decided on black tactical pants, a black T-shirt, and black combat boots. It wasn't the armor she would have worn in service, but it was close enough.

She came back out to find Titus in the living room, wearing a very similar outfit in desert tan. She smiled. "Great minds, huh?"

"Yeah. Also? This whole SWAT look? Very hot."

"Thanks." She grinned despite the anticipation running through her. "You look pretty hot yourself."

They settled in to read while they waited for Ingvar to arrive, but Jenna found herself staring at the same page in the magazine, unable to concentrate on the words.

Thankfully, Titus's doorbell rang a few minutes after they'd sat down.

Jenna closed the magazine she wasn't reading. "Ingvar."

He nodded. "I'm sure." He answered the door. The seer stood on the other side, the car service she'd used pulling out of his drive. She was all in black and wore all the same jewelry, except she'd added a circlet around her head made of tiny vertebrae. He moved out of the way. "Come on in."

She shook her head. "I have already prepared myself. I don't want to fight the energy of your home."

Jenna jumped up. "Hi, Ingvar. Where do you want us to meet you, then? Around back? We can go into the forest from there."

She nodded. "That's fine."

As Ingvar started down off the porch, Titus closed the door. "You ready?"

Jenna took a breath. "Yes."

"Then let's go."

They went out the back and down the steps. Ingvar was just coming around the side of the house. Dusk approached, darkening the horizon. She had a large cloth bag with her. Supplies for her work, no doubt.

"Take me to where you saw the wraith last. I'll need some time to prepare the trap. Alone. When you return, the wolf must stay as far away as possible."

"So you said." Titus didn't look happy.

Jenna did her best to intervene. "No problem." She smiled at Titus. "I'm not sure I remember how to get there from here."

His gaze was still on Ingvar. "Just follow me."

They started into the woods, Titus in front.

Jenna dropped back to walk beside Ingvar. She started to ask her friend how she was feeling, but Ingvar was chanting softly to herself. More preparation for what was to come? Jenna could only assume so.

She picked up her pace to join Titus. "I don't want to mess with Ingvar's concentration."

He nodded. He looked tense.

Jenna slipped her hand in his. "It'll all be over soon."

He glanced at her but didn't smile. "I hope so. In the best possible way."

Silence settled over them again, and they made the rest of the trek like that. What had taken a few minutes to run took about twenty to walk. Dusk fell hard, and within the cathedral of trees, it seemed far darker than it should have been.

In the distance, the familiar rushing water of the falls thrummed like white noise.

"We're here," Titus said as he came to a stop. "This is where we saw it."

Ingvar closed her eyes and stretched out her arms.

She stood that way for a few seconds, then opened her eyes and nodded, letting her arms drop. "I can feel he was here. Leave me to work now."

Titus glanced at Jenna. "We can walk down to the falls."

"Okay." She waved at Ingvar, who was chanting again. "When should we come back?"

Ingvar stopped chanting and glanced in Jenna's direction. Her eyes were completely black. "You will know."

Jenna backed up, bumping into Titus. "Let's go."

They started walking, and she shuddered.

"What's wrong?"

"Nothing." She sighed. "Nothing I can put a name to. I'm having some doubts, that's all. That's normal, I suppose."

"Doubts about what?"

"Our success rate."

"That seems normal." He took her hand. "How are we going to know when to go back?"

"Beats me. She said we'd know." Jenna shrugged. "Whatever that means. In the past I always stayed with the seer, but her skills have probably advanced with all her recent training. This might be a new technique. Hey, I know you have to stay back and all that, but I was thinking, just in case, maybe you should be in wolf form. Not that anything's going to happen, but...you know."

"Yes, I know. I'm faster that way. And the wraith is afraid of the wolf." He squeezed her hand. "I'll be ready."

"Thank you. I figure as long as he can't see you, it should be okay."

They went down a small embankment and came to the water's edge. The falls were to their right about thirty yards away. The sound was so much louder here.

Titus picked up a flat stone and skipped it down the river. Then he turned and pointed in the opposite direction. "Let's go upstream a little. Maybe we can find the right angle to see the moonbow."

"All right." She picked her way up the bank with Titus right behind her. At a small bend, they saw the moonbow appear in the mist. It was beautiful, and Jenna took it as a sign that the night would go well. "That's really cool. I've never seen it before. Heard about it, always wanted to see it. Never had the chance."

"I'm glad it was with me."

She nodded. "Me too."

She looked farther upstream, then behind them. "Do you hear that?"

He listened, brow furrowed. "It's just the water. I think."

"I don't know."

The low, gravelly rumble grew louder and more distinct.

He shook his head. "That's not the water."

They turned to look behind them in time to see the wraith emerge from the trees.

Titus's first instinct was to snarl back and send the foul creature running, but he had to keep the end game in mind, and for that, they needed the wraith to stick around. He spoke quietly, not sure how much the apparition could understand. "What do you want me to do?"

She kept her eyes on the creature. "Go down and around, back toward where Ingvar is setting up the circle, then get in your hiding spot. I'll go back directly. You just keep your distance like Ingvar said."

"I will. Be careful, Jenna."

"You too."

As he backed away, hating that he was leaving her but having no other choice, she spread her arms in a defiant gesture. Titus hung back in the trees, unwilling to get too far away.

"I see you, wraith. I know what you want. Come and get it."

The creature started down the bank toward her, but Jenna was faster. She darted up and around him, plunging into the woods. She stood in the gray space between moonlight and forest depth. "Come on, you dumb, dead thing. You want me? Chase me."

The wraith, much more solid and bigger than he had been previously, lumbered to turn and follow her. It was easy to see now what a mountain of a man he'd been as a berserker. His limbs that had once been more fog than flesh were now as thick as some of the tree trunks.

When he disappeared into the forest as well, Titus shifted into his wolf form. Thought after thought went through his head. The preparation he'd done hadn't been enough. He should have done more. Should have called upon his entire pack. Should have filled the woods with wolves, ready to go to battle.

But Jenna wouldn't have liked that. Nor would Ingvar. Already, his presence bothered her. And if something he did caused tonight's effort to fail, he'd never forgive himself.

He worried Jenna might not either.

But he'd also never forgive himself if tonight left Jenna injured. Or worse. Because no matter how she tried to play it off, he sincerely believed the wraith was a real threat. It wanted her dead, after all.

Whatever happened, Titus was going to do everything in his power to keep her safe. And if Ingvar didn't like that, he'd deal with that later.

Titus jogged through the underbrush, his ears twitching and turning to capture every sound.

The site was just up ahead. He edged farther out until his stomach started to ache. Too far. He came closer, inch by inch, until the ache disappeared.

Finally, he went past the trap Ingvar had set up. He looped around and went higher to where the elevation allowed him a better view.

He'd chosen a spot on an outcropping of rock. He was hidden by the trees, but he could see perfectly.

Ingvar had scratched out a rough circle in the dirt and leaves, cutting through a few mossy patches and around trees. Something filled the circle. Salt? Silver? It reminded him of the things Alice had pulled from her shelves when she'd tested their blood.

Five of the trees within the circle had runes etched on them in red paint. At least he hoped it was paint.

Ingvar stood at the very back of the circle behind one of the largest oaks, probably where she'd be hidden from the wraith.

Jenna wasn't quite at the circle yet. She was backing toward it, the wraith crunching through the underbrush as he followed her.

The breeze shifted, and a gust came up the face of the rock. For the half second it lasted, Titus got the scent of something bitter. Then it was gone. He chalked it up to whatever Ingvar had used on the circle.

His ears pricked up at the faint footfalls behind him. He lifted his nose into the air and inhaled, picking up familiar scents. He woofed softly in greeting.

Woofs answered him back.

Then three wolves joined him on the rock.

Birdie, Hank, and Bridget.

Maybe this kind of backup wasn't what Ingvar wanted, but Titus didn't care. All that mattered was Jenna.

He had to keep the woman he was going to spend the rest of his life with safe.

Jenna's pulse raced with the thrill of the moment. Battle was battle, no matter if her opponent was flesh and blood or air and spirit. This was her calling, her life's purpose. To defeat evil and rescue the worthy and in need. To help those incapable of helping themselves.

It was why she'd become a sheriff's deputy.

But it was also the first time she was the one in need of rescuing. Leif wanted to kill her. She knew that.

Helgrind knew that. The weapon thrummed and whined for release, sending ripples of bladesong through her. But it wasn't time yet. Not until she and the wraith were contained within the circle.

She'd done this a handful of times before with three different seers. Most often Ingvar, but after she'd left for seer school, Jenna had been paired with a fledgling seer named Gren, then lastly with another, more practiced seer, Sola. Jenna had thought they'd end up as a team, but Sola had had a penchant for the darker things and had lost her way. She'd been dismissed from service. That was the last Jenna had heard of her. The last Jenna had thought of her, too, because she'd left the service not long after that herself.

She stepped over the circle. "Come on, wraith."

He hesitated. Did he know what awaited him in the circle? Could he sense the magic at work?

If he needed coaxing, she knew just what to do.

She reached back and unsheathed *Helgrind*. The sword sang out with a bright, clear zing that seemed to fill the forest. The moonlight through the trees was sparse, but *Helgrind* gleamed anyway, vibrant with the joy of eminent battle.

She looped the blade around her body in a slow figure eight, showing it off, teasing the wraith. Displaying the resurrection stone.

His ember eyes seemed focused on it. He stepped inside the circle.

Jenna danced away, swinging *Helgrind* up over her head, then bringing it down in front of her again. She held it still, letting the wraith get a good look at the stone that could return him to this mortal world for good. "Is that what you want, Leif?"

He picked up his head. Looked at her.

"Surprised I know who you are? Of course I do, berserker. But now it's time for you to give up this quest and travel the path you were meant to." She couldn't very well tell him Valhalla awaited when it didn't. He had not earned glory, had no right to the halls of the valiant and brave.

He was a traitor to his own kind, and traitors didn't get happy endings.

She passed the center of the circle. She caught movement out of the corner of her eye as Ingvar stepped out from behind a tree.

The seer cast a handful of powder into the air and spoke ancient words, the secret language of the seers from centuries ago.

Jenna recognized some of the sounds, but none of the meaning.

As the last syllable fell from Ingvar's lips, a wall of light sprang from the circle, closing them in. It glittered and pulsated with the magic used to build it.

Ingvar stretched out her hand toward the wraith. "Now."

The wraith clenched his fists, tilted his head back, and roared.

The sound shook the trees and made *Helgrind* vibrate in Jenna's hand. She gripped the blade tighter as she went into battle stance.

The wraith lost what little translucency he had left, turning into a solid wall of living death in the form of a man.

An incredibly large and dangerous man. But a man who could now be killed. He pointed at Jenna with an arm like a steel beam. "You killed me."

His voice was a husky scrape of sound. Concrete on rusted metal. But it was Leif's voice all the same.

Panic sluiced through Jenna, but only for a moment. She leveled *Helgrind* at him. "I did what I was commanded to do. You went too far.

You destroyed the righteous for your own gain. You lost your way, berserker. Lost the right to that revered name."

He took a step toward her. "You're the one who went too far, valkyrie. Now you will pay."

He swiped at her, but she dodged his sluggish attack easily. His speed would increase soon enough. She sliced her blade across his ribs as a warning. The flesh split, and oily black fog spilled out and disappeared into the air. A second later, the wound closed.

Odin's eye, that wasn't good. He might be solid on the outside, but his interior wasn't. And that meant collecting his soul was going to be very difficult. But she could at least slow him down until Ingvar did her thing. Time to get medieval.

Jenna backed up and raised her sword to deal a potential death blow, but Ingvar stepped closer, arms outstretched, ancient words spilling from her lips again in a stream too fast to be understood.

She was too close. Leif could easily strike her at this range.

Jenna turned her head to tell Ingvar to back up, then realized she couldn't move. Not her arms, not her hands, not her feet. At least she could speak, but she couldn't bring her head back around either. She could see Leif advancing only from the corner of her eye. "Ingvar, what are you doing? You're supposed to freeze the wraith, not me."

Ingvar's eyes were still solid disks of black. Jenna didn't remember a seer's eyes looking like that before.

Her mouth kept moving as she continued the incantation.

Leif moved closer.

"Ingvar, *help* me. I can't move. What have you done?" Jenna's panic returned. Nothing like this had ever happened to her before. Nothing like this was supposed to happen. *Helgrind* quivered, bound by the same immobility that held her.

Ingvar remained oblivious, lost in the spell she was casting.

Leif was only a few feet away. Another step or two and he'd be able to take *Helgrind* from her.

Through the shroud of magic encircling them, she saw movement. The feral pacing of the most magnificent beast she'd ever had the pleasure of knowing.

With every ounce of energy she had, she yelled for the one person sure to come to her aid. "*TITUS!*"

An eerie howl went up, splitting the night with its haunting cry and ending Ingvar's chanting. Even Leif stopped moving.

Titus, in wolf form, came flying through the wall of light, shattering it. All at once, the wall disappeared, Leif dissolved into black threads of vapor, and Ingvar backed up.

Jenna's body began to tingle as the ability to move returned to her.

Titus stood between her and Ingvar, hackles raised, teeth bared. He snarled for all he was worth.

Beyond the circle, three more wolves snapped and growled.

Finally able to move, Jenna lowered *Helgrind* to her side and looked at the seer. "What's going on, Ingvar? This didn't go the way it was supposed to."

"No, it did not." Ingvar glared at Titus. Her face seemed to twitch and stretch for a moment as if her skin wasn't her own. She dug into a small pouch at her waist and came out with another handful of powder. She quickly tossed it into the air, muttered a single word, and just like Leif, she vanished into the night.

Jenna stared at the blank space where her friend had just stood. "What in the name of Freya is going on?"

Titus looked over his shoulder at her, let out a whimper, and collapsed.

She opened her hand, dropping *Helgrind* to instantly return it to her back, and fell to her knees beside Titus.

"Get him out of there!"

Jenna looked back to see Birdie, Hank, and Bridget standing where the wolves had been.

Birdie motioned to her. "You've got to get him out of there. There's wolfsbane in the circle. A lot of it. And he's been exposed. We've got to get him out of here."

Jenna didn't know exactly what wolfsbane was, but she understood that Titus was hurt. Because of her. She scooped the wolf into her arms and staggered out of the circle. She was strong, but Titus was a lot of wolf to carry. The runes would have to be closed, but she could deal with that later. Titus was all that mattered now.

Hank took Titus from her and immediately started toward Titus's house. "We need to get him to the hospital."

"It's that serious?" She felt sick as she followed along. What had he done to save her? "It wasn't supposed to go down like that. Ingvar's spell to freeze the wraith froze me instead. Something went wrong."

Bridget slanted her eyes at Jenna. "Ya think?"

"I didn't know any of that was going to happen."

Birdie looped her arm through Jenna's. "Of course you didn't know. I'm sure he'll be all right. Just needs some fluids to flush out his system. Wolfsbane takes about twenty-four hours to clear a body."

"If he didn't get a lethal dose," Bridget snapped.

Hank growled at his sister. "Deputy Blythe didn't do this. Don't take your anger out on her."

"Titus did what he did because of her," Bridget shot back.

"I'm sorry, Bridget." Jenna's next exhale was ragged. "I would never want him to be hurt. I love—"

Bridget looked at her. "That's just the spell talking."

Jenna shook her head. "Maybe it was a day ago. But not now. I would die for your brother."

Bridget's hard expression softened. "I just hope he's not about to do the same for you."

There was something horrifyingly full circle about being back in the hospital. Jenna sat by Titus's bed, wishing with everything she had that he was going to be okay while also wondering what in the seven hells had happened with Ingvar and the wraith and the trap that had gone completely belly up.

At least he'd regained consciousness long enough to shift back to his human form before they'd arrived at the hospital.

Birdie strode into the room without knocking. "How is he?"

Jenna looked up from her thoughts. "Still out."

She nodded and sat beside Jenna. "He probably will be for a while. It's all right. His body is working that poison out. Have you had any sleep? It's nearly three in the morning. Security only let me up here because I told them it was official sheriff business. That and Darnell Mansfield has always been a little sweet on me."

"No, not sleep. I can't. Not with him like this."

Birdie nodded. "I understand." But then she gave Jenna a hard look. "It's just as well you're awake. We need to talk."

Jenna sighed. "I know you're mad at me. I am so, so sorry. I swear on my sword that I don't know what—"

"Take a breath, Deputy. That's not what I want to talk about. I know you're not to blame."

"You do?"

Birdie laughed softly. "Honey, you love him. You said as much. No woman who's newly in love with a man, especially a woman who's been keeping men at arm's length for a while, is going to do anything to jeopardize that budding relationship. Not on purpose."

"But Bridget said—"

"Bridget is just being protective of her brother. Weren't you like that when Tessa got involved with Sebastian?"

Jenna sighed. "Yes. But I don't want Bridget to hate me."

"She doesn't hate you. She's probably already mad at herself for snapping at you."

Jenna frowned. "I hope you're right."

Birdie tipped her head. "Am I ever wrong?"

"Not often, no. I owe all of you a thank-you for showing up tonight. You weren't supposed to be there, but I'm so glad you were. I couldn't see much of what was going on outside the circle. What happened exactly?"

"We met Titus on the hill above the circle. There's an outcropping of rock there. Made a great vantage point. Anyway, as soon as she lit that thing up, we came down. Titus was antsy. But we could all smell the wolfsbane. I don't know how much she used in her magic, but she used a lot. I don't know if it was supposed to be a part of the spell or if she was trying to keep him out. It was enough that it should have."

"But it didn't. Because of me."

Birdie put her arm around Jenna's shoulders. "Fire wouldn't have kept him out."

Jenna groaned. "Why would she do that? I told her Titus wouldn't interfere. And he didn't. Until I called for him."

"He wasn't going to let you be hurt."

Jenna was at a loss for words. Then her brain kicked in. "If me being to blame isn't what you wanted to talk about, then what is?"

Birdie's brows went up, and her mouth puckered. "I did a little deep dive on your friend. Ingvar."

Jenna sat up. "You did? And?"

"And something seems off. Her pattern changed." Birdie pulled a file from her enormous floral handbag. She opened the file to reveal several printouts.

"Pattern?"

Birdie looked at the first sheet as she spoke. "Up until a week ago, her routine was so consistent you could set your watch by it."

Jenna stared at the paper, but lack of sleep and too much worry made it hard to focus. "Show me."

Birdie pointed at the first line. "If you look at the dates, you can see she does the same things every day, based on her credit card receipts. Every Monday morning, she fills her tank at the same gas station. After that and on all other mornings, she gets a tall chai tea at the Green Leaf Tea House. In the middle of the day, she buys what I'm assuming is lunch at the Peas and Love Café, which happens to be across from the Norse Studies Institute. Every third day, around six thirty, she makes a purchase at the same grocery store."

She looked at Jenna. "Ingvar's a creature of habit. Most of us are. That's not the unusual part. Now look at last week."

She flipped to the second sheet. "No chai, no lunch, no groceries all week. She gasses up at a different station and orders takeout almost every night. And look at this." She tapped a line item. "Three times this week, she bought an iced latte at Starbucks."

Jenna shook her head. "Ingvar's never been a coffee drinker that I've known. Where did she order takeout from?"

Birdie read off the names. "Peking Express, Bowman's Steak House, Fat Sam's BBQ, and Mello's Pizza."

Jenna's whole system went on alert, buzzing from what she was seeing, but she needed the full picture before she could accept what had happened. She pointed to the next couple of things. "What are these?"

244

"A large purchase at a metaphysical store. I looked them up online. They're basically a witchcraft-supply place. Then there's a handful of gas stations, budget motels, and fast-food stops on a route that leads to Nocturne Falls. Since we know she came here, the destination isn't the interesting part."

"But the coffee is. The takeout places may be even more so."

"I agree." Birdie frowned. "Wait, why are the takeout places interesting?"

"Because Ingvar's a vegetarian. Not saying it's impossible to eat that way at a steakhouse or a barbecue place, but…it's not the easy choice. It seems more likely that she would have chosen restaurants with broader selections." Jenna got up and stood at the end of Titus's bed, the steady hum of the machine monitoring his vital signs suddenly the most bothersome sound in the world. He shouldn't be here. This was her fault.

"True," Birdie said. "I'm not quite sure what to make of it yet, though. On the surface, it looks like someone stole her credit card, but to let it go on for a week? And while she's traveling?"

"No, Ingvar wouldn't have ignored a thing like that." She thought back to the trap and how unlike Ingvar all that magic had seemed. Ingvar was a perfectionist. She would never have gotten a spell so wrong. And then Jenna thought about how off Ingvar had looked since she'd been here. Jenna shook her head. "Something's wrong. Deeply wrong."

"What?"

Jenna paced a few steps away, then came back. "It's like Ingvar isn't herself. Like…she's—oh, Birdie, I just had the most terrible thought."

"What?"

"Could Ingvar be possessed? Who could do something like that? Who has a reason? The capability?" One name came to her. It was a long shot. But a long shot was better than nothing. "We need to go to the station, now. I need to get to a computer."

Birdie stood. "You can't. The binding spell."

Jenna ground her teeth together. "Loki on a stick. No, I can't. Okay, I need you to go back to the station and do something for me."

"Anything."

"You know how you just did the deep dive on Ingvar? I have a new name for you. Sola Skarsgard."

"On it." She yanked her purse straps over her shoulder. "You think that's who stole Ingvar's identity?"

"More than that." Jenna looked at Titus. "I think she's stolen Ingvar's body."

Birdie raced out, and as she left, Jenna pulled a chair next to the bed so she could hold Titus's hand. His skin was like fire. She went into the bathroom and found a washcloth, rinsed it in cold water, then came back and mopped the sweat off his forehead.

A few times, he muttered something unintelligible. He'd groan. Or growl. Once, his wolf flickered across his face.

But mostly, he lay still as death.

She held his hand and rested her head on her arm on the bed. He was strong. He'd pull through this. He had to. Because if he didn't, *Helgrind* would taste blood in retribution. She didn't know whose blood just yet, but she'd find out.

She drifted off to dreams of battle.

"Jenna?"

The gruff whisper pulled her from sleep. She lifted her head to see Titus blinking at her. She sucked in a breath. "You're awake. How do you feel?"

"Like I was poisoned. Did you get the wraith?"

She shook her head, smiling a little to soften the blow. "No, he and Ingvar disappeared. I haven't had a chance to close the runes on the trap, so there's a very distinct possibility he's still out in those woods, wandering around. The runes are meant to draw wraiths in. Hopefully, he's the only one out there. Otherwise…" She took a breath. "I'm rambling, sorry."

"No, it's nice. Your voice." Breathing seemed to be taking some effort. "Wolfsbane, huh?"

"Yes. I'm so sorry. I had no idea she was going to use that. I've never even heard of it." She gripped his hand tighter. "I'm so glad you're awake."

"You're not mad at me?"

Her mouth fell open. "Why would I be mad at you?"

"For asking Hank and Bridget and Birdie to come."

"No. I'm not mad at you for that. You did what you thought needed to be done. Obviously, you had a better feeling about what was going to happen than I did." She swallowed down a lump of emotion. "I never imagined it would go so wrong."

"How could you?"

"I just should have."

"Jenna. Stop blaming yourself. I don't blame you, so you shouldn't either."

"Thanks." She gave him a quick smile. "Your aunt was here around three."

"What time is it now?"

She checked the clock. She must have fallen asleep for a bit. "Almost six in the morning."

His eyes were closing. "Full moon's getting closer."

"It is. But I might be on to something. Birdie's doing some research for me at the station." She wasn't sure he was awake enough to comprehend what she had to tell him, but she could always tell him again. "She'd already done a little research on her own."

"Mm-hmm. Who?"

He was falling asleep, but that was okay. Rest was what he needed. "On Ingvar. Found an interesting change in her pattern of behavior. The kind of change that points to a few possible things going on. One being her identity was stolen. While giving that some thought, I came up with another idea."

"Hmm."

She smiled at his sleepy attempt to listen. "Go back to sleep, my brave wolf. I'll fill you in later."

"No." His eyes opened a slit. "Another idea. What?"

"That Ingvar isn't really Ingvar. Remember how you asked me if she's always had those dark circles? Even you noticed without realizing it. I think another seer from our division, a woman who delved too deeply into the darker parts of our traditions, is behind all this."

His eyes opened a little more. "Who?"

"Her name is Sola Skarsgard. She was dismissed for practicing the dark arts of her craft. Birdie is researching her. I'm hoping she finds some link that might connect her with Ingvar."

"Is she powerful enough to build that circle?"

"She could be. I don't know what happened to her after she was kicked out."

"Does Ingvar know her?"

Jenna nodded. "Better than I do. They were in school together. Both studying to be seers."

"Isn't that a link?"

"It is. But not enough of one. Why would she suddenly take over Ingvar's body to work all this dark magic? Why not just be herself? What does posing as Ingvar get her?"

Birdie pushed through the door, papers in hand. "I know what posing as Ingvar gets her. Closer to you, Jenna. Sola Skarsgard is definitely behind this, but that's not her name anymore."

"She changed it? That already sounds suspicious."

Birdie shrugged. "She changed it because she got married. And now she lists herself as a widow."

The small hairs on Jenna's neck went up. "Birdie, what's her married name?"

"Guddersen. Husband's name was Leif. Does that mean anything to you?"

Jenna's blood went cold, and *Helgrind* sent an angry whine through her bones. She pushed to her feet. "Yes. That's the berserker who became a mercenary. The berserker I was tasked with eliminating. The very one who's come back as a wraith to do the same to me."

Titus struggled to get up. The wolfsbane still had more control of his body than he did, making every movement a battle. He pushed to his elbows, raising himself as much as he could. "They're working together."

Jenna came to his side. "I have no doubt they are, but that's not your concern right now. You need to rest and kick this poison out of your system so you can be a hundred percent again. Come on, lie down."

Birdie nodded. "Titus, honey, she's right. I know you want to help, but you're not in a position to do that. You've got to rest."

"Women," he muttered as he fell back against the pillows. He wasn't sure how much longer he would have been able to hold himself up anyway. His head was spinning ever so slightly. "The two of you are so bossy."

Birdie laughed. "If you're listening, that's all that matters."

He looked at Jenna. "I'm sure you agree with her."

She crossed her arms. "Yes, I do. Your health comes first."

"You realize you can't leave the hospital either."

She smiled at him, uncrossing her arms to plant her hands on the edge of his bed and lean in. "I do, but I also know that means more time with you."

He smiled back at her. It was hard not to when she was being this sweet. And he *was* madly in love with her, a truth that couldn't be denied. "That's very kind, and I appreciate it, but the full moon is coming. We're running out of time." Although he was starting to care less about being permanently bonded to her. Yes, it would make their lives harder, but at the same time, this incredible woman would always be with him.

If that wasn't a win, winning no longer existed.

"I know, Titus. But I can work on things from here. It's not like I'm going to be sitting around idle."

"It won't be the same. You'll be hampered. Speaking of…" He glanced at the IV in his arm. "This seems unnecessary."

Birdie clucked her tongue. "No, it isn't. It's speeding up the detox process. You remember when Ivy had the incident with wolfsbane? Being in the hospital made all the difference."

"But she ingested it. I was only exposed to it."

The look Birdie gave him said that made no difference. "And for all we know, your exposure was worse."

252

She was a stubborn old woman, but he knew she had his best interests at heart. "Aunt Birdie, I'm not asking to go to the firehouse. Just home. It would be easier for Jenna to get things done from there. Please, get the doctor. I want to be discharged."

Birdie looked at Jenna. The nerve. Like Jenna was in charge of his recovery. He was a grown man, fully capable of—a wave of nausea and weakness came over him. He suddenly exhaled, hard, like he'd taken a hard punch to the gut.

Jenna's eyes narrowed. "Are you okay? You're white as a sheet." She put her hand on his head. "I think your fever is spiking."

She nodded at Birdie. "We definitely need the doctor."

"I'll get him." Birdie ran out the door.

Jenna bent and kissed his forehead, then pressed her cheek to his. "It's going to be okay. You're going to get through this. You have to. I need you."

He put his hand on the back of her neck and turned to kiss her cheek. "I need you, too, Jenna. Thank you for being here with me. I know you don't have a choice, but…"

She pulled back a little so he could see her face. "There's nowhere in the world I'd rather be than with you. Although there are other locations I'd prefer."

"Me too." He smiled up at his beautiful valkyrie.

Birdie returned with Dr. Navarro. "Chief Merrow, how are you feeling?"

"A little nauseous. And warm."

Dr. Navarro scanned Titus's forehead with the infrared thermometer. He checked the readout and nodded. "One-oh-three. I'll have a nurse give you something for the nausea. The best prescription I can give you right now is rest. Sleep will make this easier."

"I can sleep at home. I'd like to be discharged." But he already knew the answer.

Dr. Navarro shook his head. "I'm not discharging you until your fever's gone."

Titus sighed. "Understood."

With a nod, Dr. Navarro left.

Titus growled softly. "I hate this."

"I know, honey." Birdie patted his leg. "We'll just set up a command center here."

"Doesn't Hank need you at the department?"

"Yes, and that's where I'll be. But not until I bring Jenna a laptop she can work on."

"Thank you," Jenna said.

Birdie nodded. "What else do you need?"

"Laptop and charger. Pen and paper. Phone charger wouldn't hurt either." She tapped her fingers on the bed. "I'm sure I'm forgetting something."

"Breakfast, anyone?" Bridget walked in, carrying a shopping bag from Mummy's Diner in one hand and a drink tray in the other.

"Doesn't that smell good?" A nurse came in behind her with a syringe.

"No," Titus groused. Not only was he burning up, but feeling like he might barf at any moment was making him grouchy.

The nurse went right to Titus's IV line and injected the solution into the port. "This should help with the nausea."

"Oh, sorry," Bridget said. "Are you sick to your stomach, Titus?"

"A little."

Bridget's brows went up. "Just a little? Because you sound ready to snap. You want me to take this food out?"

He took a breath and tried to exhale some of his bad mood. "No, Jenna needs to eat. And I'll feel better in a minute, right?" He looked at the nurse.

She nodded. "You should, yes. Need anything else?"

"No, thanks."

"Call if you do." She left.

Bridget didn't come any closer with the food. Thankfully. She looked at Jenna. "I'm sorry about the way I reacted in the woods, Jenna. I was mad that Titus got hurt, but that wasn't your fault. I shouldn't have taken it out on you."

"What did I miss?" Titus asked.

"Just your sister being worried about you." Jenna smiled at him before looking at Bridget. "Thank you, Bridget. I really appreciate that."

"So we're friends again?"

Jenna nodded. "We are if there's a cinnamon roll in that bag."

Bridget laughed. "Is there any other reason to go to Mummy's?"

Jenna winked at Titus.

He winked back, the pull of sleep almost too much to ignore.

"Hey," Jenna said softly. "Why don't we take this down to the visiting room? I think I can make it that far without the binding spell kicking in. Titus needs to sleep."

Birdie nodded. "And I need to go get your things. I'll walk with you."

"Okay," Bridget said. "See you later, bro."

"Bye, honey," Birdie said.

"Back soon," Jenna added.

"Later," he whispered, eyes already closed. He drifted off, unable to do anything else.

The visiting room had a small dining area with three round tables. Jenna and Bridget set up at one of those, but Birdie didn't sit.

"You girls enjoy your breakfast. I should run and get that stuff for Jenna."

Jenna pushed a chair out with her foot. "You can stay for a little bit. Twenty minutes isn't going to change anything. Come on, eat with us. Besides, we need to make a plan."

"Yeah," Bridget said. "Plus, I got a ton of food."

She had too. Pancakes in three varieties—peach, chocolate chip, and plain. A side each of bacon and sausage links. Two cinnamon rolls, which might have been overkill, considering they were the size of dinner plates. Two breakfast platters of scrambled eggs, bacon, hash browns, and biscuits. And a yogurt parfait with fruit and granola.

She also had a tray of coffees and two bottles of orange juice.

Birdie hesitated. Then sat. "All right, but just for a few minutes."

Jenna nodded. "We have a lot of work to do, I know that. But fueling up will help. All right, let's figure out what needs to be done."

Bridget dumped the packets of utensils in the middle of the table, and they dug in. Jenna went for the peach pancakes and a couple of strips of bacon, plus a coffee. Birdie and Bridget took the breakfast platters and the OJ.

"Okay," Bridget said. "Where do we start?"

"With Alice," Jenna answered. "I need to talk to her. She said if she knew who built the spell, it would make it easier for her to undo it. I will tell her everything I know about Sola. It isn't much, but at the very least, Alice will know the origin of the magic used against us. That has to be worth something."

"Okay," Birdie said. "That's a phone call. And one you should make in about an hour. I don't think Alice is an early riser, and it's still plenty early. You could try her now, but I'm pretty sure it'd just go to voicemail."

"Voicemail is fine. At least she'll know I'm trying to reach her." Jenna took her phone out and tapped Alice's name on her contacts list. The phone rang four times before going to voicemail. She nodded at Birdie and pointed at her phone, mouthing the word *voicemail* while she listened to Alice's brief message. Then she spoke. "Hi, Alice, it's Deputy Blythe. I know who built the spell. A disgraced seer by the name of Sola Skarsgard, now Guddersen. Please call me and let me know what else you need to know about her that will be helpful. Thank you."

Jenna hung up. "That's done."

"Good," Birdie said.

Jenna went back to her food. She cut into her pancakes with her plastic fork and knife. "Birdie, do you think you can do more of your computer magic and find out where Sola is staying? She never told me. Which brings me to the matter of Ingvar."

Bridget reached for the little packets of salt and pepper. "That's the woman you met at Howler's?"

"Yes. At least on the outside." Jenna stared at the triangle of food on the end of her fork. "I don't know what it takes to possess someone the way Sola has possessed Ingvar. What kind of damage it does. Sola must be a very powerful seer." She had a terrible sinking feeling about the whole thing. "I hope my friend is still alive, but I'm not sure."

Bridget's eyes held a world of sympathy. "We'll find out. We'll get Hank on this as soon as Birdie figures out where they are."

"You know…" Jenna put her fork down and pulled out her phone again. "I was texting with Ingvar before I knew what was going on. So really, I was texting with Sola, I guess. Birdie, let's get that cell number tracked."

"On it, so long as she hasn't turned the phone off and pulled the SIM card."

"Let's hope. But first, let me give this a shot." She took a moment, formulated her thoughts, then dashed off a quick text to the number she'd thought was Ingvar's. *What happened? Are you okay? We need to talk.*

She set her phone down next to her food. She hated playing dumb, but it was worth it if it got her a response. "Let's see if she replies and, if she does, what she says."

"The sun is barely over the horizon," Birdie said. "Do you think the evil get up this early?"

Jenna chuckled. "I know it's a long shot."

"I bet she doesn't reply," Bridget said. "For one thing, she knows you're not stupid. That you've by now figured out she's not only gone to the dark side, but she married it. Even if she thinks you still believe she's Ingvar, at this point you'd have some serious problems with Ingvar's behavior."

"We all do," Birdie said around a mouthful of home fries.

"That's the other thing." Bridget pointed at Birdie with her fork. "Sola saw us all there last night. Not only didn't Titus keep his distance, he brought three other wolves along with him."

That gave Jenna an idea. "Hey, wolves have highly attuned senses of smell. Could you guys track Sola down and figure out where she's staying that way?"

Bridget glanced at Birdie before answering. "We already tried that. Birdie and I went back to the circle as soon as we knew Titus was going to be all right."

"You did? The runes are still open. Did you see the wraith? Or any wraith?"

Birdie sighed. "No wraiths, but the site is so saturated with wolfsbane, we couldn't get closer than twenty feet before our sinuses started burning." She frowned, and her eyes lit with the golden wolfy glow that Jenna had come to appreciate. "We're going to have to do this the old-fashioned way. Research and police intuition."

Jenna's phone vibrated. She flipped it over and read the new text.

You're right. We do need to talk.

Jenna stared at her phone screen in disbelief. "You guys. She answered."

"Who?" Birdie asked. "Sola? Or Alice."

"Sola. As Ingvar." Jenna chewed on her lower lip. "I don't know if I should take that to mean she doesn't think *I* know who she really is, or if she's fishing to see what I know, or maybe even trying to set me up, but I can't let this opportunity pass by."

Bridget looked confused. "How are you going to do anything about it? You can't be more than a hundred feet away from Titus, and he's not going anywhere for a while. And even when he gets out of here, he's still not going to be in fighting shape."

"Yeah, that's definitely a problem." Jenna thought out loud. "If I learned anything from last night's experience, it's that Leif's wraith form continues to get stronger. Wraiths generally can only exist in dark places until they get stronger, but Leif's got Sola working with him. As badly as he wants my sword, there's a very good chance they could hunt me down here at the hospital. They won't care what collateral damage they cause."

"Great," Bridget said.

"Exactly. I'd much rather control the location where that battle happens." Jenna ate a bite of pancake. "Wolfsbane takes twenty-four hours to clear a wolf's system?"

"Typically," Birdie answered. "It may not take quite as long with him since he didn't ingest it. He probably inhaled some, though, so it might be six of one, a half dozen of the other."

Jenna's brows rose. "Any way to speed that up, other than the fluids he's getting?"

"Not really." Bridget put her fork down, picked up her OJ, and looked at Birdie. "Unless you know some ancient wolfy secrets about dealing with wolfsbane that I don't."

"I wish I did," Birdie said. "But we need to think about this. If we're going to run some kind of sting on Sola, deal with this wraith, and try to save Ingvar, we have to find a way to at least make Titus mobile." She glanced behind her at the other people in the visiting area. "We do not want some kind of magical showdown happening in the hospital."

"No, we don't." Jenna frowned. "Especially not with the havoc a wraith can cause."

Birdie looked at Bridget. "You think your brother will help?"

"Titus? I'm sure he'll do anything to go home."

"I meant Hank."

Bridget shrugged. "He might not be happy about it, but I'm sure he will if it means less trouble later."

"Which it would," Jenna said. "If we win. We're in a war now. We have to go forward with that mentality."

Bridget frowned. "I might be a werewolf, but I'm also just an ordinary restaurant owner. I'm not a battle-trained warrior woman like you."

Jenna gave her a quick smile. "Understood. And I wouldn't expect anyone else to do the heavy lifting. But you're also a strong, capable werewolf. And the bottom line is, I can't do this alone."

Bridget nodded. "Just tell us what to do."

Titus opened his eyes to see the Four Horsemen of the Apocalypse standing at the end of his hospital bed.

He blinked again and realized it was Jenna, Hank, Bridget, and Birdie. "Am I dying? Why are you all staring at me like that?"

Jenna smiled. "No, you're not dying. We were just talking, and you sighed, and we thought you might be waking up. And then you did. How are you feeling?"

He took a second to make a personal assessment. He didn't feel warm anymore. Or achy all over. Or like he was about to puke. "Pretty good. What were you talking about? Me getting discharged, hopefully."

Hank nodded. "You are. But you're not going to get much rest. We have business to take care of."

Titus sat up a little. It was a lot easier than last time. "Business?"

"Wraith business," Jenna answered.

"Right." He hadn't forgotten that. Just thought Hank had meant something else. "That means you made progress while I was asleep."

"We did," Jenna said. "A good amount. Enough that we're moving forward."

"Did you talk to Alice?" He knew there was hope in his voice, but Jenna had said they'd made headway. Hard not to want that to include all aspects of their troubles.

"A few times. And she had some good news and some not-good news. I can explain more in the car, but here's one thing we know: The bomb was meant to make me fall in love with Leif so that I'd feel compelled to give him my sword. And in case I didn't, the binding spell was so that I couldn't get away from him and he'd have an easier time killing me and taking the sword."

She smiled at Titus. "That means you being in the attic with me saved my life. If I'd been alone and ended up stuck with the wraith, I'm not sure I'd be standing here right now."

"I'm really glad you are," Titus said.

"We all are," Birdie added.

That was for sure. Now Titus wanted nothing more than to get out of this place and do whatever was necessary to make sure the wraith never bothered Jenna again. He glanced toward the window. The light had changed since the last time he'd been awake. "How long have I been asleep?"

"Almost twelve hours."

"Wow. I guess that explains why I feel so much better."

"Do you?" Jenna asked.

He nodded. "I feel pretty much like myself again." Mostly. Enough that he could function and get back to being useful.

Birdie rubbed her hands together. "Then let's get you out of here."

The discharge process moved slower than Titus would have liked, but within the hour, he was walking into his own home again. He felt good, but he knew he wasn't completely rid of the wolfsbane.

He also knew he couldn't let that stop him from helping Jenna. He stood in the hallway and faced his family, who'd all come back to the house with him. "I need to take a shower before I do anything else. Then I need to eat. I'm starving and probably a little weak from lack of food. But after that, I'm all yours."

Bridget spoke before Jenna or Birdie could. "What do you want? I'll run to the restaurant and get it."

That was an easy answer. "Double bacon cheese-burger and fries. Also onion rings."

"Ohh," Birdie said. "I could eat that too."

Hank stuck his thumbs in his pants pockets. "None of us have had dinner."

Bridget laughed. "Okay, give me the full order, and I'll bring back enough food for everyone. I'll even call it in on the ride there so we don't have to wait."

Titus raised his hand. "You know what I want. I'm off to shower."

He left them to work out the details and went back to his bedroom. He cranked the water on in the shower and let it run while he shucked his clothes. The weight of what was to come lay heavy on him. Tonight would decide everything.

Jenna had told him in the car that she'd been in touch with Alice about Sola being the source of the magic and that Alice had worked on the spell all day, only to discover breaking it would be impossible without Sola's blood. At least for him, anyway.

Jenna had quoted Alice. "Blood balances blood."

He looked at his hand where he'd scratched it on the nail in the attic. Of course there was no trace of the mark now, but the memory remained. Was he destined to be bound to Jenna for the rest of his life?

If that was his lot in life, he was at peace with it. Was she?

He stepped into the shower and let the water rain down over him, the heat washing away the remnants of the hospital. Whatever happened tonight—whatever happened between him and Jenna—he was ready.

By the time he got out, shaved, got dressed, and went back to the living room, Bridget had arrived with the food. Fast service was just one of the benefits of having a sister who owned a restaurant. They sat down at his dining room table, Titus at one end with Jenna to his right, Hank at the other with Birdie and Bridget flanking him.

Titus inhaled. "Everything smells so good. I should have ordered more."

Bridget used her elbow to point to a bag on the kitchen counter. "I got peach cobblers for everyone too. I figure if we're going to war tonight, we should go well fed."

"I like that plan." Titus picked up his burger. They all dug in and ate in silence for a while. Bridget had gotten a few extra things, too, like more onion rings, potato skins, and stuffed mushrooms. They plowed through the spread like they'd never seen food before.

When they were mostly done, he finally asked the question he'd been wanting to. "So what is the plan?"

Jenna was just finishing her burger. "In a nutshell, I've set up a meeting with Sola back at the circle, where I hope I'll be able to convince her to reopen the trap for the wraith. I need him to show up. Of course, I'll be doing all this while pretending that I know nothing about Ingvar being possessed by Sola. And while that's going on, Bridget and Birdie are going to find wherever Sola's been staying and see if they can work things from that end."

"Work things? What does that mean?"

Jenna swallowed the bite she'd been chewing. "The way Alice explained it to me, Sola's spirit might be possessing Ingvar's physical form, but Sola still has a physical form, too, and that body has to be somewhere."

Birdie used a fry to punctuate her words. "Bridget and I are going to find that body and take it into custody. At the same time, we're going to try to neutralize whatever magic she's using to control Ingvar."

Titus frowned. "Where are you going to look? There have to be hundreds of places she could be staying. And how are you going to neutralize the magic?"

"Well," Birdie said, "I used my computer superpowers to narrow down the possibilities of where she might be staying, and Deputy Cruz and I eliminated a few of them this afternoon, which means we've only two final places to check. Bridget and I will track her down, don't you worry. As for the neutralizing, Alice gave us something for that."

"And the part about you taking someone into custody?" Titus looked at his brother. "Don't tell me."

Hank sighed. "Yes, I deputized Birdie. But I am also sending Deputy Lafitte with them."

Titus wiped his hands on a paper napkin from Howler's. "Remy's a good guy. And you can't go wrong with a vampire as backup." But he wasn't sure he liked how that left the odds. "That means it's just me, Hank, and Jenna in the woods?"

"Not exactly," Jenna said with a smile. "I called in some backup of my own."

The doorbell rang with the most perfect timing ever. Titus started to get up, but Jenna stopped him. "I got it."

She answered the door, opening it wide. "You guys all know Tessa, my sister, and Pandora Williams, witch extraordinaire and rock star Realtor."

Tessa and Pandora waved to the gang.

The gang waved back.

Titus nodded. Both women were dressed in black, hair up in ponytails and looking very much like they were ready to throw down. "That's some good backup right there."

"They've already been briefed." Jenna smiled, but there was a little reserve there. Probably because she was feeling the seriousness of what they were about to attempt. "They know their parts."

"Excellent." Titus pushed back from the table. "Peach cobbler is going to have to wait for the victory celebration. I say we do this now."

Jenna checked the time. "We have an hour yet before I'm supposed to meet Sola, but we can definitely head out there and get into position."

Birdie stood. "You all go. Bridget and I will do a quick cleanup, then we'll swing by the department, pick up Remy, and get started on our search. According to what Alice told us, we can't do anything until we know Sola's actively engaged in possessing Ingvar's body, so as soon as she reaches Jenna and the circle, we'll be good to go."

Pandora raised her hand. "That's one of my jobs. Keeping Birdie and Bridget in the loop on our end of things."

Titus nodded at Jenna. "You really do have this all worked out."

"We do," Jenna said. "Still lots that could go wrong, but I think we've got most of that covered. I hope."

He hooked a thumb toward the bedroom. "I'll get my boots on, and I'm ready. Jenna, could I see you for a sec?"

"Sure." She walked with him to the bedroom.

He opened the door and went in, motioning for her to do the same.

When she'd entered, he closed the door. He had to tell her how he felt now, before things blew up. "Look, before we head out there, I want you to know that when the spell is lifted later tonight, I don't expect my feelings for you to be any different. I want us to still be us. I want us to be a couple. We're good together. I see no reason to change that just because we aren't magically bonded anymore."

She smiled and gave him a little nod. "Me too."

He exhaled. "Yes?"

"Yes."

He grinned. "I love you, you know."

She smiled. "I know." Then she laughed for a second before her expression went back to a serious, but happy, smile. "I love you too. And it scares me more than anything we're about to do, but I figure we're in this together, right? Just the way we have been."

"That's right," he said. "And I'm not going to let you get hurt." He cupped her face in his hands and kissed her, a solid, full-on promise of a kiss. He held her there for a long moment until he knew he had to let her go.

Her arms stayed wrapped around him. "I'm not going to let you get hurt either."

"Good," he said. "Now let's go kick some wraith ass."

The plan was that, to Sola, Jenna would appear as if she were alone in the woods, desperate to meet her friend and find out how things had gone so wrong with the trap to catch the wraith.

Except none of that was true. Well, maybe the desperate part.

Jenna knew exactly what had gone wrong with the trap.

She also wasn't alone. Titus, Hank, and Tessa were on the outcropping of rock just above the circle, the same place Titus had been last time. Pandora was an equidistance away in the opposite direction, hidden in blackberry bramble. Not that she really needed the coverage.

Marigold had made a camouflage spell for Pandora that allowed her to blend into the forest. Marigold, Pandora's sister, was a florist by trade but a green witch by practice.

Jenna had tried twice to spot Pandora, and even though she knew where the witch was hiding, she couldn't see her. That was good. It meant Sola wouldn't see her either.

Just like Jenna prayed Sola wouldn't see or smell or sense the wolves waiting on the ridge. Hopefully, the seer would be too preoccupied with her own devious plans to give much thought to Jenna having backup.

Although Jenna had had some last time, and Sola was no fool. But Jenna had a plan for that.

As the meeting time approached, Jenna pushed all other thoughts out of her head except for what she had to focus on. Defeat the wraith. Take Sola captive. Free Ingvar.

Helgrind sizzled with energy, the same energy that ran through Jenna's blood and bones, the same energy she'd felt on the battlefield or while transporting worthy souls to Valhalla or pursuing a criminal.

Which, in all honesty, didn't happen that much in Nocturne Falls. She loved being a deputy, but most of the things they did day-to-day was deal with speeders, the occasional drunk or cranky tourist, and, every once in a while, a shoplifter.

There was the yearly noise ordinance violation from old Mrs. Morris, a banshee well into her years who, on her birthday, liked to play her death metal a bit louder than the neighbors cared for, but really, that was about it.

And generally, Jenna found her work to be just fine. An uninteresting day when you were a sheriff's deputy was also a safe day.

But safe could get boring pretty easily.

Facing off with Leif wasn't something Jenna was looking forward to, but tasting battle again would be…okay, to be brutally honest, she was kind of looking forward to that part of it. It would be a lie to say she didn't miss her time in service. The sense of duty, the thrill of battle, the accomplishment of being on the winning side.

Which wasn't to say she wasn't on the winning side every day, but being victorious in battle was something else. Was there anything like the feeling of victory? Yes, actually there was. Love.

She smiled. Tonight, if all went well, she'd have both.

She waited, losing herself in her thoughts and the sounds of the forest as the shadows grew longer. She kept a tree at her back and the breeze in her face.

Leaves crunched underfoot. She turned slightly to face the sound and saw Ingvar coming toward her from the direction of the river.

Jenna pushed off the tree and raised her hand in greeting, just as she would if the woman approaching actually was Ingvar and not the shell of her friend currently possessed by a disgraced seer. "Ingvar."

The seer smiled and waved back. "I'm so glad you could meet me."

"Same. Are you all right?" Jenna kept up the pretense that she had no idea what had gone wrong. "After what happened last night, I wasn't sure if you'd been injured or overcome by the wraith or if the magic was bad. What on earth happened, Ingvar?"

The woman who looked like Ingvar stared at her, and for a split second, her eyes flashed green with hatred. In that split second, Jenna saw Sola.

Her own face twisted into a mask of revulsion before she could stop herself. She shook her head suddenly and dug deep for a way to cover. "I hate that I almost lost you."

"You didn't." Sola was gone now, hidden in Ingvar's pale beauty. "It was all my mistake. I used one wrong ingredient in the casting of the circle." She sighed. "You'd think after all my years of training that such a thing should not be possible, but becoming a seer means being a student for a lifetime. I guess it had been too long since I'd cast that spell." She looked around. "Where is the wolf?"

"He didn't make it. Passed just a short time ago." There was no other lie Jenna could use. Saying he was sick wouldn't be enough. Not with the binding spell connecting them.

"What a shame. But not unexpected." Ingvar shrugged. "I told him to stay away. Wolfsbane is deadly to their kind."

She'd never once uttered anything close to that. Jenna's anger bubbled up, and she wanted to punch her, but that was Ingvar's face. No sense in hurting her friend further. She'd punch Sola once she was in custody.

Sola tipped her head, her bone earrings rattling softly. "Was he your friend?"

Jenna kept her face blank and uncaring. "Just an acquaintance."

"I see."

Sola seemed to have bought it, so Jenna prodded her toward the next step. "While that really is a terrible shame, shouldn't we try again? I don't see why the wolf's death should hold us back. I'm here, and we need to deal with this wraith once and for all. More now than ever before."

Sola looked genuinely surprised. "You really want to try the trap again? You're not too distraught?"

"Because of the wolf? I didn't really know him that well. If anything, my desire to end the wraith has increased. He can't be allowed to roam free. Losing the wolf was awful, yes, but the wraith wants to kill me, too, Ingvar. I'm sure of it." Jenna got a little worried Sola was having second thoughts. That wouldn't do at all. Jenna decided to work on the woman's ego. "Unless you're too weak after last night. Or you're not sure how to fix the thing that went wrong. Do you need more time?"

"No," Sola snapped. "I can do it now. I just hope you're ready."

"I am. Absolutely." Jenna took a few steps toward the river. "You need time alone again?"

"Yes."

Was Sola's grasp on Ingvar slipping? Her short, snippy comments weren't doing a whole lot to keep up her pretense of being Jenna's old friend. Was it possible the seams were splitting on this tightly sewn spell?

Jenna wanted to see if she could rip out a few more stitches and make Sola fray even further. She stopped her retreat toward the water to peer closely at her.

"Are you positive you can do this? You look tired, my friend. Maybe I should go hunt the wraith myself. I know that's a job best done by two, but I can always call my sister."

The other woman's eyes went wide. "I am fine. We will do this now." Her hands were clenched at her sides. "I need time to cast the circle, lay the runes, and speak the words of summoning. Leave me."

"You're sure?"

"Yes," Sola hissed.

"Just make sure you freeze the wraith this time and not me, right?"

Sola glared.

"Okay, you got it. But if you need me, just call." Jenna started to walk away again, watching Sola as closely as she could.

"I won't."

"Cool." Jenna gave her a thumbs-up. "You got this, Ingvar."

The seer ignored her and walked on toward the remains of last night's circle, muttering under her breath.

Jenna turned away, barely containing her grin, and jogged toward the water's edge. This time, she stayed at the top of the bank. Right around the same place the wraith had appeared. She kept her head on a swivel and scanned for any signs of the creature. A few stars twinkled overhead, and here and there, the water caught the moon's light.

A large blackbird landed on a big rock at the river's edge. It was a beautiful bird, feathers iridescent and gleaming. Jenna looked more closely, realizing it was too big to be a blackbird. That was a raven. It looked up at her with a gaze that seemed wise beyond any typical bird's. Jenna took a few steps toward the bird and kept her voice low. "Cole?"

The bird nodded.

Cole Van Zant was Pandora's husband and her familiar. He was also a shifter who could take on this raven form. Most important, his presence actually allowed Pandora's magic to work and work very well. In fact, since he'd entered Pandora's life, her magic had been usable for the first time since she'd come into her powers.

Cole was also a professor at Harmswood Academy, where Tessa was the dean of library studies.

"I assume you're here to help Pandora?"

He peered at her intently, cocking his head.

"And me?"

He nodded again.

"Thank you."

He made a clicking sound, then took to the air. He let out a sharp caw as he rose into the darkening sky. The call seemed like a warning. Jenna turned in time to see the wraith lurching along the bank toward her.

Leif was still a ways out, but he looked more like a soot-covered man than a creature of smoke and shadow. Nothing about him looked even slightly nebulous. There was no doubt he'd gotten stronger, more solid. This had to happen now.

Good thing she genuinely looked forward to a battle, because she was definitely going to get one. What worried her was that practice, which she did a lot of, was no substitute for real in-the-moment fighting.

It was like riding a bike, though, right? She pondered the idea of drawing her sword here and starting without waiting for Sola to have the circle's magic functioning, but they needed Sola fully engaged, or Bridget and Birdie were going to have a hard time freeing Ingvar from her clutches.

Besides, if Jenna got into trouble this far from the trap, her team wouldn't know what was going on. And wraith killing *really* was best done in teams of two. Or more. Especially when that wraith had a warped seer on his side.

No, she needed to stick to the plan.

With that in mind, she took a few careless steps, deliberately displacing rocks and making noise.

The wraith looked in her direction. And growled. His eyes went red-hot.

Jenna went into full battle mode. She peered back at him with her chest out, chin down, and gaze fully engaged. "You ready to try again, wraith?"

The creature picked up speed, such as it was.

"Come on, then. See if you can catch me." She crooked her finger at him, then made her way up the bank to the edge of the forest again. When he was below her, she started toward the circle.

She kept going, glancing over her shoulder every once in a while to make sure Leif was still following.

He was. In a few more feet, Sola's chanting reached her ears. Everything was proceeding as planned, except tonight there was going to be a very different ending.

"Ingvar," she called out. "Ready?"

The seer wasn't bothering to hide herself this time. She still stood near the back of the circle, but she was plainly visible. Arms outstretched, eyes black with the magic she was working, she nodded without breaking the rhythm of the words she was chanting.

Jenna hated being between Leif and the Sola-controlled Ingvar. She couldn't keep an eye on both at the same time. Thankfully, Jenna wasn't truly alone.

With that thought lifting her up, she began her slow retreat into the circle. Leif lumbered after her with all the grace of a drunken bull.

Helgrind quivered for release, but it wasn't quite time, although her hands itched to grip the handle of her beloved sword.

The moment he was within the confines of the ring, two things happened.

The first was that Sola stepped forward, speaking the same words as she had before to close the circle. Light sprang up all around them, and Sola reached into the pouch at her waist and again drew out a handful of powder. She tossed it into the air.

Everything progressed exactly as it had the first time, but the circumstances weren't the same as before because Alice had been here earlier and cast a spell of her own, to prevent Sola's magic from working.

The second thing was Jenna reached back and pulled *Helgrind* free. The blade sang out its joy, shushing through the air as Jenna brandished the gorgeous weapon. "This is what you want, wraith. Come closer. I'll give you a taste."

Leif snarled and swiped at her, but he was still too far away.

She moved back and forth from one foot to the other, staying light and ready. As she did, she danced to the right just a little every few steps. Slowly, she put the seer in her peripheral vision. In her current position, she could also see the spot where Pandora was hiding.

Tessa, Hank, and Titus were above and behind her now.

This was a stronger position than having Sola behind her. At any moment, Sola would attempt her second spell, the one that would freeze Jenna in place and allow Leif to land a killing blow.

She had to work fast, because as soon as Sola realized Jenna wasn't frozen, she'd know the game was finished. Jenna said a little prayer that Birdie and Bridget had been successful in their quest, because things were about to blow up.

Jenna smiled a smile she didn't really feel as she leveled *Helgrind* at Leif. "All right, wraith. Playtime is over."

Leif charged, but he still didn't have the speed of a living berserker. Jenna dodged him without too much effort. He kept moving forward, nearly going headfirst into a large oak.

He caught it with one hand and used it to pull himself back around, ember eyes crackling with anger. He came at her again, hands grasping for the thing he wanted most.

Helgrind.

Again, she danced out of reach.

"Blythe," he growled. "You cannot escape me. I grow stronger with each passing moment."

"Stronger, but also easier to kill." *Easier* probably wasn't the right word. *More possible to be killed* was a truer statement.

He swiped at her again, and again she evaded him.

Her time was ticking down. At any moment, Sola would cast the spell that was supposed to freeze Leif in place so Jenna could deliver the killing blow.

Of course, Sola would once again attempt to freeze Jenna instead.

But it wouldn't work this time. Once Sola realized her magic no longer had any potency, that would be the end of it. The house of cards that Sola had built would come tumbling down. Sola with it.

Until then, however, Jenna had to do her best to end Leif. It wasn't impossible to kill a wraith who'd not yet achieved a solid state. But it was very, very hard.

Valkyries knew all about hard, though.

She was going to have to get his sword if she was going to transport his soul once and for all to the underworld.

He came at her. She ducked his swinging arm and sliced her blade across his ribs as deeply as she could.

He yowled at the cut, most likely at the indignity. Neither wraiths nor berserkers felt pain in a tangible way.

A dark, oily, sooty fog escaped from the wound before it closed. Not much change since yesterday, then. Odin's eye. Was he still so insubstantial? What was taking him so long to become fully corporeal?

But maybe the wound *had* healed slower this time? And had there been a hint of actual blood? Possibly. He had to be closer to being completely solid. If so, the time for the death blow was coming. But he clearly wasn't solid enough. Not yet. How much longer was it going to take?

She'd hoped not much longer, or her chance was going to pass. The thought occurred to her that Sola might have done something to keep him from becoming fully corporeal in order to protect him from Jenna.

Sola stepped forward. Jenna frowned, knowing what was about to happen. She had to act now. One final attempt to remove the wraith from this plane of existence.

In that moment, time sped up, but it also stood still.

With both hands on the hilt of *Helgrind*, Jenna whipped around with the blade at chest level and drove toward Leif with every ounce of force she had.

Sola began to speak as *Helgrind* pierced Leif's chest. The blade slid through him, and the momentum carried Jenna and the sword forward, pinning Leif to the first solid thing behind him. A pine.

A low, angry rumble vibrated out of him. "You think you can end me?"

She honestly wasn't sure anymore, but he couldn't know that. "I know I can. And once I do, I'm going to carry your soul straight to the underworld where you belong. There will be no Valhalla for you, Leif."

Growling, he swiped at her.

She couldn't let go of *Helgrind*, so she couldn't escape. The best she could do was rear back. His ragged nails caught her cheek and caused a brief moment of searing pain before it subsided.

The wounds stung, but she'd suffered worse. And it was nothing compared to what she was going to do to him.

But if *Helgrind* piercing his heart wasn't enough to finish him, she was in trouble.

He sneered at Jenna as he wrapped his hands around the sword sticking out of his chest and pulled, seemingly oblivious to the blood spilling from his hands as they were cut by the blade.

His hands were *bleeding*.

Encouraged by that realization, Jenna kept her grip firmly on the hilt. She dared not let *Helgrind* go, or Leif would take control of it. His eyes were already fixed on the resurrection stone.

If his hands could bleed, that meant he *was* becoming corporeal. Just not fast enough. And with every wraith, the heart was the last thing to solidify. She was just going to have to be patient.

Not the easiest thing to do.

Behind her, Sola chanted louder now. Almost angrily. But any second, she would realize her spell wasn't working. Jenna had to move faster. Still holding on to *Helgrind*, she kicked her feet up and planted them on Leif's chest on either side of the blade, then yanked the sword free and backflipped away from him.

At least he'd been solid enough for her to do that.

The hole in Leif's chest where *Helgrind* had been spilled black smoke. A second later, it started to close. She snarled in rage. Stupid wraiths. So hard to kill. At least he was contained in the circle.

Unfortunately, so was Sola.

With a thunderous roar, Leif came away from the tree. He reached back and unleashed his own blade.

Finally. *Kirsgut* was free. The sword made *Helgrind* look like a child's toy. A large child, but still. Berserker swords were legendary and sized to match the men who wielded them.

He raised the sword to strike.

"My spell," Sola snarled. Realization had come to her.

Blade up for protection, Jenna spun away from Leif, putting Sola between herself and the wraith. If he struck now, he'd hit Ingvar's body, and Jenna didn't think he'd do that with Sola inside her.

But the game was over. There was no reason left to pretend that everything was as it should be. She only prayed that Bridget and Birdie were successful on their end very soon. She pointed her weapon at Sola. "Not working, is it?"

"No, it's—" The seer's mouth pulled back in a sneer. "What have you done?"

Jenna brought her blade up slightly, enough to push Sola closer to Leif. "Realized the truth, that's what."

Unable to use his blade in such a small space, Leif let it go. It disappeared, no doubt returning to his back.

Jenna supposed that was one less thing to worry about, but she couldn't spare a glance to see where the rest of her team was. If they hadn't already started for the circle, now was the time. "Titus, Pandora, Tessa, *now*."

"I'm here." Pandora reached the circle first, but the howl of wolves accompanied her. She threw her hands toward the seer and began a spell of her own to break the circle.

Titus and Hank, in their wolf forms, ran up to flank Pandora. They snarled and snapped at Leif and Sola, pulling the pair's attention away from Jenna.

Then Tessa showed up, sword raised.

Leif snarled at them, but Sola retreated.

The light that encircled them, protecting Leif and Sola, began to waver.

Leif stopped snarling the second he noticed the magical glow sputtering like a flame about to go out. He looked at Jenna. "I will kill you, valkyrie. I will kill you and take that stone."

Then he glanced at Sola, eyes wide and edgy with fear. He shook his head at her. A second later, he disintegrated into worms of smoke that burrowed into the air and turned to nothing.

"No," Sola shouted.

The light vanished, the magic broken. Titus, Hank, and Tessa all lunged forward, but the wraith was gone.

Instinct drove Jenna's actions. She grabbed the seer's arm and shoved the tip of *Helgrind* under her chin. "I know it's you, Sola. I know what you've done. How you're using Ingvar. How you've enchanted Leif to keep him from becoming fully corporeal to spare him from my blade."

"You know nothing." Sola tried to pull away, but Jenna held firm.

She looked at Pandora. "Any word from Birdie and Bridget?"

Pandora nodded. "They got her. Taking her to Alice now. Which is where we need to bring Sola. Ingvar. Whoever this is."

Hank and Titus returned to their human forms. Hank unhooked a pair of handcuffs from his belt. "These'll help."

"I'm not so sure," Jenna said. "She poofed away just like Leif did last time. Her magic skills are obviously pretty strong."

Hank dangled the bracelets off his index finger. "These aren't my regular cuffs. These are the ones Alice fixed up for special circumstances."

"In that case, be my guest." The sooner Jenna could put *Helgrind* away, the better. Not only were the runes still open, but having the sword out would only further entice the wraith to come back. She wasn't ready to face him again. Not without a plan.

Titus came to Jenna immediately. "Are you all right? Your cheek is bleeding. You've got some pretty nasty-looking scratches."

"It's just a flesh wound. I'm good. Should you be in here? What about the wolfsbane?"

"It's been neutralized. And Sola, thankfully, didn't add more when she rebuilt the circle." He frowned, his gaze still on her cheek. "If it's just a flesh wound, why hasn't it healed yet?"

"A wraith's touch contains death. Just means it's going to take longer to heal. But it will." She sighed and scanned the surrounding woods. "I am *not* happy about Leif getting away, but it couldn't be helped."

Hank cuffed Sola's hands behind her back. She hissed as the metal touched her skin and instantly seemed to shrink down inside herself.

Jenna turned to her, staring into her friend's eyes, looking for any glint that Ingvar was still in there. "Ingvar?"

"Jenna." The word was a whisper, and a second later, her knees buckled, her eyes rolled back in her head, and she went down.

Hank caught her. "You think the bad one's gone?"

Jenna shook her head. "No. At best, she's been subdued by whatever magic Alice put in those cuffs. At worst…she's licking her wounds and planning her revenge."

"She won't get that far," Pandora said. Cole, in raven form, landed on her shoulder. She reached up and stroked his head. "The coven will see to that."

"Speaking of…" Hank walked out of the circle with Ingvar in his arms. "We should get her to Alice's as soon as possible so whatever needs to be done can be done."

Pandora nodded. "Yes. Removing Sola may not be easy. I'm thinking she's had possession of that body for far too long."

"Don't forget," Jenna said. "Alice needs Sola's blood to break the spells we're under."

"Right." Pandora gave her a quick smile, but it turned to concern. "Your cheek doesn't look so good. You should get that checked out."

Jenna waved her concern away. "It's fine. I've had wraith damage before. Just needs time. But I will go back to the house and clean it. That'll help. Then we'll meet you at Alice's. We'll just be a few minutes behind you. Go ahead."

"Why don't you come with us?"

"Because you need to get Ingvar to Alice's, and I need to close these runes. This circle may be broken, but it's still open. The last thing we need is a portal in the middle of the Nocturne Falls forest calling wraiths in from all over the place."

"Yeah, that sounds like a bad idea." Pandora's brows lifted. "You want help?"

"You know how to close ancient Norse runes by writing their opposite over top of them?"

Pandora shook her head. "Not even a little bit." She hooked her thumb over her shoulder. "I'll go with Hank. See you guys at Alice's."

Titus waved. "See you there." He turned to Jenna. "We'll get him next time."

"I hope so." She went to the first rune. This was typically the job of the seer, but as a fell maiden, she knew the runes. It had been a long time since she'd used them. Really long. She had to think hard to remember which rune closed each successive rune.

Finally, she had them all finished. "Okay, we can go."

Titus was looking around as they started walking back to the house. "Is he still out here?"

"I don't know. Maybe. But if I had to guess, I'd say probably not. He's more likely to seek out Sola at this point. Especially if she's got him enchanted to keep him from turning corporeal."

"If she does, and the coven strips her of her magic, breaks the spells we're under, and removes her control of Ingvar, what happens to the spell she's protecting him with?"

"It'll go away." Jenna already knew his next question. "So then what becomes of Leif?"

He nodded.

She smiled. "He becomes a lot easier to kill."

29

"Hold still." Titus dabbed at the scratches on Jenna's cheek with a gauze pad soaked in hydrogen peroxide. She sat on the counter in his bathroom.

She pulled away. "I don't like the fizzing."

He slanted his eyes at her, trying not to chuckle. "That's what you don't like? The fizzing?"

"It's like having tiny bees on my face," she protested.

He stopped trying not to laugh. "Imagine that. Jenna Blythe, wraith-killing valkyrie, transporter of men's souls, sword-wielding warrior...bothered by fizzing."

"I haven't killed the wraith yet, but go ahead, yuck it up, Merrow. It's just more fuel for me to beat you in that 10K."

He kissed the top of her head. "You're adorable. Sweetheart, I'm a wolf. You know what we're really good at? Running."

"So are valkyries. You'll see when you watch me cross the finish line ahead of you."

"Well, if you're in front of me, at least I'll have a nice view."

She snorted and swatted him on the arm.

"Hey!" But he snickered, catching her and pulling her in close for a second kiss, this one on the mouth.

When it ended, she held on to him. "Does this mean I'm all healed up and ready to go?"

He inspected her cheek. "I can still see the scratches, but they're definitely looking better."

"Good. Thanks."

"Anytime." He sighed contentedly. "We should get going."

"We should." She seemed as reluctant as he felt. She smoothed the front of his shirt. "Funny, but I care a lot less about having our spells removed than I do about how Ingvar's going to come out of all this."

He liked that Jenna wasn't so concerned about their spells being lifted. But he understood her concern for her fellow valkyrie. "She got the short end of this, huh?"

"She really did." Jenna hopped off the bathroom counter and glanced at her face in the mirror. "I really hope she's okay. I want my friend back. And not just so she can tell me how Sola pulled this off."

He put his arm around her shoulders. "Ingvar is in good hands. Come on, let's go see how the coven is progressing."

He drove, and while he did, she reached over and took his hand. "Thanks for everything. You've been really amazing about this whole mess, and I know I'm not easy to live with. So…thanks."

He smiled at her. "You're very easy to live with. You only rearranged my fridge once."

She laughed. "I have some organizational issues."

"Some might say it's a gift to be that organized." He chuckled. "And some might say you need therapy, but I'm cool with it."

"Good thing for me."

He glanced at her and was surprised to see she didn't look all that happy. "What's wrong?"

She shrugged. "It was nice having coffee with you in the morning. Nice having a beer with you at night too."

She was bummed about leaving? He was bummed about it too. "You should just stay tonight. It's already eleven o'clock. By the time we get through with the spell removal, who knows what time it'll be? Just crash at my place this evening. You'll have plenty of time in the morning to pack up. Plus, we could hit the hot tub one last time."

"That would be nice. I might have to get one for my house." She smiled. "Okay. I'll stay."

He pulled into the drive to Elenora's estate a few minutes later, feeling much better about the evening. Cars filled the large circular drive on both sides. The coven was definitely in session. That was good. It was all good. And yet he had some trepidation about the removal of the love spell. What would that do to them? Would it take them back to square one, like an emotional reset? Or would they still be crazy about each other?

He found it hard to believe they wouldn't be. They were pretty perfect for each other. But the chance that things would go back to how they'd been…that bothered him. There was nothing he could do but hope for the best.

He found a spot, parked, and glanced at Jenna. She seemed lost in thought. "Hey. You okay?"

She looked at him and nodded. "We're still going to like each other, right? I'm okay if we aren't in love. That takes time, and it'll come back if it's meant to be, but I'm worried we're going to go back to square one, and I don't want that."

He laughed. "I just had that same thought. I think the fact that we're both thinking about it is a good sign."

"So what do you think will happen?"

"Getting rid of the spell isn't going to erase the last few days. Everything we've been through, everything we've learned and come to appreciate about each other, that's all still going to be there."

"Right." She smiled. "Which means we'll still like each other."

"That's what I think." They might even still love each other, but he wasn't going to push it. What happened happened. And they'd recover from it, because he wasn't about to give up on something this good. "Come on. Let's go get untethered."

The door opened as they walked up, and Pandora greeted them. "Hey, good timing. We're pretty much ready to start."

Jenna bit her lip. "How's Ingvar?"

"That's what we're about to start, the separation. One of our members, Kelly, is a nurse, and she checked Ingvar's vitals, just to see how she's doing, and discovered she's pretty dehydrated, so Kelly started her on an IV."

"Oh. Okay." Jenna growled softly. "I hate this. I hate what Sola's done to her."

Titus took Jenna's hand, and she gripped his, hard. "She's going to be okay."

Jenna seemed to steel herself. "How did she get so dehydrated?"

Pandora's eyes held all kinds of sympathy. "The truth is, Sola wasn't taking very good care of the body she was inhabiting. If your friend makes it through this, she's in for a long recovery."

"If?" Jenna lifted her chin. "Ingvar is one of the strongest women I know. She's going to get through this."

Pandora nodded. "Of course she is. I should have said when. Come on, we're all gathered in Alice's practice."

They followed Pandora back to the room they'd visited when they'd given blood for tests.

It looked a little different now. The rug was gone. So was all the other furniture, except for the large worktable Titus had made. It had been moved to the center of the room and the top cleared off. Now Ingvar and Sola lay side by side on its surface. Ingvar looked paler than normal and lay very still. An IV had been hung from a coatrack beside her.

Sola's hands and feet were in restraints, and there was duct tape over her mouth. She looked like she was trying to cast spells with her eyes. Her deep auburn curls were a tangled mess around her bitter face. She looked like she'd been pretty once, but Titus wondered if giving herself to the dark side was to blame for that no longer being true. Something had cast an undeniable ugliness over her.

Jenna grimaced. "Duct tape, huh?"

Alice stood at the head of the table. "Yes. We can't have her casting counterspells in the midst of our work."

Jenna pursed her lips. "No, we can't."

A circle of what looked like salt and silver surrounded the table. Beeswax candles sat at even intervals, their flames flickering and sending the warm scent of honey into the air.

Runes just like Titus had seen on the trees in the circle marked the four directions. Alice had done her homework.

Women stood shoulder to shoulder around the walls. Titus knew many of them. Corette Williams and her other two daughters, Marigold and Charisma. Agnes from the bookstore. Dominique, who was also on the town council.

He nodded at them, hoping they knew how much he appreciated what they were doing for him and Jenna.

Alice lit the single candle at the head of the table. "Let us begin."

She pointed to Jenna. "Deputy Blythe, please come hold your friend's hand. I believe the connection will increase the magic's power. Step over the circle so it remains unbroken."

"Sure." Jenna did as she was asked and went to Ingvar's side. She took her hand. Ingvar was ice-cold, and this close, Jenna could see just how much of a toll Sola's control of Ingvar's body had taken. There were lines in her face that Jenna didn't remember. And tiny spider veins in her cheeks. Her skin was chalky. "I'm here, Ingvar," she whispered.

There was no response, but Jenna hadn't expected one.

Alice spread her arms and began, but as Jenna looked into Ingvar's face, she was lost in memories. They'd had so many good times together. Some bad ones, too, but getting through the hard moments together had only made their friendship stronger. How many times had they gone into battle together? Taken souls to Valhalla? Celebrated their victories? Cried on each other's shoulders?

The women surrounding them joined in with Alice's chanting, lifting their voices as one. The sound washed over Jenna, but she remained in the past.

From battle camp to the battlegrounds, she and Ingvar had been inseparable. So what had happened? Life? Was that one-word answer really enough?

No. It wasn't. Life happened to everyone. It wasn't an excuse.

The candle flames flickered and strengthened as the chanting increased.

Guilt settled in Jenna's stomach like a knot. Why had she let so many years go by with so little contact? Sure, they'd both been busy. Ingvar even more than Jenna. So really, the blame was on Jenna for not reaching out. She wasn't going to let this happen again.

"Come on, Ingvar," she said quietly. "Come back to me."

The moment stretched out, the chanting around her filled with positive energy and a buoyancy that Jenna recognized but just couldn't connect to. Her heart hurt too much for her friend.

Jenna held on. Ingvar's hand felt warmer, but maybe that was because Jenna had been holding on to it.

"I need you to come back. *Vikka* needs you to come back." Jenna wasn't sure Ingvar's sword would respond to someone else speaking its name, but maybe it was enough to send a little bolt through her.

Anything to wake her up.

But nothing seemed to be working.

Alice sprinkled something into the flame of the candle on the table, sending sparks into the air. The sparks seemed to twist and turn before landing on Ingvar and Sola like tiny fireflies. A glow lit each woman from within, causing them to arch skyward as the light filled them.

Sola howled and fought against the magic. Ingvar looked like she was floating in a warm bath.

Then they went prone again, and the light disappeared. Jenna held her breath, waiting…waiting…

Ingvar's mouth opened, and she gasped for air. She blinked without any obvious focus.

Jenna leaned down. "Ingvar? Can you hear me?"

The seer's gaze settled on Jenna. She calmed and took a few more breaths. "Jenna?"

Jenna nodded, smiling. "You're back. How do you feel?"

Ingvar exhaled. Already, her coloring seemed better. "Tired. And angry. Sola…Sola cast a spell…took control of me…"

Jenna squeezed Ingvar's hand. "We know. It's all over now."

Beside her, Sola squirmed and twitched like she'd been struck with a live wire.

Alice stepped back from the table. Her shoulders dropped. "It's finished. Well done, my sisters. Well done." Her eyes fixed on Sola, who was still writhing in protest. "Now, we just need to collect the offender's blood."

Ingvar nodded. "Good," she whispered. Then her eyes rolled back in her head, and she passed out.

The next minutes passed in a blur of activity. Jenna was clearly thrilled to have Ingvar back, but it was obvious she needed medical attention. And soon. But neither she nor Titus could leave until their spells were removed. The full moon was fast approaching.

Pandora, along with her mom and sisters, jumped in to help. They rushed Ingvar to the hospital. Alice, having already taken what she needed of Sola's blood, went to work finishing the spell that would free Jenna and Titus.

The rest of the coven quickly returned Alice's practice to its usual setup, then, at Alice's request and with her thanks, went home. Not only was it late, but according to her, some things were better done without an audience.

Several of the members carried Sola out and handed her over to Deputy Remy, who'd been called back out. He assured everyone that she'd be tucked safely away in the special supernatural holding cells in the Nocturne Falls Basement until she could be dealt with properly.

Then it was just the three of them—Alice, Jenna, and Titus. When Alice was ready, she had them stand facing each other in front of her worktable. She loosely wrapped a white silk cord around their hands. Titus stared into Jenna's eyes, and she stared back. There was nothing else for them to do.

Alice lit a candle on the table, then held a small metal pot over the flame by its long handle. She added things to the pot. Pinches of this and that. A sprinkle of something. A sprig of something else. Then finally, three drops of Sola's blood.

As the drops hit and sizzled, smoke poured out of the little pot. Alice fanned it toward them. "Inhale."

So they did. Jenna coughed at the acrid, bitter smoke. Titus wrinkled his nose. Smoke was one of his least favorite smells. And not just because he was the fire chief.

Finally, the smoke died away, and Alice set the pot on a stand before coming around to their side of the table again. "It's done. The spells are removed."

"Just like that?" Jenna said. "I didn't feel a thing."

"I didn't either. Are you sure it worked?" Titus said, then added, "Forgive me. I'm sure it did. I just thought I'd feel something."

"Magic doesn't always work that way." Alice unwound the cord from their hands and held it up. "But yes, I'm sure it was successful."

The cord was now black.

"Wow," Jenna said. "I guess it did." She looked at Titus and smiled.

He looked back at her. Really looked. Nothing about the way he saw her had changed. She was still incredibly beautiful. And something—everything—about her still made his wolf sit up and howl.

She took a breath. "I still like you."

He grinned. "I still like you too."

They both turned to Alice. She looked pleased but also worn out. No wonder. She'd worked so hard for them.

Jenna pressed her hands together in front of her heart. "Thank you so much. We appreciate everything you've done on our behalf. But I especially appreciate you helping Ingvar."

Alice nodded, a soft smile bending her mouth. "You're welcome. It was my pleasure to help a seer such as her. I hope the best for her. And for you too. Now, if you'll excuse me, I am very tired. Do you mind seeing yourselves out?"

"Not at all," Titus said. He grabbed Jenna's hand, happy he could still do that because nothing had changed. "Come on, let's go check on Ingvar."

They practically ran out of the house. When they got to the hospital, though, security wouldn't let them in.

Jenna didn't have her badge and told Titus she wasn't sure it would have worked anyway. It was after midnight, and visiting hours were long over. She wasn't Ingvar's family, and she certainly wasn't Birdie.

Titus had a little talk with the security guard, whose brother was on the volunteer squad. The man took pity on them and called up for a report.

Ingvar was sleeping and holding her own.

Jenna seemed to take comfort in that as she and Titus left the hospital lobby to return to his truck. "I should have known we weren't going to get in."

"It was worth a shot." He went ahead of her and opened her door. "Holding her own is good."

"It's really good." She climbed into the truck, her hand on the dash. "This feels weird to say, but I'm suddenly starving."

He nodded. "I could eat. Let's get something."

"Can we take it back to your place? I'm not in the mood to be around people."

He smiled. There was only one person he wanted to be around. "So…dinner in the hot tub?"

"I've never heard a sentence I liked more."

With a laugh, he went around and got in the driver's side. They decided on cheesesteaks from Mummy's, since it was open twenty-four hours. He got mushrooms, and she got peppers. Jenna called their orders in as he drove, then he went in and picked them up.

He grabbed a few extra items while he was in there and came out smiling. The bag was bigger than what she'd probably expected, so what he'd done wasn't going to be a secret for long.

He got into the truck, handing the bag over to her.

"This is way heavier than just two cheesesteaks."

He started the truck. "I also got fries, onion rings, and two molten lava cakes."

"I love their onion rings. Good job. But since when does Mummy's have molten lava cakes?"

"They don't usually, but they're trying them out. I figured after everything we've been through, we could survive a little chocolate experimentation. Plus, I thought they'd go well with some of that ice cream we still have."

"I like that kind of thinking. Man, this all smells good." She inhaled. Her stomach rumbled in response. She laughed. "Drive faster."

"Hey, I don't want to get a ticket."

She shot him a look. "Right. Like the brother of the sheriff has to worry about that."

"All right, then." He stepped on the pedal, happy to oblige and pushing her back in her seat with the force.

She let out a little squeal that sounded like pure joy. It made him happy. And she seemed happy. Sure, there could be better news about Ingvar, but Titus believed Jenna would get that tomorrow. After all, Ingvar was in good hands and had already survived Sola. She was a valkyrie like Jenna. And they were strong women. She'd recover.

She had to. They still had a wraith to vanquish.

A few minutes later, he pulled into his driveway. He parked but looked at Jenna before getting out. Even after the day they'd had, she still beamed light and beauty. Removing the spell had done nothing to take away his desire for her. "I'll grab a couple of Warhammers, then get the jets going. Will you take the food to the kitchen?"

"Sure. I'll get plates out."

"That would be great. I have a tray that hooks on the edge of the hot tub. I'll set that up to use as our table."

"Hot-tub picnic. I love it."

"I'll meet you in there after I change into my trunks." He smirked, suddenly wondering what she'd be changing into. "Will, uh, Miss America be making an appearance this evening?"

She laughed. "I think that can be arranged."

He opened the truck door, grinning so hard his cheeks were starting to ache. "This might be the most epic night of my life."

"It might be." She said the words so softly he almost didn't catch them.

When he looked over at her, she just grabbed the bag and got out. Did she have plans for this evening? Plans for what might happen *after* the hot tub? Now that they were no longer under the influence of any magic, there was no reason to hold back. Not if she gave him the green light.

Maybe it was time to see just how compatible he and the valkyrie were. With the same grin still stuck to his face, he disappeared into the garage.

Jenna headed for the kitchen. She put the bag on the counter, then went to her room to change. She slipped into the star-spangled bikini, smiling the whole time. Some men were easy to please.

So far, Titus was one of those men. And she liked that. She'd always thought she wanted a guy who was more like his brother. Kind of a gruff, super-focused, no-fluff kind of guy. Which wasn't to say she was attracted to her boss. She wasn't.

In fact, she couldn't imagine being attracted to anyone but Titus right now.

She also didn't mean that Titus was the opposite of those things. He certainly wasn't a fluff kind of guy. Not at all. He was just more easygoing than his brother. He seemed open to all kinds of things.

And yes, easy to please. At least he was that way around her.

She laughed. She wouldn't have said he was easy to please last week when they'd butted heads over where the water stands should be along the race route.

Now, however, she couldn't see them having an argument like that. So what had changed?

They'd gotten to know each other. And she'd fallen for him. Head over sword.

She went back out to the kitchen and started removing the food containers from the bag. She took two plates down from the cabinet and set them out. She was dividing up the fries when she heard his outside door open and then close a short while later.

He was behind her a minute after that, leaning past her to sneak a fry. She didn't have to look to know he was in swim trunks and nothing else. His bare chest brushed the back of her arm as he went for a second fry.

"The food smells great." His hands went around her waist, and he kissed the side of her neck. "If I wasn't so hungry, I'd suggest dessert first."

"Really?" she teased. "You'd rather have the molten lava cake than the cheesesteak?"

He nipped her throat playfully. "I'd rather have the hot-as-lava valkyrie in my arms."

She leaned into him, putting her arms on top of his. "Be careful. You might get what you wish for."

He took a deep breath, and a soft, needy growl vibrated against her skin where his mouth was. "Blythe, don't tease me."

She turned in his arms, planted her hands flat on his chest, and stared into his wolfy, glowing eyes. "Do I look like I'm teasing?"

He stared back for a moment without saying a word. "No. You don't." He swallowed. "Let's eat. I think we're both going to need our strength."

"Agreed." She wasn't about to argue with that.

They grabbed their plates and headed for the hot tub. The jets were bubbling away, and he'd set up the tray just as he'd said.

He took her plate while she got in. "Did you build that tray?" It looked like his work, and she'd never seen anything like it.

"I did."

She took her plate back. "You have a lot of women over for hot-tub picnics, do you?"

He shook his head as he joined her in the water. "Not a one." He put his plate on the tray. "Not since Zoe."

"Is she who you built that porch swing for?"

He nodded. "I should probably take it down."

She ate a fry. No wonder why it had been a sore subject. "Or you could just sit in it with someone new. Make some new memories."

He smiled. "Or that."

He was so handsome. "How have you not dated anyone in all this time?"

"It's easy to be too busy with work and family stuff." He cracked open a beer and set it next to her plate, then opened a second for himself. "But then, you already know that, don't you?"

"I do." She tilted her bottle in his direction. "Here's to not being too busy anymore."

He clinked his against hers, smiling. "Cheers to that." He took a sip, then put the bottle back down and took hold of the first half of his cheesesteak. "I told you we'd still like each other."

"You did. And you were right." She picked up her cheesesteak as well. "I'm really glad."

"Me too."

They ate for a bit, satisfying part of their appetites. When they were halfway through, Titus leaned against the tub. "What are we going to do about the wraith? He's still out there."

She nodded. "I've been thinking about that. With Sola out of the picture, he might not still be out there. She's the reason he's here and as strong as he is. Or was here and was as strong. There's every chance he was so weakened by the loss of her magic that he won't be a problem anymore."

He ate a fry. "And if that's not the case?"

"Then the best thing to do would be to wait until Ingvar's well enough to build the trap Sola was supposed to. That's really the best way to take down a wraith. Draw them into a trap, where they're frozen solid by the seer who opened the circle, and then run them through the heart with a fell maiden's blade."

He nodded. "So we're in a waiting game."

"Just a brief one." She brushed her hands off over the side of the tub so she didn't get crumbs in the water. "If there's the slightest indication that he's still around and causing problems before Ingvar's on her feet, I can always call in another seer."

Titus went for the second half of his cheesesteak. "Good to know."

"There is one other possibility."

He stopped just shy of taking a bite. "One I'm not going to like, based on the tone of your voice."

"If it makes you feel any better, I don't like it either."

He frowned. "What is it?"

"Sola had a spell on Leif to keep him from going fully corporeal. When that happens, a wraith is the most dangerous because they're at their strongest. It's like they've returned to their mortal berserker form. They have that kind of strength and speed again."

"You're right, I don't like it."

"There are two factors that make this stage hard for them. First, they still aren't mortal. They still feel the constant pull of the underworld calling them. As a reminder of that, their touch eventually brings death.

Think about that. What would your life be like if touching something too much caused it to die?"

He grimaced. "I see your point. And the second thing?"

"The biggest drawback, for them, is they can be killed. Yes, they're already dead, but in that form, a second death is a final one. A blade through the heart and the wraith's soul can finally be transported to its final resting place."

"You did that in the circle."

"I did, but he wasn't solid. Not fully. More like a hard candy shell with a soft nougat center."

"Okay, that's a little gross. But I get it. She kept him from reaching that stage to protect him from being killed."

Jenna nodded. "It was smart. Or maybe 'diabolical' is a better word. But now that her magic has been nullified, he could reach that stage on his own. No clue how long it might take him. Or if he's lost his way without her."

Titus sat back. "I'd like to know for sure. I don't want to have to worry about him wreaking havoc in this town. Or coming after you."

"I understand. I don't like the idea either. But I think we'll know soon enough, because if he's at that point, he's not going to sit idle. He can't get his full life back without the resurrection stone from my sword. Trust me, he'll make his presence known."

Titus's gaze shifted past her to the far end of the deck. "I think he just has."

Jenna followed Titus's line of sight.

The wraith stood at the end of the deck, just a shadow creature at the moment, but fast becoming solid before their eyes.

Her worst fear realized.

Every fiber of Jenna's being went on battle-ready alert. She jumped out of the tub, flinging water everywhere. She landed on the deck between the tub and Leif. "You don't belong here, wraith. Not at this house, not on this plane."

"You took my wife." He was fully corporeal now and every inch the berserker, except for those glowing ember eyes. "I want her back."

Jenna had no doubt he was solid through and through without Sola's magic to protect him. This was going to be a test of skills like she'd never encountered before. "Sola hurt Ingvar. And even if she didn't do that, she still broke the vows of the seer."

Just like he'd broken his oath as a berserker to become a traitor to their kind. He and Sola made a fine couple in that regard.

He roared at her. "She was helping me."

"To do what? Kill me? Not a great argument." *Helgrind* itched for release, but he hadn't drawn his sword yet. She didn't want to force that next step. Not until Titus could get to a less vulnerable spot, and from the sound of sloshing water behind her, he was moving.

"You killed me." Leif's eyes beamed as he held his hand out. "Give me your sword, and I'll let you live."

They both knew that was a lie.

She shook her head. "You know how this is going to end, Leif."

He smiled, a gruesome sight. "Yes, valkyrie. I do."

Titus growled softly, but it seemed to have no effect on Leif. "Jenna," he said quietly. "Should I shift?"

"I don't think it'll make a difference now. He's too far gone." As she spoke, Leif reached back and pulled out *Kirsgut*. The mammoth weapon gleamed in the light spilling out of the house. She went for hers at the same time, freeing *Helgrind* with the sweet, metallic bladesong that had so often announced Jenna's foray into battle.

"I'll call for help," Titus said.

"You can," she answered. "But I don't intend for this to last that long." She whipped *Helgrind* around her body. She was vaguely aware of the sliders being opened and Titus going inside. "This is your final chance to leave, berserker. Accept your fate and take your place in the underworld."

"Never," he snarled.

She didn't wait another second. She swung her sword to drive him back. He counterattacked, their blades meeting in a clash of metal that sent tremors down her arms and into her bones.

The beeps of Titus's phone as he called for backup barely registered. She was focused on putting an end to Leif.

They fought on, sparks flying when their blades met, sweat trickling down her back and mingling with the water from the hot tub.

Leif's sword was bigger and heavier, but she wielded *Helgrind* like it was an extension of herself. She caught him across the thigh. Just a slice, but enough to make him rage harder and fight wilder.

And it bled.

She realized something as she connected again, thanks to his sloppy swordplay. He was so far gone that the rage that should have been his greatest strength was making him reckless. And a reckless fighter was often the loser.

He would soon slip up and leave himself open enough for her to get her sword through his chest. That's all she needed.

So she pressed harder on the metaphorical wound she'd found. "Sola always used to say how someday she was going to find some idiot berserker to practice on. I guess she did."

He growled, overreaching with his next swing and missing wildly.

"She said she'd find one who'd do anything for her. One she'd pretend to love, all in the name of manipulation."

He charged, but she stepped aside as if she were a matador and Leif a bull blinded by the mania of the fight. He tossed his sword into the air and caught it, reversing his grip on the hilt.

Then everything happened at once.

Titus stepped out of the house. "Hank is on his way."

Leif threw his sword like a javelin, sending it straight at Jenna.

Titus shoved her out of the way.

She fell, twisting in the air as she reached for the weapon that was no longer aimed at her. She landed flat on her back as *Kirsgut* flew overhead and buried itself in Titus's chest.

The scream that ripped out of her left her throat raw. Her vision went red. She leaped to her feet and charged Leif, flinging herself into the air and driving her blade into his heart.

His mouth came open, and his eyes flickered red-hot, then they burned out. Dead coals. He fell to the deck beneath her and, a second later, disintegrated into ash and smoke.

Helgrind in hand, she ran to Titus, tears blinding her.

He lay sprawled a few feet from the hot tub, Leif's sword still jutting from his body where it had pierced his heart. She dropped her sword to return it to her back as she knelt beside him, cradling his head in her lap. She didn't need to take his pulse to know she was losing him. "Titus," she sobbed.

His smile was weak, his eyes unfocused. He tried to reach for her, but his hand fell back. "Hey. Should have ducked."

How could he joke at a time like this? She sniffed hard. She was about to watch him die. She couldn't let that happen. "Yeah, you should have. I love you. I'm not losing you. Do you trust me?"

He managed a nod. "With my whole heart."

"Good. This is going to hurt for a second." She eased his head back to the deck, then steeled herself to do the most terrible thing she'd ever done. "Close your eyes, baby."

They were already closing. She had no time to waste. She pulled Leif's sword from Titus's chest and tossed it aside, then unsheathed *Helgrind*, raised it high and plunged the blade into the heart of the man she loved more than life itself.

He gasped, eyes coming open. He started to say something, but she didn't have time to explain.

She wrenched *Helgrind* free, ripped the resurrection stone from the pommel and shoved it into the gaping wound left behind.

Light exploded from Titus's chest, filling him with the sharp green glow of ancient magic. He seemed to levitate a few inches off the deck. She rocked back on her heels, sending every ounce of energy she had left toward him. Tears still streamed down her face.

If she lost him…Sola would not live either.

In the glow of the stone, Jenna realized Hank, Birdie, and Bridget were watching from the open slider. They looked paralyzed by what they were seeing. She understood. She wasn't sure when they'd arrived or how much they'd seen, but there was blood everywhere and light spilling out of Titus, and she could only imagine what they were thinking.

The glow began to subside, and the wound closed, but Titus was very pale and not moving.

"Titus?" Bridget said softly.

Jenna couldn't speak. She knew how this must look to his family. There was blood everywhere. She reached out and took his hand. His fingers wrapped around hers. That was all the sign she needed.

She looked up at his family, laughing through her tears. "He's going to be all right, but we should still probably get him to the hospital."

"Hey." Titus's voice was thin and reedy. "Am I alive?"

"You are." She leaned over him, kissing his cheek. "But I think you're going to need some serious rest so you can finish healing. The stone can only do so much, you know?"

He stared up at her a little blankly. "You plunged your sword into my heart."

"What?" Birdie screeched.

Jenna just nodded. "Yeah, I did. But it was to save you, and now you're going to be okay."

He smiled at her. "I love you. You saved my life. We should get married."

She laughed. "How about we talk about that after you're fully recovered?" She looked up at Hank. "Hospital. Now."

That lit a fire under the sheriff. He bent to take Titus by the arms. "You got his feet?"

She nodded. "Your car?"

"Yes."

They lifted at the same time, carrying Titus through the house. Bridget and Birdie looked like they were about to explode with questions.

Jenna caught Bridget's gaze. "Do not touch the sword on the back deck, and do not let anyone else touch it. Touching it will release the wraith, and I need him in there so I can take him to the underworld. Got it?"

"Underworld. No touching. Got it." Bridget nodded as she ran ahead to open the front door.

Birdie wrung her hands. "Should I call Tessa?"

"No, just keep an eye on things here. I'll be back as soon as I can. Remember, no one touches that sword."

"No one touches the sword," Birdie repeated. Then she gasped and put a hand to her heart. "I can't. I have to go with Titus. I need to know he's going to be all right."

"Go on," Bridget said. "I'll stay and guard the sword."

"Call Remy," Hank grunted as they went through the front door.

Birdie went ahead again and opened the passenger door of Hank's SUV.

"Might as well call Tessa too," Jenna said over her shoulder. Tessa wouldn't let anyone touch the sword, and she wasn't sure Bridget was going to stay at the house, considering the way she was looking at her brother being loaded into Hank's vehicle.

"Jenna?" Titus's voice still had no strength.

"I'm right here." She grabbed hold of his ankle, the first part of him she could reach.

"Stay with me."

She didn't need to be asked twice.

Hank looked at her across the seat from where he was standing on the other side of the SUV. "Ride back here with him."

She nodded and climbed in, positioning herself so that Titus's head was on her lap again.

Birdie got in the front. Bridget was already on her phone.

Jenna looked down at Titus. His coloring looked a little better. She smiled at him. "You're going to be okay."

"Thanks to you," he whispered. Then he fell asleep.

She finger-combed his hair off his forehead. There was no point in telling him that he'd actually saved her life by pushing her out of the way of Leif's sword. That he was the real hero. And that she'd just done what any woman in love would have done.

Just like there was no point in explaining that the resurrection stone restored life, but he still had a lot of healing to do to hang on to that life. There might even be surgery in his future.

However long his recovery took, she'd be there. Yes, there were a few other things that needed doing, like transporting Leif's sword to the underworld to ensure that he was never released into the mortal world again, but she'd handle that as soon as Titus was being cared for. And then there was the 10K charity relay race coming up.

"Couple more minutes," Hank said as he drove on.

"Okay," Jenna answered.

Titus was going to be mad about missing that race. Which he would, because you didn't run a race two days after you had a berserker's sword through your heart.

Wouldn't matter that he would miss it because he was in the hospital, trying to stay alive. He'd still be mad. She shook her head.

Then she smiled as an idea came to her. She bent and kissed his forehead. Funny that they'd put so much effort into getting untethered, and now all she could think about was how to never be away from him again.

Hank looked at her through the rearview mirror. "Blue duffel bag has sweatpants and a sweatshirt in it."

Jenna frowned at him for a second. "For Titus?"

"No." Hank's gaze shifted, and he looked back at the road.

Birdie cleared her throat as she twisted around in her seat. "Not that I wouldn't wear the same thing if I had your body, but you might be a little chilly in the hospital, Deputy."

Jenna looked down, suddenly realizing she was still in her Old Glory bikini. "Oh. Right."

Someday, this would be a very funny story.

When Titus was a little boy, Aunt Birdie told him stories about how after you died, if you were a good werewolf and ate all your supper and obeyed your parents, you went to the most beautiful forest you could ever imagine, where there were rabbits to chase and clear blue streams to splash in and more places to run than you could cover in a thousand years, and all your friends and family became part of your pack.

She'd never said anything about a soft beep-beep-beeping or the smell of disinfectant or the cold.

So while he was pretty sure he'd died, he was starting to think he hadn't been a very good werewolf.

He cracked one eye open. And saw an angel. Then he smelled lemons. Maybe he'd done all right after all.

The angel looked at him. "Titus? Oh, you're awake. I'm so glad."

Aunt Birdie popped up behind the angel, and he realized he wasn't actually dead. He opened both eyes. "Jenna?"

She nodded. "It's me. Hi there, handsome."

"Hi." He smiled despite the dull ache in his chest. "Hi, Aunt Birdie."

"How are you feeling, honey?" Birdie leaned in, looking like she might burst into tears or song, depending on his answer.

"Like there's an elephant sitting on my chest."

"You had surgery," Jenna said.

He squinted at her, trying to remember what had happened. An image flashed through his head. "Because…you stabbed me?"

She smirked. "Technically, that's true. But Leif's sword stabbed you first. And I did it to save your life. It's just that the resurrection stone works best on those whose life was also ended by *Helgrind*. I know. It's complicated Norse magic. Best not to question it. The gods get touchy about that."

He looked around. "I've been in the hospital a lot since going into that attic with you."

She laughed. "That's true. But I promise that after this, your hospital visits are over."

"That would be nice."

Birdie pressed a hand to her chest. "I should call Hank and Bridget and let them know you're awake."

"Don't bother them if they're working," Titus said.

"You hush," Birdie answered. "They're in the cafeteria. They went to get coffee." She walked toward the door to make her call.

Titus snorted. "Glad to see she's not going to baby me or anything."

Jenna smiled. "That's my job now."

He smiled back, liking the sound of that very much. "So if they went to get coffee, I'm guessing I've been here overnight?"

"You've been here for two overnights. About two and a half days."

"What?"

She put her hands on her hips. "You did have a sword through your heart, so…"

"Yeah, but I'm a werewolf. I heal very fast."

"Sure, but you were also just getting over wolfsbane poisoning."

He exhaled. "Thanks for reminding me what a dangerous woman you are to hang around with."

"I know. I've been terrible for your health. Sorry about that."

Another thought occurred to him. "The race!" He groaned. "I missed it."

Bridget and Hank walked in with their coffees, smiling at their brother.

Bridget went straight to the other side of his bed. "It's good to see you awake."

"Likewise," Hank said.

"Thanks, but I missed the race." Titus let out a sigh that sounded grouchy even to his own ears, but he gave himself a pass for being in pain. And being stabbed twice in the heart with a sword. That had to be worth a little bit of crankiness. He looked at Jenna. "I suppose you won, since I wasn't there to beat you."

322

"I did." She smiled like she knew more than she was telling.

"Of course. Another trophy for the sheriff's department." Titus shook his head and rolled his eyes at his brother.

Hank sipped his coffee. "Actually, the trophy went to the fire department."

Titus stared at Hank for a second, then looked back at Jenna. "I don't understand."

Her smile got a little bigger. "I switched teams and ran anchor in your place."

All his grouchiness disappeared. "You did?"

She nodded, then winked at him. "But next year? I'm totally winning back that trophy for the NFSD."

He laughed, which hurt but was worth it.

Birdie nudged Hank. "Let's give these two a little time alone, okay?"

Bridget squeezed his arm. "See you later, bro."

"Bye, sis."

When the door closed, leaving just the two of them, Titus took Jenna's hand as best he could with the IV sticking out of him. "Are you okay? Did you get hurt at all?"

"A couple scratches. Nothing serious. Speaking of, Ingvar's out of the hospital. Doing pretty well too. I've moved her into my place. I think she might stay in Nocturne Falls for a while. After everything the coven did for her, she feels a little indebted, you know?"

"I do know. Did she tell you how Sola took her over?"

"She did." Jenna took a breath. "As best she can figure, Sola finally worked out the magic to raise Leif as a wraith, then they located me and decided to bring him all the way back. She knew Ingvar and I were friends, so she put Ingvar under a spell, took possession of her body, and used her as a decoy to lure me in." She smiled at him. "You were just collateral damage."

He nodded a little. "Wow."

"Yep."

He loved the warmth of her hand in his. "Listen. I'm well aware that you saved my life with your actions. I don't remember it all too clearly, but you used the resurrection stone on me, didn't you?"

"I did. But you saved me from getting skewered by pushing me out of the way. We're basically even."

He squeezed her hand. "Are there any consequences from being resurrected by that stone? Any side effects I should know about?"

She pursed her lips. "I was trying to figure out how to break this to you... You can't be more than a hundred feet from *Helgrind* at any given moment, or the stone stops working and—"

He went very still. "Are you serious?"

She laughed. "No. But it was worth it to see the look on your face."

He snorted, then frowned. "Did you take Leif's sword to the underworld yet?"

"Not yet. I needed to know you were going to be okay. But it's in safe keeping, don't worry."

He exhaled. She'd stayed. For him. "I really do owe you my life. I probably shouldn't be too far away from you anyway."

She smiled. "I'd like that."

"And when I get out of here, we can try that hot-tub picnic again."

Her smile went from ear to ear. "I'd like that even more."

Want to be up to date on all books & release dates by Kristen Painter? Sign-up for my newsletter on my website, www.kristenpainter.com. No spam, just news (sales, freebies, releases, you know, all that jazz.)

If you loved the book and want to help the series grow, tell a friend about the book and take time to leave a review!

Other Books by Kristen Painter

PARANORMAL ROMANCE:

Nocturne Falls series:
The Vampire's Mail Order Bride
The Werewolf Meets His Match
The Gargoyle Gets His Girl
The Professor Woos The Witch
The Witch's Halloween Hero – short story
The Werewolf's Christmas Wish – short story
The Vampire's Fake Fiancée
The Vampire's Valentine Surprise – short story
The Shifter Romances The Writer
The Vampire's True Love Trials – short story
The Dragon Finds Forever
The Vampire's Accidental Wife
The Reaper Rescues the Genie
The Detective Wins the Witch
The Vampire's Priceless Treasure
The Vampire Dates the Deputy

Can't get enough Nocturne Falls?
Try the NOCTURNE FALLS UNIVERSE books.
New stories, new authors, same Nocturne Falls world!
www.http://kristenpainter.com/nocturne-falls-universe/

Nothing is completed without an amazing team.

Many thanks to:

Design & derivative cover art: Janet Holmes using
images under license from Shutterstock.com
Interior formatting: Author E.M.S
Editor: Joyce Lamb
Copyedits/proofs: Chris Kridler/Lisa Bateman

About the Author

USA Today Best Selling author Kristen Painter is a little obsessed with cats, books, chocolate, and shoes. It's a healthy mix. She loves to entertain her readers with interesting twists and unforgettable characters. She currently writes the best-selling paranormal romance series, Nocturne Falls, and the cozy mystery spin off series, Jayne Frost. The former college English teacher can often be found all over social media where she loves to interact with readers.

www.kristenpainter.com

Made in the USA
Columbia, SC
29 July 2020